FROM INTERNATIONAL BESTSELLING AUTHOR

DAVID B. LYONS

IN THE
MIDDLE OF
MIDDLE
AMERICA

Print ISBN: 978-1-9160518-8-1

 Created with Vellum

PRAISE FOR DAVID B. LYONS

"Keeps you guessing right until the end" – **Mail On Sunday**

"Simply outstanding" – **The Book Magnet**

"Impossible to put down" – **The Book Literati**

"So clever" – **The Writing Garnet**

"Lyons is a great new voice in fiction" – **Bestselling author John A. Marley**

For

the O'Hanlons

—AMERICA PAST—

When lives entangle, webs will weave...

ONE

THE LIMOUSINE STRETCHED AS LONG as the three yellow cabs belching exhaust fumes toward the overcast sky as they lined up at yet another red light behind it. At the far end of the limousine, by a cracked open door, stood posture-perfect, a kind-eyed man whose snow-white hair puffed out like clouds from under his tightly fitted, navy peaked cap.

It was a dull afternoon in the city, dry and still; yet a chill would still cut through the layers of those rushing by whenever the sun would inevitably peek behind the annoyingly consistent and persistent conveyor belt of loose, gray clouds.

"Good evenin', Ma'am," the kind-eyed man in the navy peaked cap said, bowing his head. He took a step forward, pulling the door wider open with him, before motioning to them with a sweep of his free hand, an invitation to the cream leather, U-shaped interior.

"Ya don't gotta call me no *Ma'am*," she said, tapping him on the shoulder as she passed him. "Sarah-Jane will do."

She slid, ladylike, into the back of the limousine, before Phil clumsily clambered in after her. Then the man with the peaked navy cap shut them inside, muting the rush and the hum of the city. Phil looked scruffy against the crisp, clean interior, even though Sarah-Jane had presented him with a newly purchased double-breasted winter jacket that very morning.

Sarah-Jane had, over the previous days, considered suggesting he comb his unkempt hair, or at least trim his scruffy, patchy beard. But, designer double-breasted jacket aside, she ultimately decided she didn't want Phil to change much at all. She was content for him to be the same, oddball, practically mute, middle-aged, scruffy-looking shy guy she had driven every street of northern Kansas with over the previous three years.

They met on the morning of her very first day at Kansas City PBS. She had used the local public broadcasting service for work experience during summer breaks of her completing a degree in journalism and, after becoming a hit with the few dozen local viewers who bothered to tune in, was offered a full-time role as a reporter covering the suburbs of northern Kansas. When she walked into the damp and disappointing PBS studios for the very first time, like a supermodel — all bright-eyed and undeniably attractive — Sarah-Jane's station manager led her into a stuffy office no larger than the closet she packed her shoes into back home. In that stuffy office, staring down at his worn-out meshed New Balance sneakers, stood Phil—his hair just as unkempt and his beard just as patchy and shabby as it was the day he clumsily clambered into the back of that limousine after her.

"This is Philip Meredith," her station manager said. "He'll be your cameraman slash producer."

"Cameraman slash producer?" Sarah-Jane said, snorting a laugh through her nose. "Is that what it says on your business cards?"

Phil glanced up from his sneakers at her, then blinked his eyes slowly. Phil always blinked slowly. In fact, Phil did everything slowly.

"I ain't got no business cards," he mumbled.

Sarah-Jane glanced at her new station manager, then back at Phil. Neither of them were laughing.

"Aren't we like just four blocks from Times Square?" Sarah-Jane said as the limousine vibrated and hummed to a stop behind yet another line of yellow cabs.

"Dunno," Phil said, scratching at his beard.

After sighing heavily, Sarah-Jane reached into her oversized purse, removed a notepad and then sat back into the cream-leather seat. As she flicked through the notes she had scribbled back in her hotel room before she had been informed her driver was downstairs waiting for her, Phil looked her up and down; from the point of her high-heeled leather shoes, all the way up to her marble eyes. Then he fake coughed into the back of his hand nervously. It was unusual that Phil would feel nervous, but he was nervous in the back of that limousine because he felt a need to speak. And Philip Meredith was not a man who enjoyed speaking. It's why Sarah-Jane loved working with him. She could control him. From day one of meeting him in that stuffy little office in the bowels of the PBS studios, Sarah-Jane adopted a career puppy dog; a puppy dog who would leap to her every command.

"Just wanna say," Phil said, before nervously coughing again, causing Sarah-Jane to slap her notebook closed because she knew more than anyone that when Phil spoke, it was because something needed to be said. "Thank you for taking me with you."

"Oh, you've thanked me enough," Sarah-Jane said, batting him away with a wave of her hand.

"But I haven't said it properly, 'cause I'm not really good with words. But thank you. You didn't..."

He paused, to scratch at a patch of his scruffy beard again, shrugging his shoulders.

"I know I didn't *have* to take you with me to New York," Sarah-Jane said. "But I *needed* to take you with me." She leaned toward him, and as she squeezed his elbow, she winked one of her beautiful, mirror-like eyes. "And look at you now, Phil, huh? A producer on one of the biggest networks in America. Business cards and all."

Sarah-Jane waited for Phil to snort his usual hoarse chuckle, then she leaned back in the leather seat and sighed, because the limousine had stopped, yet again, behind another line of stationary yellow cabs.

"It's one, fifty-five," she said, pulling at the cuff of her left sleeve. "Screw this. Come on, Phil."

She snatched open the limousine door and stepped into the

vibrating hum of the stalled traffic, where she waited on Phil to join her.

"We're gonna run," she said, slapping at the driver's window before darting between the rows of stalled traffic. Phil jog-walked after her, carrying her oversized purse under his arm as if it was a football.

They were headed toward the lights. The brightest lights the city had to offer. The brightest lights in all of America. Lights that seemed to shine brighter and glow more magical the closer they raced toward them, especially so for Phil. He hadn't been to New York City before; had only ever seen these bright lights through the screen of his bulky television set back home. Whereas this wasn't Sarah-Jane's first time in Times Square. She had visited on both occasions she had come to New York to audition for stage roles during her late teens. It had been mentioned to her more than once that her looks would be enough to elevate her to the boards of Broadway, from where she would inevitably be offered a first-class ticket to the hills of Hollywood. Only she was turned down without any feedback whatsoever for the two auditions she managed to book, simply because she didn't possess anywhere near the talent required to be treading the boards of a Broadway stage. When the second casting director she auditioned for squinted at her as if she had two heads and ranted, "Have you even taken the time to consider the nuances that might emanate from within the character you are auditioning to portray?" she shook her head, dropped her script to the floor and slowly shuffled her shoes toward the exit—ending not just that particular audition, but her aspirations of becoming the next Michelle Pfeiffer.

Although she quit acting that day, she didn't quite quit on her ambition of finding fame. And so, after long consideration, she decided she would study journalism when she eventually graduated high school. If being the next Michelle Pfeiffer was too far of a stretch for her, then perhaps being the next Katie Couric was within her grasp.

"How hard can reporting the news actually be?" she once

asked her journalism professor. "S'not as if anybody is gonna expect me to consider the nuances that might emanate from within the character I'm wishing to portray, is it?" The professor barked out a laugh, then placed a hand to her shoulder. He liked touching her shoulder. In fact, he did so as often as he could without, hopefully, coming across as too creepy. He had a wife and three children at home in his three-story townhouse and could do without the damage being labeled a sleaze would inevitably bring. His infatuation with this particular student never ran so far beyond the line that he blatantly came on to her, but it ran far enough for him to award her A grades and glowing feedback even when she didn't, perhaps, deserve such acclaim.

The hum of atmosphere around Times Square rarely pauses even as the sun revolves around the high-rise buildings. In the very early hours of the morning — between the hours of three a.m. and five a.m., and under the darkest navy of the smog-filled skies unique to New York City — Times Square can be somewhat deserted, save for the street cleaners who go about their business of sweeping up the previous day's mess. But in every other hour of the day on either side of those two hours, bodies continually squeeze through this intersection almost shoulder to shoulder, as lights dance and blink around them.

By the time Sarah-Jane skidded to a stop outside the Virgin store, Phil was already struggling for breath. He bent over, resting his hands on his knees and sucked in as much of the polluted air as he possibly could from between those bodies rushing by almost shoulder-to-shoulder.

"It's gonna be this one here," Sarah-Jane said, patting him on the back as he remained bent over.

Phil looked up, following the direction of Sarah-Jane's finger, to the biggest and brightest lights across the busy street. There were three billboards on the opposite side, stretching as high as the twenty-story building next to them. A Coca-Cola ad was beaming from the bottom screen, blinking its "Enjoy" logo behind a silhouette of the bodies veering off in all directions in front of it. On top

of that, on another large screen, equal in size, shone an advertise-
ment for Samsung — flashing a blue-and-white striped logo onto
the rooftops of the cabs lined up underneath. On the highest of the
three billboards squinted the piercing blue eyes of Leonardo
DiCaprio, staring down at Times Square from beneath his
curtained center-parted haircut, before his face disappeared and
the words "*Titanic*. January, 1998" flashed instead.

"Which one?" Phil asked, standing back upright.

"The top one. The *Titanic* one. It's due to change at two p.m."
She curled a finger into the left cuff of her blazer and hooked it
back. "It's past two, now. It should be up already."

Phil turned down his lips while he continued to stare at the top
billboard, watching Leonardo DiCaprio's pretty face advertise
what was being regarded as the most eagerly anticipated movie of
the decade. Sarah-Jane had already been distracted from the
Hollywood star's piercing eyes by the hum of the people way
below as they swarmed across her and by her in every conceivable
direction. She noted not one of them was staring up at the billboard Phil was staring at, and began to wonder if it was wise for the
network to have spent thirty-thousand dollars just to blink a shiny
ad high above the oblivious tourists below in Times Square.

"There," Phil said, pointing.

Sarah-Jane glanced up from the sea of bodies in front of her, to
see her own teeth shining bright.

"Ahhh," she squealed, as she slapped both hands to her face. "I
can't believe it!"

"Zdanski," flashed up under her chin. "Tonight 7 p.m.,
Eastern."

Phil, who participated in the art of body language as irregularly
as he participated in oral conversation, lifted his arm and placed it,
gingerly, across the back of Sarah-Jane's shoulders. She was
touched by this gesture so much, that she grabbed his hanging
fingers and gripped them as tightly as she could, just as a tear
spilled from her eye.

"Do you think I should be smiling?" she asked. "I probably

shouldn't be smiling." Phil, as always, took her question as rhetorical, and remained silent. "Doesn't matter," she said, shaking her head. "My name up in lights in Times Square. I can't believe it. Okay..." She reached into her pocket, took out a yellow box camera and then wound it to its setting. "Take a picture," she ordered Phil.

He removed his arm from her shoulder, placed her purse between his New Balance sneakers on the filthy sidewalk, and then squinted through the square lens, taking a full-length shot of Sarah-Jane Zdanski making a peace sign in front of Sarah-Jane Zdanski beaming a wide smile.

"Cool," she said, taking the camera from him. "I'm gonna get that one developed first thing in the morning. That's one for the scrapbook."

"Get more than one developed," Phil said, picking up Sarah-Jane's purse.

"Yeah," she replied, as she stuffed the camera back into her coat pocket. "I should send a copy of that back to my folks in Kansas."

"Hey," a voice called out. "That you? Are you Zdanski? Holy shit. It's you. You're Sarah-Jane Zdanski."

"Shhhh," Phil cut in, holding a hand to the man's chest. "Keep it down."

"Sorry, dude," the man said. "Can I... can I get your autograph, Sarah-Jane?" He reached inside his bomber jacket, removed a balled-up Footlocker receipt from the inside pocket and held it toward the blonde beauty.

"You got a pen?" she asked.

"Damn it, no!" the man replied.

Then Phil pressed his thumb to click a pen in front of his boss's face before she uncreased the man's receipt and scribbled her name on the back of it.

"Best of luck with your show tonight," the man said, taking the receipt from her and grinning at it as though he had just gotten her phone number. "I'll be watching."

She offered the stranger a thin smile, then walked away swiftly, with Phil jog-walking behind her, her purse tucked back under his arm.

"First autograph," she side-mouthed back to Phil as they weaved around the shoulder-to-shoulder bodies.

"First of many," Phil said.

LUCY DECKER

It don't feel right to place your hand between your legs while you're peeing. But every time I do this, there's always a wave of optimism sloshing around inside me that recedes the annoyance of urine misting my fingertips.

I shake the stick into the toilet when I'm done while, at the same time, I stretch both my underwear and my sweatpants upward with my free hand until they snap back to my waist.

"Please. Please," I whisper to the stick. I place it, carefully, down onto a prepared sheet of toilet paper before turning to the sink to rid my fingertips of mists of urine. After I dry them, I read the back of the box one more time, as if I don't already know with absolute certainty that it will take two minutes for a result to show.

When I reconfirm to myself that it does indeed take two minutes, I spin on my bare feet and head for the kitchen. Well, it's a combination kitchen-living room. Open-plan living, if you will. But open-plan living if you're a family of either three elves or one average-sized lonely human being. Which is ideal for me. Because that's exactly what I am. One averaged-sized lonely human being.

I stab my finger at the TV as I walk past it before pacing into the kitchen, allowing the last news channel I was watching late last night to blink itself back to life. Before I go through my two cupboards in search of something to eat, I snatch at the receiver of my phone hanging from the kitchen wall and speed dial seven.

Only out of habit. I really don't care what the message says. It's just... I'm still paying for the monthly subscription and I may as well check in every now and then. Just in case...

"Hello, Lucy," the robot barks down the line. "You have....." Long pause. "Zero dating requests."

I sigh a routine sigh that seems to always accompany my speed dialing of the number seven, then hang the receiver back to the phone on the wall.

The cupboards are as bare as I really should start expecting them to be. I don't know why I look through them with renewed optimism every day, as if Santa Claus arrived overnight to pack them full of groceries. I grab at the battered box of Oreo O's, then stretch for the fridge door to get some milk... when... What? What did that CNN reporter just say?

I crane my neck to take in the TV, then shuffle my bare feet closer to it, my mouth hanging open, my neck still craning.

"It is believed the Princess's car was traveling at considerable speed and, according to eyewitnesses, was being chased by a number of paparazzo at the time of the collision."

Holy fuckin' shit!

I collapse into my worn couch and drag my security blanket all the way up to my chin.

"Holy. Fucking. Shit."

I stare, wide-eyed, at the TV — soaking in the episodic updates from the studio; the live broadcast from two pompous, even when mourning, royal experts in London; and the live links from a Parisian reporter who is gripping his microphone with pale knuckles just yards from the tunnel in which the crash reportedly happened — until my stomach growls, reminding me there's a dry bowl of Oreo O's waiting for me on the kitchen countertop.

I feel numb as I open the fridge before smelling the top of the milk carton. Then the image of the prettiest princess that's ever lived leaves the forefront of my thoughts momentarily, just so I can take a mental note to buy a carton of milk from Ladow's Market later today. Sometimes I remember these mental notes. But most times I don't. It's why I really should start learning to expect the cupboards to be bare every time I look inside them.

"Fuck me," I say to myself as I slouch back into the couch, a bowl of dry Oreo O's pressed against my bony chest.

When CNN opts for a commercial break, after their two hosts purse their lips in sorrow through the screen at me, I switch over to FOX News.

"It is believed she had been spending time in Paris with her rumored boyfriend Dodi Fayed, son of the billionaire owner of Harrods, Mohamed Al-Fayed."

"This is nuts," I say to nobody, spitting miniature shards of Oreo O's onto my blanket.

Then FOX News decides to take a commercial break too, and as I switch to the next channel to hear Sarah-Jane Zdanski teasing her new upcoming interviews, I think about ringing Mia, wondering if she's yet heard the news. She loves Princess Diana. Lov*ed* Princess Diana. Holy shit. I can't believe I'm talking about Princess Diana in the past tense. But I shouldn't disturb Mia. Not on the weekends. She has her children to—

Holy shit!

Children.

I sweep my security blanket away, tossing my bowl of dry Oreo O's to the carpet, and sprint as fast as I can, skidding from the kitchen-living room into my tiny bathroom.

"Please."

Please.

As I reach for the stick, I hold my eyes closed; a routine I've adopted over the past eighteen months of peeing on sticks and then waiting two minutes for the results to show.

"Please. Please," I whisper.

Okay, Lucy. On three, open your eyes.

"One... two..."

CAOIMHE LARKIN

"Jesus... is that it?"

"Don't use the Lord's name in vain, Caoimhe!" Mam snaps at me. Though I can tell she's just as let down by this as I am. Her eyes are squinting and her hands are getting all fidgety. She does that when she's uncomfortable — shuffles one hand inside, then outside the other over and over again. She did it for the entire flight over here.

"It's just a bloody triangular bundle of bricks," I say. Then I tut. A really loud tut; loud enough for Dad to hear it, even though he's on the other side of this... this... triangular bundle of bricks.

"The geographical center of the United States of America," Dad reads out loud, as if we didn't already know why we were stood around the triangular bundle of bricks. He has one foot on the edge of the monument, his forearm resting on his knee, and is squinting at the fading bronze plaque screwed into the bricks. "Lebanon, Kansas." Then he looks up at the stars and stripes flapping above us.

"Have to say, I agree with you, Caoimhe," he says, cocking his head around the flagpole to take in my moody face. "I thought there'd be a bit more fanfare. Y'know Americans... they normally have fanfare for anything. They even have bigger bloody St. Patrick's Day parades than we do at home. Sure, they call the baseball final the World Series... even though America is the only country that takes part. But for some reason, to mark the actual geographical center of the land of the whole country, all's they've got is... is this... this...."

"Triangular bundle of bricks," I say.

And then Dad laughs. Which makes Mam laugh. Which makes Aine laugh. And I know they're all waiting for me to join in with a laugh, just so we can be one big happy family again. But I don't. Cause I'm not in the humor of laughing. Not today. In fact, I may never be in the humor of laughing again for the rest of my whole shitty little life.

I'm not annoyed by the triangular bundle of bricks. I'm annoyed by everything else around it. I'm annoyed by the flapping of that bloody flag above our heads. I'm annoyed by the little prat wearing a baseball cap who hasn't stopped cycling around the triangular bundle of bricks on his rusty mountain bike while we stare at it like the blow ins we are. I'm annoyed by the smell of the air around here. I'm annoyed by the food. Everything's way too greasy. I'm annoyed by the fake "Have a nice days" we get everywhere we go. I'm annoyed by the fact that every road around here seems so flat. Like, really flat. It doesn't look right. No road back home in Tipperary is *this* flat. It just makes everything feel and look weird.

"Are we not even going to get a smile out of ye today?" Mam asks.

I huff... then flash her a smile. All of my teeth. All of my gums.

"A proper smile," Dad says. I drop the fake smile from my face, then shove my hands into the pockets of my hoodie. "You got that psychic reading in Esbon tonight, right? You love that sort of thing. That's something to look forward to, isn't it? Whatsername did you say to me? Funny name she had. Madam...."

"Madam Aspectu," Mam says, answering for me.

"Fuck sake," I mouth, just past my breath; past it enough for both of my parents, and my younger sister, to snap their faces toward me.

"Excuse me?" Dad says, raising his eyebrows.

"We're in the middle of nowhere," I say, taking my hands from my pockets and slapping them against the sides of my thighs.

"You're not in the middle of nowhere," Mam says. "You're in the middle of America. The greatest country in the world."

"Mam, look up and down this road... go on. Take a good look about yerself. There's nothing around here... not as far as our eyes can see. Does this look like the greatest country in the world to you? Does it? It's hardly the America we've watched on TV back home, is it? It's not New York. It's not LA. I'm hardly gonna bump into Jason Priestly round here, am I? I doubt he lives in Lebanon, Kansas." I slap my hands against the sides of my thighs again, and huff. "I mean.... I never even heard of Lebanon, Kansas before. I don't even know where in America Kansas is."

"It's in the middle," Aine says, pointing at the triangular bundle of bricks. And then Dad laughs, followed by Mam. I can't help myself this time. I snort out a cackle that I didn't want to come out. The little wench. She's only eleven years of age. And already smart as a whip. And as funny as a fart at a funeral. I love her. I love them all. I'd just rather love them all back home in Ireland rather than here... wherever here is... the bloody middle of middle America.

"Tell ye what," Dad says, throwing his arm around me and giving my shoulder a squeeze. "When you're going to your psychic reading tonight, why don't you take the wheel, huh? How about that?"

"Really?" I say, my voice all high-pitched. "What if the police see us?"

He squeezes me tighter.

"Dunno...." he shrugs. "I guess you'll just have to put your foot down."

I drive carefully. *Really* carefully. As if there are other cars on the road. Which there aren't. Not really. It's so bloody quiet round here, though I guess that makes it the perfect place for me to learn how to drive properly. It's certainly easier here than it is on the narrow, cobbled streets of Tipperary.

Dad has been holding on to the handle of the door with both

hands all the way to Esbon, but he hasn't said anything to panic me or annoy me like he usually does when I'm behind the wheel. He has promised me he'll buy me a car as soon as I turn sixteen. Which is only eight weeks away, now. Being able to drive at sixteen was the only cool thing about moving to America. I just pictured, in my head, being able to drive into school... and well, that was that. Who wouldn't want to drive to school? So, my mind was made up. I was finally won over.

Esbon seems to be a smaller town than Lebanon — which I wasn't sure was possible — so it doesn't take long for us to find the yellow-bricked bank we were directed to the back of by Madam Aspectu over the phone this morning.

I indicate, then pull over and stare at the little tent down the end of the back lane way.

"You stay in the car," I say to Dad. He holds his hands up immediately, as if he's being arrested. Then he offers me one of his cheesy dad smiles. I know he feels bad for me and Aine, because he knows he ripped us away from our lives. But that kinda makes me feel bad for him. I can understand why he did this. He has to live his life as much as we have to live ours. He couldn't have turned this opportunity down. And I should never have expected him to. Even if it was heart-breaking to leave my friends behind.

"Of course I'm staying in the car," he says. "You've made your intentions on that perfectly clear... numerous times, Caoimhe. Now, in ye go. Let's see what this Madam whatever-her-name-is thinks life has in store for you in America, huh?"

I huff out a sigh then offer him a wink and a grin. I know he doesn't believe in this psychic reading stuff 'cause he used to make fun of me back home when I would go and see Philomena for readings. But he's trying to act excited for me now because he wants me to be happy. He's desperate for me and Aine to have something to look forward to; a reason to be excited about our new lives in the middle of America.

I get out of the car and then take a look around myself as if I'm expecting to see anything other than flat roads filled with nothing. It really is so bloody quiet around here. Then I step slowly into the narrow lane way before walking toward the red curtains across the front of the tent, above which, I can now make out, is a chalkboard sign that reads: "Madam Aspectu."

"Hello," I say, inching closer to the sliver of a gap in the curtains.

Nothing.

"Hello," I say again, a bit louder this time.

"Is that you Kow-im-hay?" a high-pitched voice says, butchering the pronunciation of my name.

"It's eh... it's actually pronounced Kwee-Va," I say.

"Really?" the strange voice replies, even more high-pitched this time.

"It's eh... it's an Irish name," I tell her.

"Ah, yes. Well, my little Irish doll... why don't you just brush those curtains aside and step right in. Ma crystal ball is already bubbling for you."

MERIC MILLER

I bend over and rest my hands to my knees, just so I can take in a deep breath. Don't think I've ever ridden my bike so fast. Or so far. It took me forty minutes to get here—without stopping.

I'm still bent over and still trying to catch my breath, with my bike stood up against the yellow-brick wall at the back of the bank, when a woman sweeps open the curtains and rushes out; her eyes heavy, a tissue pressed against her nose.

She looks at me, then jogs quicker, leaving me alone to stare at the gap in the curtains. I walk closer and poke my nose in. It's dark inside. But she's sitting there with her eyes closed, a deck of cards fanned out on the table in front of her, a crystal ball that she probably bought at the two-dollar store sitting behind the cards. And, there's steam rising from a plugged-in machine in the far corner of the tent for some reason.

"Can I help you?" she says, without opening her eyes. Her voice is funny and high-pitched, like she's some cartoon character.

I take a step backward, pause, and blink my eyes a few times. Then I pick up the courage to take that one step forward again, poking my nose back through the gap in the curtains.

"I uh..." I walk through the curtains, to the sound of a bell jingling above me, and then I wave away the steam coming toward me. "I uh..."

"You're not here for a reading. I can tell," she says.

I raise an eyebrow. Maybe that crystal ball isn't from the two-dollar store after all.

"No. Not for a reading," I say. "Just looking for a favor, is all."

Her eyes open and, as they do, I have to take another step backward. They're black. Not just the pupils. The whole of her eyeballs are black.

"A favor you say?" she screeches. It doesn't sound funny this time. It sounds scary. "I don't believe I've listed favors as one of my services, boy."

"Well it's... it's ah... it's ah..."

"Speak boy!" she says. "I can tell you are a man of few words. My crystal ball is sayin' you practically mute."

I stare at the crystal ball, then back into her black eyes. *How'd she know I do all my talkin' inside ma head and not out through my mouth like everyone else does?*

"It's ah...."

"Stop stutterin' boy and tell me why you here if you not here fo' a readin'.

"It's ah. ..." She twists her face toward me, her black eyes widening. I take off my baseball cap and hold it against my chest. "It's about a reading. A reading you have scheduled in for later." I feel my palms get all sweaty, so I curl and dig my fingernails into them, just to stop myself from being such a pussy for once in my life. C'mon, Meric. You biked all the way here. Spit it out already. "She's a red-haired girl. I don't know her name. I saw her, y'see, down by the central monument in Lebanon. She's European judging by her accent... or maybe Canadian. Don't some Canadians talk really funny sometimes?" I wait for an answer. But her big black eyes just continue to stare through me. "Anyway..." I shake my hair. "We never get new girls round here and well... I overheard her down by the monument saying that she was coming to you for a reading tonight and I just wondered if... if you would do me a favor?"

She stands. Really slowly; the wooden seat she's sat in creaking and cracking as her heavy ass lifts from it.

"What's your name, boy?"

I cough. A fake cough. Then I wave more of the steam away from my face.

"Miller. Meric Miller."

"And you wish for me to do you what kind of favor, young Miller?"

"I uh... I need you to tell this girl that she needs a boyfriend. And that that boyfriend should be me. I know how girls work. If she thinks a psychic said it in a reading, then she'll believe it and then she'll just have to fall in love with me and she won't have a choice, and then I'll finally have a girlfriend and—"

"My boy," she says, holding her hand up. "I am a psychic. Not a matchmaker."

"I'll pay you," I say.

She sits her heavy ass back down on to her creaking chair and then taps her long fingernail against the tiny chalkboard on her table next to the crystal ball.

"Forty dollars? But where am I supposed to get forty dollars from?"

Her head shakes and as she sighs, she spreads her fingers wide on the table.

"Well how much money do you have?" she says, her voice changing; the scary high-pitchiness gone, replaced instead by a woman who sounds pretty much like my momma sounds. Normal. With a hint of irritation.

I shovel my hand into my jeans pocket and then drop all of my coins — as well as two empty candy wrappers — onto the table in front of her.

"That much," I say.

KAI CHAYTON

The key slides into the lock just as I'm putting on momma's lipstick and it makes me turn my head so sharply that the lipstick draws across my cheek.

Holy Hell. Poppa's home!

I'm still standing in front of the mirror, my body in shock, when the first step on our stairs creaks. So, I have to shake my head back to real life and find a place to hide. Quickly.

I move to run toward my bedroom, but he might see me racing across the landing. So I fall to my knees, lower my face to the carpet and then snake my way under Momma and Poppa's bed.

His leather shoes squeak as they walk across the landing toward the bedroom and when he enters, his shoes are all I can see of him. His black leather shoes, his black socks, the hem of his always too-short black pants.

He begins to whistle. A light tune that should offer a contrasting feeling to the manic thudding in my heart. But it's not helping me calm down. Of course it's not helping me calm down. If he sees me like this... Holy Hell, if he sees me like this...

I try to steady my sharp breaths as I press my cheek to the carpet, my mind racing as I stare at his shoes.

What's he doin' home this early? He's supposed to be at night church.

Then, he stops whistling, sighs deeply, and I see his knees

lower to the carpet. Holy Hell. He's bending down. He's heard me breathing. He's gonna see me...

A hand creeps under the bed, patting around while I hold a deep breath in my cheeks. I twist my head in the cramped space, to see what he's feeling around for. His tie! He forgot his tie for church. I must've dragged it under the bed with me when I snaked my way here to hide. I pinch it between my two fingers, then bring it closer to his patting hand.

"Ah got ya," Poppa says.

I hold my eyes closed in relief and let out a slow, grateful, silent sigh through my nostrils as he stands back upright.

He whistles again as he strolls out of the bedroom and begins to trot down the stairs. When I hear him reach the bottom, I snake out from under the bed, only for Momma's dress to catch against one of the slats. I hear it tear a little, just before the front door slams shut and the whistling stops.

"Damn it," I say, dragging the seam of the dress toward my face and squinting at it. It's nothing major. A split of two stitches inside the waistline. Momma won't notice. So, I flatten down the dress, steady my breathing after such a fright, and then walk toward the mirror in the corner of their bedroom. I look pretty in this. Prettier than Momma does. Though a lot of folk say me and Momma look alike. I guess I can see what they're saying sometimes. I have long black hair like she does; though a lot of native American men wear their hair long, so I'm hardly unique. But I do have high cheek bones and long eyelashes like Momma has too; a couple of feminine features on my face to match my feminine fashion tastes. It's just a shame I don't have the female genitalia to go along with it all, too. For something so small, my penis sure does cause me a big problem.

I push out a laugh when I look in the mirror and see my face. Then I suck on my thumb and begin to rub it along the lipstick mark smudged across my cheek.

"Holy Hell, Kai," I say to my reflection. "That was close."

LUCY DECKER

While he taps away at his keyboard, after offering me the deepest and rudest sigh I think I've ever been offered straight to my face, I distract myself from his frowning forehead by thinking about the mess back home.

I couldn't bring myself to clean it up last night. I was too upset. I should have left the mess as just another white pregnancy test snapped in two and lying on the tiles of my bathroom floor. But no. I had to pander to my rage by tearing down my shower bar, causing all of my shampoos and conditioners and bodywashes to tumble and crash to the tiles. I noticed when I brushed my teeth this morning that one of the shampoo bottles had burst at the bottom, and thick green liquid had formed a puddle under my sink. The thought of cleaning that mess up later is making my temple throb almost as much as the frowning of this ignoramus's forehead.

"Nope," he says after tapping ridiculously loudly against the keyboard in front of him, using just his two stubby forefingers. "There's no chance. You've been awarded your yearly increment already, Lucy. That's it. This isn't a place you can come crying to for a pay raise. It's not how it works in this profession."

"Firstly, Mister... Mister..."

"Thompson," he says with an eye roll.

"Yes... well, firstly Mr. Thompson, I am not crying, and I resent you even mentioning the word crying when that is literally an inaccurate description of what I'm doing right—"

"Well, not crying but..." He sweeps his hands like the ignoramus he is; as if a sweep of his hand is enough of an apology for his misogyny. He really is insufferable. An arrogant, ignorant little toad of a man, with tiny little hands that have tiny, stubby forefingers he can barely type with.

"Mr Thompson," I say, before letting a deep exhale release through my nostrils in an attempt to temper the rage bubbling inside of me. "I need a pay raise. It's for very personal reasons. If I don't get a pay raise, I'm not sure I'll be able to continue working here."

He sits back clasping his hands behind his head, before gently swinging side to side in his office chair, offering me his sweaty armpits.

"We simply can't afford to offer you a pay raise. Now, if you'd like to give your notice, I can detail the procedure for you and we can take it from there—"

"It doesn't matter, Thompson," I say, picking up my box of paperwork from his desk before spinning on my heels. "You just have a good day, huh?" I beam a sarcastic grin at him, then leave his office, slamming the door shut behind me as loudly as I can.

BRODY EDWARDS

Sarah-Jane Zdanski curls her thumbs into the top of my boxer shorts and yanks them down; down past my thighs, over my knees and out of only one foot, leaving them dangling from the other. Then she flicks her hair away from her perfect face and stares up at me. Those eyes. Big and bright; staring right into my soul as she gently lifts my throbbing cock away from my belly and begins to slowly run her hand up and down it.

"You're a filthy ho," I whisper.

She smiles and then, keeping eye contact with me, lowers her face, her mouth opening, before she takes me inside of her, her tongue slowly running around the rim of my helmet. Then she begins to lower and suck, as if she has been gasping for this blowjob as much as I have.

I grip the bedsheets with my left hand, and roll my eyes into the back of my head.

"Oh...I'm gonna cum," I whisper, gripping the bedsheets tighter. "I'm gonna... I'm gonna..."

"What the hell is going on in here?" Mom says, swinging my bedroom door open. "You're moaning before you're even out of bed this morning?"

I cross my legs as quickly as I can, grab a fistful of my bed cover and pull it over me.

"I uh... I'm uh... just watching the news," I say, sitting up against the steel rail at the head of my bed, dragging the duvet with me, and nodding toward the tiny TV in the corner of my room.

She stares at it, and as she does, I hold my eyes closed. Mortified. A cringe racing around my stomach. *She didn't see me... did she?*

"Watching the news? But the TV is paused. That's on VHS. What are you doing? Watching a recording of the news? Did you tape-record the news, Brody?"

"Gee, mom. Which one of those million questions do you want me to answer first?"

She stares at me, then back at the paused image of Sarah-Jane Zdanski with white lines of worn tape blinking just under her perfect jugs.

"That girl's blouses are way too low-cut for a news reporter," Mom says. Then she snatches at the boxer shorts dangling from my foot and picks up the dirty socks I wore yesterday from my bedroom floor. "Come on, Brody. Summer's over. Get your ass outta bed."

I pull back the covers as soon as she leaves my room, stare at my limp dick, then back up at Sarah-Jane paused on the tiny TV before mumbling to myself, "Fuck it. I'll do one later."

I try not to think about Sarah-Jane as I shower. I finish, get dressed, go downstairs and then I grab some OJ and a slice of toast before leaving the house without saying goodbye to Mom. She's used to it... us not talking. We've never fallen out or anything. It's just... well... I can never really think of anything I want to say to her. Fifteen-year- old boys don't tend to have too much in common with middle-aged moms. I love her and all that kinda thing. I just never tell her I love her. Same way she never tells me she loves me, even though I'm pretty sure she does. She picks up my stained boxer shorts and socks from my bedroom floor every morning. Surely nothing says "I love you" more than that.

"Dude, my mom walked in on me jacking off this morning," I tell Stevie as soon as he has stepped outside his house and we have perfected our handshake greeting.

"No way, man," Stevie says, adjusting the straps of his back-pack on his shoulders. "What happened?"

"I was whacking out..."

"To SJZ."

"Of course, to SJZ," I say, nodding, "and I was just about to squirt a whole juice carton-load up my stomach when the bedroom door sweeps open. 'Brody. Get up. Get up. Time for school.' I was like, 'Hey, Mom get the fuck outta my room,' y'know? Bitch never knocks. Anyway, get this, dude. She stares at the TV and I have Sarah-Jane Zdanksi paused... Y'know the one where she's wearing that green top that cuts right down to here?" I point to my belly button.

"Yeah... yeah." Stevie says. "Oh man, I've jerked off to that a hundred times. Maybe a thousand. I dunno. So did your mom... did she, like, did she know what you were doing? Where was yo dick, dude?"

"I'd pulled the duvet over me when she walked in. I've no idea if she knows what I was doing. She just stared at the TV, stared at me and then I was all like, 'Yo, get the fuck outta ma room, bitch,' y'know?"

Stevie holds his hand to his mouth and giggles into it like Michael Jackson giggles. He only ever giggles like that around me. It's straight up, deep, heavy man-laughs and slaps on the back around everybody else. Stevie's got a reputation to live up to. He's supposed to be the man of the students. The *main* man. Our football team's quarterback. You can't be heard giggling like Michael Jackson if you're the QB.

"Y'know who I jerked off to this mornin'?" he says to me as we turn on to Walnut Street.

"Not SJZ?"

"Not Sarah-Jane this morning, no," he says, shaking his head.

"Was it um... one of the chicks from *Baywatch*?"

"Uh-uh," he says, still shaking his head.

"One of the Spice Girls? Baby Spice?"

"Uh-uh." His head still hasn't stopped shaking.

"Gee, uh... Princess Diana?"

He punches my arm.

"Dude. She just fuckin' died, man. You think I'm sick?"

"I dunno. She just popped into my head because she was all over the news yesterday. Have you uh..." I lean into him. "Have you ever jerked off to Princess Di... ya know when she was alive?"

"Nah, dude," he says. "You?"

"Nah... too flat for me. And high-class. Not my type at all. Anyway... tell me — who *did* you jerk off to this morning?"

He stops walking, holds a hand to my chest, and grins.

"Toni. Braxton."

"Toni Bra— but she's black. I ain't never whacked off to a black chick."

"I'm all for equality, bro," he says. Then he slaps me on the back and laughs one of them deep man-laughs. Only because we have stopped where Walnut Street merges on to Grove Avenue and other students strolling from that direction are probably, by now, within earshot of us. "Think there'll be any new chicks in our class this year?" he says out of the corner of his mouth when we continue walking.

I raspberry through my lips.

"Doubt it, dude. Been the same faces ever since we were in kindergarten, hasn't it? Ain't nobody new ever moves to Lebanon. All folks ever do around here is move out."

"No wonder we gotta jerk off to celebrities all the time. Ain't nobody around here worth wasting a tug on, right?"

I laugh. A big husky man-laugh. But only because lots of students are, by now, definitely within earshot as we approach the school pathway. We both have reputations to keep up. Stevie may be the QB. But I'm the left tackle. We only each look good if we both look good.

"Think I'm gonna have to find time to jerk off in the restroom later," I whisper to him.

"Wouldn't be the first time," Stevie says, spraying one of his husky man-laughs into my face. Then we pull open the double doors to begin our lives as tenth graders by doing our cool hand-shake thing again.

CAOIMHE LARKIN

I sit, with me legs crossed, on a hard plastic chair, holding the forms the principal's assistant handed to me, while all of the other students, who know where they're going, push through the double front doors before splitting off in all manner of directions.

I try to take as many of them in as I can, without being caught staring; the two pretty girls who giggled their way up the stairs; the tall Goth with the crazy haircut who stared at me like I was an alien. Though I guess, to him, I am. The two dudes with the square heads who did a stupid handshake as soon as they stepped inside. I wondered immediately if either of their names had two M's in it. That's what Madam Aspectu told me my next boyfriend would have. "Two M's," she said, "He will be the one." The teacher rushing by with an apple clenched between her teeth, carrying a box filled with paperwork; the tiny geeky kid who must be at least fourteen to be coming here, but who only looks as if he's ten. God love him. I hope he doesn't get eaten alive in here. Jeez, I hope I don't get eaten alive in here.

Though I think I was more nervous walking to school this morning than I am now. It's relaxed me a bit to finally get inside; to feel a sense of the place. I might actually like it here. The building's a lot brighter and much more modern than my school was back home. And the teachers look like normal people —well... in that they're not nuns with faces so wrinkled under their habits that they look like prunes.

I look back over my shoulder to where the principal's assistant is sitting, then cough to try to get her attention. But her eyes seem glued to whatever it is that's on her computer screen. She said she'd come over to me when I'd finished filling out these forms so she could show me to my first class. But that must've been at least ten minutes ago now.

As more students pull open the double doors and walk into the reception area, I stare at the faces of the boys in search of a face that looks as if it might belong to somebody with two M's in their name. Then a tall girl with cropped blonde hair strolls by me and it makes me think of Princess Diana. A little ball rolls itself around my stomach. It's so sad. I can't believe it. It was on the news all day yesterday. That's what they do in America. They have news channels that are on *all* day, every day. Even through the night, when we're asleep. Back home, the news comes on at six p.m. every evening for half an hour and the whole country tunes in. That's it. You get your news at six. There's a repeat of that and an update at nine p.m. But if you miss it, you miss it. Tough luck. Here, it seems as if people can't breathe unless they're being updated on the news every other minute. And the news happens to be on every other bloody channel, too, when I'm flicking through the TV.

"Cow-Im-Hay," a voice calls out.

I turn and smile politely at the principal's assistant.

"It's pronounced Kwee-Va, the MH together makes a V sound."

Her face squishes up.

"A V sound?"

I shrug one shoulder.

"Yeah... we've only been using the alphabet for, oh-I-dunno, about a thousand years in Ireland," I say. "So maybe it's us who've got our sounds all in a muddle... how many years has America been using the alphabet again?"

She raises an eyebrow at me, clearly not humored by my sarcasm. Dad actually said that about America on the flight over here. He said they don't really do sarcasm. But I thought it was a bit ironic that he said that, because he was watching episodes of *Seinfeld* on the plane, and breaking his shite laughing.

"Follow me," she says. And then she turns and almost races away as though she doesn't want me to catch up with her.

I pace after her, down a well-lit wide corridor with lockers on either side — a luxury we don't get in Irish schools for whatever reason — before she turns to walk up a winding staircase.

"Your first period is in room 2C — it's Miss Decker's room. She'll be teaching you American History. Perhaps you should ask her how long America has been using the alphabet... Oh, here she is now," the principal's assistant says. And then the teacher who raced by me a few minutes ago with an apple clenched tightly between her teeth while she was carrying a box of papers offers me an eye smile.

"Miss Decker, this is..."

"Caoimhe," Miss Decker says, holding her hand out for me to shake.

"Yes," I reply, sounding as surprised as I am impressed.

"I have family from Ireland, so when I read your name as my new student I had to give them a call, just to make sure I got the pronunciation right."

"You nailed it," I say, offering her a big smile. I already like her. She looks... well, she looks nice. Warm. Certainly warmer than a prune-faced nun whose lip-corners never so much as think about turning upward.

"Guys, this is Caoimhe," Miss Decker shouts out, leading me into the classroom. "Her name won't look like that when you see it written down, but trust me, that's the correct pronunciation. Her and her family have just moved to Lebanon from Ireland."

I look at all of the gormless faces staring back at me in what must be one of the most awkward silences I've ever experienced. This was literally the reason I was nervous walking to school this morning... this introduction. Me standing at the top of the class, while all of the students check me out, and realizing, as I'm sure they are right about now, that I am about as average looking as any girl possibly can be. I glance by the two square heads I saw doing a silly handshake in the reception area earlier sitting in the front row, whispering and giggling. I bet they've already decided I'm not pretty enough for them. Five is probably the rank they've both agreed I should have. Which is fine by me. Unless one of them has two M's in their name. Cos if that is the case, then I guess he's my next boyfriend regardless of what mark out of ten he has just given me.

"Eh... where'll I sit?" I say when the staring goes on for so long that I'm sure my face is turning the same color as my hair.

"You'll uh... you'll have to sit in that back corner," Miss Decker says, pointing her whole hand to the back of the class. As I walk toward the vacant chair I notice I'll be sitting next to a boy with a mop of so much black hair that it covers his eyes, and who has acne spots scarring across both of his cheeks.

He doesn't look at me as I sidle in beside him. As if he's shy. Which is odd. I'm supposed to be the newbie. I should be the one not wanting to make eye contact with you, mate. Then, as Miss Decker begins, by welcoming everybody back for a brand new year and asking them to fill in the blank lines on the front of the new notebooks she had left on each desk, I take a peek around the room and do a quick count. Twelve desks, each with two students. Twenty-four in total. A smaller class of students than I ever had back in Ireland. I stare at the two square heads again who are still whispering and giggling, then I inch up in my chair to see over their broad shoulders at the names they have written onto the front of their notebooks before plunking back down to my seat. Darn it. No M's in either of their names. So, I reach down, take a pen out of the front pocket of my bag and begin to fill out the front of the notebook Miss Decker left on my desk.

Caoimhe Larkin
American History
Miss Decker

As I'm placing the cap back on to my pen, I glance at the quiet, acne-scarred boy next to me, to see if he will at least, by now, acknowledge the new student sat beside him. But he doesn't lift his gaze from the edge of the desk. And that's when I look down at his notebook, and notice the name he has scribbled messily across the top.

Meric Miller

TWO

SHE WAS SO FAR AWAY that she had to yell her thank you toward the driver as she swung her legs out the open door of the limousine.

Phil followed, scooting and squeaking himself along the cream leather lounge seat behind her, without thanking the driver; not because he didn't want to, but because saying as little as possible was how Phil went about his days. It was as if his throat was controlled by a battery that was constantly running low, and so he only used it when he felt it absolutely necessary to do so.

When he finally lifted his heavy frame out of the limousine, he stood next to Sarah-Jane on the sidewalk and followed her line of vision to the very top of the sixty-story building standing proud in front of them. The sign above the revolving doors glowed an orange logo well-known to the entire population of America. CSN. The third most popular news network in the country. In fact, it had just been confirmed as the fastest growing news network in the country the month Sarah-Jane Zdanski signed a lucrative contract with them. In the first quarter of 1997, CSN found itself in sixth-place in the daily overall ratings. But by the time Sarah-Jane arrived — in the final quarter of 1997 — the network was rapidly closing in on top dogs CNN and FOX, who had held on to numbers one and two for almost two decades.

Sarah-Jane hooked her arm inside Phil's and pulled him tight against her as they glared at the famous logo.

"Ready, buddy?" she asked.

Phil nodded, and then they both — as if they were in a three-legged race — entered the revolving doors together, hip to hip, shoulder to shoulder.

"Ah, Miss Zdanski," a pockmarked face young man said, racing toward them as soon they entered the marbled lobby. "I was told you'd be here just after two p.m. Did you ah... did you manage to see the billboard in Times Square?"

Sarah-Jane stopped and squinted, trying desperately to not stare at the pockmarks splashed across the young man's cheeks.

"And you are...?"

"Thomas. Thomas Ferrie. I'm an assistant researcher on your show. I was introduced to you last week when you came in for a meeting."

"Oh," Sarah-Jane said, offering a grimaced smile. "Sorry. I met so many new faces and heard so many new names last week that—"

"It's understandable," Thomas said, nodding his head.

"Tell me, Thomas," Sarah-Jane said. "Have *you* seen the billboard in Times Square?"

"Not in Times Square itself," Thomas said. "Not yet, anyway. But I did see the artwork before it was approved."

"And let me ask you this, Thomas. Do you think I should be smiling on that billboard?"

"*Pfft...* I think you look amazing on it," Thomas said, sounding, to Sarah-Jane, annoyingly diplomatic.

"Just doesn't feel right for me to be smiling. Not today," Sarah-Jane said. Thomas didn't offer any further opinion on the subject, and instead lead both Sarah-Jane and Phil to the large gold-painted elevator double doors at the back end of the lobby, where he held the key card hanging from his neck against a sensor.

The mirror in the elevator was so large that it reflected all three of them head-to-toe as they entered. Thomas pressed at the number 55 on the large silver panel screwed into a marble wall, and after an initial clunk and a stuttering vibration, the elevator began to rise with a purr.

The walls that greeted them when the elevator doors finally slid back open were wallpapered with the orange CSN logo, and as they walked along the hallways — hallways that seemed to get darker and narrower the further they walked — Sarah-Jane took in the portraits of the well-known faces who had fronted the network over the years. Jared Astley. Monica Sleight. Jon Burrows. Matt Lauer. Matt had left CSN three years prior to take up the much-coveted position at *The Today Show* on rival network NBC, but was still considered somewhat a legend around these dark hallways, despite persistent whispers from some quarters. Sarah-Jane drummed her long fingernails against Matt's portrait as she passed it. Phil knew why. Matt Lauer was Sarah-Jane Zdanski's celebrity crush. It wasn't just his chiseled jawline or his narrow, smoldering eyes that took her fancy. It was the ease in which he presented. Talent was what turned Sarah-Jane Zdanski on.

"The studio is all set up, Miss Zdanksi," Thomas said as he continued to lead Sarah-Jane and Phil, who was still carrying his boss's purse under his arm, through the maze of dark hallways.

"Can we see it?" Sarah-Jane asked.

"Sure."

Thomas spun on his heels, then led them back through the hallways they had just walked down, past the portraits of legendary CSN anchors and to the other side of the golden double doors of the elevator before eventually coming to a stop behind a large black curtain.

"Just through there," he said. "I'm gonna go find Howie Laine and let him know you're here."

Sarah-Jane winked at Thomas, then she reached for the curtain and pulled it across.

Even though she had seen the set almost finished when she called by for a production meeting the week prior, she still gasped.

"I love it," she said. Then she slapped her hands to her face again and screeched into them.

Phil produced one of his throat chuckles, but in truth he wasn't bowled over by the set. In fact, he felt somewhat let down by it. Though he wouldn't say as much to Sarah-Jane. His assumptions had led him to believe that the major networks such as CSN or FOX or CNN or MSNBC would produce sets that looked as if they belonged on a Broadway stage. It was a disappointment for him to realize they were no bigger than the tiny, dank studios he had worked on at his local PBS network back in Kansas—the studio in which he first met and fell in love with Sarah-Jane Zdanski. News sets, to him, always looked like a well-lit desk and backdrop that seemed out of place among the mess either side of them.

The set, as was always the case, was perfectly lit and the name Zdanski blinked at them from a light-blue neon sign on the dark back wall. But for Phil, the neon sign aside, this easily could've been one of many small PBS studios he had been so familiar with. It smelled of the same wood-chipping scent as the PBS studios — as if all sets shared an open workspace with a carpentry firm. And it was surrounded by dark shadows on either side of the light, which could easily be mistaken for a trash area for large opened cardboard boxes, sheets of plastic wrapping and a gaggle of employees who didn't quite look like they were doing much. In front of Phil and Sarah-Jane, as they stood in the shadows of the perfectly lit studio, spread a web of thick cables that raced off in all manner of directions along the dark, dusty floor.

"You love it?" Sarah-Jane asked, bumping her hip off Phil's.

Phil bumped hers back. And then she placed both of her hands to her face so she could squeal into them again.

While she glided across the web of cables toward the stage, Phil tripped and stumbled his way behind her. And as she stepped up onto the stage, the men responsible for the constant smell of fresh wood chippings in the shadows to one side immediately paused their chatter and began to stare. Phil took them in as they squinted at his boss, and when one of them noticed him eyeballing them, he whispered something to his colleagues and then they all got back to scratching the backs of their necks while chatting about nothing much at all.

Sarah-Jane stood, grinning, under the neon sign that displayed her family name and then took her camera out of her pocket.

"Here, Phil," she said, "take another one for the scrapbook."

Phil, as all good puppy dogs do, obeyed his mistress without hesitation and took the camera from Sarah-Jane, wound it, then peered through the square lens to snap his boss making a peace sign in front of her own name.

"Another one to send back to your Ma and Pa in Kansas," Phil said, handing the camera back to her.

Sarah-Jane squinted at her sidekick then shrugged her shoulders before sitting in her brand new leather chair. She got to choose this one from a shortlist of three. For some reason, that decision was in the contract she had signed weeks prior without it ever popping up in conversation. She didn't know until she saw a tag hanging from the chair last week when she stopped by to see the set for the very first time that it had arrived at a cost of twenty thousand dollars.

"Sure don't feel like a twenty K chair," she said, bouncing her back off it as she sought the level of comfort she assumed twenty thousand dollars should bring.

Somebody coughed lightly behind Phil and when he shuffled his bulky frame around, moving as slowly as he always does, he saw one of the workmen who had been ogling his boss moments prior.

"I just wanted to say best of luck for your interviews tonight, Sarah-Jane," the man said.

Phil growled softly in the back of his throat as Sarah-Jane rose from her expensive leather chair to make her way toward the man.

"Thank you. Do you work here?" she said, placing her hand inside his.

"Sometimes. I'm just a tradesman, so when they need new studios built, we get called in."

"Well, thank you for helping build my new studio."

The tradesman fawned and laughed, unable to hide how unbelievably attractive he found the woman whose hand he was still holding was. She looked attractive in the teaser ads he had seen over the past couple of weeks, but up this close, inches from him, she was a knockout. As his eyes locked into Sarah-Jane's, the curtain over his shoulder swept open and in walked a tall, skinny man dressed in an overly loud patterned shirt.

Howie Laine came across more camp than any man Sarah-Jane had ever encountered back home in Kansas, yet he wasn't gay, even if most of those he had worked with over the years assumed he was. He was actually married to a sexually satisfied woman who got it at least five times a week. On occasions five times a night, although those days seemed as if they were in the past. Howie wore a loud shirt most days, as well as John Lennon-esqe round glasses that were so thin they seemed rather redundant perched on the narrow bridge of his long skinny nose.

He embraced Sarah-Jane with an elaborate hug, as if they were long-separated best friends and not two new associates who had only met each other for the first time one week ago, then dismissed the handsome tradesman with a sweep of his hand.

"You guys should've been finished three days ago. Watch'all still doing here?"

"We are all done," the tradesman said, "we're just clearing out now."

Then the tradesman slumped off, back into the shadows of the studio to where his colleagues were waiting for him in a huddle.

"Bullshit," Howie whispered to Sarah-Jane, "those guys were just hanging around to see you."

"Phil," Sarah-Jane said, "meet Howie Laine—he's the exec producer of our show."

"Ah, you must be Philip Meredith. You have a producer credit on the show, right? We haven't yet met. Pleasure to meet you." Phil shook Howie's hand, but offered no words. "Anyway," Howie said, turning back to Sarah-Jane, "this is so exciting. I can't wait for tonight." He threw his cuff away from his watch with a flamboyant flick of his left wrist. "Just over four hours till we're live. Whaddya think of the finished studio?"

"I love it," Sarah-Jane replied.

"Yeah," Howie said, nodding, "to me, they all look the same. Anyway...," he motioned to the stage, where Sarah-Jane's twenty thousand dollar chair was glowing under a strong light alongside a row of cheaper chairs that ran away from hers but along a narrow desk that looked a little like a sausage in how it curved. It was from this sausage-shaped desk that Sarah-Jane would question her first guests later that night.

She sat in her expensive chair, and while Howie sat in the cheap one next to hers, Phil took up a standing position among the web of cables in the shadows, with his arms folded and his boss's purse resting between his New Balance trainers.

"You haven't heard the projected audience number for tonight, have you?" Howie said, tapping his fingers together repeatedly to produce a silent applause.

Sarah-Jane's lips stretched into a beautiful smile.

"No. Is it big? Are we expecting a big audience?"

Howie formed a steeple by pressing his fingers together and then lifted it to his chin.

"Oh, I shouldn't say. I shouldn't create any anxiety for you ahead of going live."

Sarah-Jane sat forward in her chair.

"Is it bigger than the usual seven p.m. audience?"

Howie slapped his hands back down to his knees.

"Oh yeah. Higher than our usual seven p.m. Sarah-Jane," he said, "it's higher than any audience number we've ever had at CSN."

"What? Get the hell outta here," she said.

"I'm serious. All the projections point to this show being the most-watched show in CSN history. In fact, it's likely to be the second-most watched show across the whole nation this year... apart from the Super Bowl, of course."

"And what about... what about the viewing figures for, like, Princess Diana's funeral?" Sarah-Jane said, shaking her head and squinting in disbelief.

"Well, that was news for everybody wasn't it?" Howie said. "Every news channel had that story, so the audience was split. But this... this is exclusive content... and America is hungry for it. America is hungry for you."

Sarah-Jane slapped her hands to her face, but she didn't squeal into them this time. Instead she just subtly shook her hair and soaked in her reality.

"But you're not gonna tell me the figure?"

Howie winked, shook his head, then tapped her on the knee — a move that made Phil subtly growl — before he reached to the back pocket of his jeans from where he produced a tiny, but ragged, notepad.

"I won't tell you the figure, because I was told not to. But I know Walter Fellowes is particularly excited and I ain't ever heard of him being excited before. He called down to my office earlier today. Says he wants to have dinner with you."

"Today?"

"Uh-huh."

"Where?"

"Up in his office. It's only five more floors up."

"Oh," Sarah-Jane said.

"And he wants you in wardrobe before dinner."

"*Before* dinner?" Sarah-Jane said, her eyebrows narrowing. "But that'll be hours before we go live."

Howie shrugged his shoulders, then licked his thumb so he could flick through the pages of his notebook.

"He's Walter Fellowes," he said. "Anyway, what else was it I had to tell you?" He whistled as he continued to flick through the pages while Sarah-Jane took the time to glance at Phil. He was still peering at them from the shadows, his boss's purse resting by his feet. "Oh, yeah. We've got the next three shows booked. You hear?"

"Nope," Sarah-Jane said, snorting out a laugh.

"Next week, we've got a panel that consists of William Cohen —he's Bill Clinton's defense secretary. Newt Gingrich is also confirmed. And we are waiting to hear back from Al Gore's representatives... but all the signs are good. That'll be an incredible second show to follow this one."

"Hmm... hmm," Sarah-Jane said, nodding. She already knew the second show would focus on the political trial of Ramzi Yousef who had been suspected of bombing the World Trade Center some four years prior, in the spring of 1993. It was just a matter of who the researchers could assemble as the best panel of guests to discuss such a topic.

"And then, on show number three, you're gonna be interviewing..." Howie raised his eyebrows and then mirrored Sarah-Jane by swinging left to right in his chair.

"Go on..." Sarah-Jane said.

"Six of the cast of *ER*"

Sarah-Jane gasped.

"Including Clooney?"

Howie sucked on his own lips, then popped them open while nodding his head.

"Including Clooney."

"Holy shit!" Sarah-Jane said. "I love him."

"Meh... he's just another John Stamos. But *ER* is the biggest show in America right now, so it's quite the coup."

Sarah-Jane placed both hands over her face and squealed as loudly as she could into them.

"Hear that, Phil?" she shouted into the darkness. "I'm gonna be interviewing George Clooney."

Phil shuffled his heavy frame slowly onto the stage, making a heavy clunk, then nodded his head once at his boss.

"Do you not speak, Phil?" Howie asked.

Sarah-Jane discreetly reached under the desk to touch Howie's knee, and when he glanced at her, she subtly shook her head. It was becoming abundantly clear to Howie that questions to Phil weren't going to be answered.

"Anywhooo," Howie said, standing his streaky figure upright under the glare of the studio lights, "we gotta nail this first show. You ready to go through the notes on each of tonight's guests?"

Sarah-Jane swiveled back in her chair so that her notes were staring up at her.

"You betcha!" she said.

BRODY EDWARDS

Stevie squints over his shoulder at her, then shakes his head.

"Nah-huh, dude. She may be fresh meat, but she ain't hot meat. I wouldn't touch her with your cock, bro."

I shrug.

"Me neither, dude. Do any guys like chicks with red hair?"

He turns around, his face all scrunched up.

"Dunno, dude. What about Ginger Spice?"

"Oh yeah." I say. "Great jugs."

We've been back in school sitting beside each other in every class — because we purposely chose all the same classes as each other — dismissing all the chicks we can think of from school that we don't wanna have sex with because they're just not hot enough for us. Stevie and me don't just talk about sex. We do it, too. Three different chicks I've had sex with — Lily Newhart, Jessica Downes and a girl from Esbon called Claire whose last name we never found out. Stevie's had sex with her too. All she wanted was Stevie's Walkman. If he gave it to her, she said she'd both let us do it with her. So we did. Separately, of course. She was sixteen, too. A year older than us. It was so awesome to do it with someone who knew what they were doing. In fact, that is really the only time I've ever done it for real. When I was with Lily and Jessica, none of us knew what we were doing and I'm not quite sure if anything went in anywhere. But we did try. So I count it as sex... I guess.

"I dunno," he whispers to me when Decker turns around to write on the chalkboard. "There's just no girls at this school I wanna bang no more, ya hear me, dude?"

I nod my head and fold my fingers up into a ball so he can bump me.

"Totally," I say, before leaning back in my chair, stretching my hands high above my head.

"They're all too easy anyway," he whispers. "If you're the quarterback and the left tackle on the school football team, then all the chicks are just automatically into you, ya know? There's no challenge in it for me and you."

"Yeah, yeah," I say, before letting a little burp jump from the back of my throat.

"Boys!" Decker calls out, raising her eyebrow at us.

I've jerked off thinking about Decker before. I don't know why. She looked hot one day. It was actually the day she stayed back with me after school just before our end of ninth grade finals to teach me something about the Watergate scandal that the thought of fucking her brains out popped into my head. I'd never seen her that way before. Decker's not sexy. Or hot. It's just I got horny when she sat next to me that day. So when I got home, I went straight to my bedroom and jerked off thinking about her. I came pretty quickly, too. But I never told Stevie about it. Cos he'd just think it was pretty weird to jerk off to Decker. Anyway, when I got into school the next day and looked at her, I couldn't believe I had wasted a jerk on her. She's super cool and all, and funny, for a teacher. But she's not hot. I coulda had that jerk about Pamela Anderson. Or Sarah-Jane Zdanski. Instead, I wasted it on a teacher as plain looking as a woman can get. I sometimes wonder how long we'll jerk off for. Will we still be doing it when we're eighty? Or is it just something you do all the time as a teenager? I wonder if my Dad still jerks off. What's he now? Forty-two? Forty-three? I wonder if he finds the time to jerk off while he's over in Iraq doing... well, whatever the hell it is he is doing over in Iraq. He sleeps in a tent. I know that much. With one other solider. So, I can't imagine they find it easy to jerk off. Though maybe by that age, men don't give a shit... so they just whack their dicks out in front of each other and jerk away. Who knows? I guess I'll find out when I'm older.

"Tell ya what?" Stevie says, leaning into me and whispering while Decker goes on and on about what we'll be learning this term. "Why don't we each pick out a chick as a dare for the other one. We've already had sex with the hottest girls at school and there's not much meat left. You choose one for me to have sex with. And I'll choose one for you."

"Really?" I say, a little too loudly; loud enough for Decker to spin back around from the chalkboard to eyeball us again.

"Sorry, Miss Decker," I say, holding my hand up.

When she turns back around and continues to talk about media or whatever it is she's talking about, Stevie leans into me again.

"We'll give a time limit, okay? You chose a chick for me and I have to have sex with her by the end of October."

I grin. That's a fucking great idea.

"Cool," I say, then I hold my fist to him and he bumps me again before I begin to look around the room.

"It can't be the goth," he says, when he notices me eyeball Vanessa.... "And it can't be Wendy the hippo either," he says when my gaze flicks to the fattest chick in the room. "But anybody else... go on. Choose one."

"Her then," I say, flicking my head backward.

He stares over his shoulder.

"Who? Irish?"

"Yep," I whisper.

"Deal," he says, holding out his fist for me to bump. "Now, my turn to choose one for you."

"Not the Goth," I say. "And not Wendy either."

"Her," he says, stretching his finger towards the chalkboard.

LUCY DECKER

Stevie and Brody giggle into their hands as they leave my classroom. They sure do make me laugh, those two. Fifteen going on six. And both about as smart as a bloodhound with no nose. I wonder what they're up to now. I turned around from the chalkboard earlier to see Stevie pointing at me. And then they both just convulsed into laughter. I've been long since done with trying to second-guess what fifteen-year-old boys talk about when my back is turned, but I am seriously starting to worry about the evolution of man. And by man, I literally mean *man*. Men. Boys. I've been teaching tenth grade for eleven years. I'm pretty certain fifteen-year-old boys are getting more and more regressive as each year passes.

"Oh, Principal Klay," I call out as I catch a glimpse of his brown beard in among the stampede of students changing classrooms.

He pauses, probably taking a moment to roll his eyes, before turning to face me and offering a sterile smile.

"I know you've been wanting to see me Miss Decker, it's just that this new year has gotten off to such a frantic start and I'm spinning so many plates. I really must rush to give this assembly..."

"I won't keep you long, Principal Klay," I say, noticing his beard has grayed a little over the summer. "It's just..." I say and then nod my head into my classroom. He looks up and down the hallway at the students rushing by, and then enters my room while producing an obvious sigh through his nose. "I spoke with Mister... Mister... what's his name again? The man who looks after the school accounts?"

"George Thompson," Klay says.

"Yeah, Thompson. It was about a pay raise."

"Oh now, Miss Decker," Klay says, immediately looking uncomfortable. "I don't get involved in discussions with staff here at Median High about salaries. And pay raises really are not a conversation for right now—"

"Principal Klay, I'm only mentioning it to you because I need the money for a very personal reason. A reason I would be uncomfortable opening up to you about. But you can be rest assured it's very personal and means the world to me. I just—"

"I'm sorry Miss Decker," he says, backing away. "If Mr. Thompson says there's no money in our budget for a pay raise, then there simply is no money. He deals with the school accounts. So he... he... *actually*... that reminds me." Klay steps toward me. "Mr. Thompson is currently looking at the accounts to see how much the school can supplement the trip to Europe."

"Trip to Europe?" I say, my eyebrows dipping, aware Klay has already skilfully averted the subject of a pay raise.

"Yes. It's all top secret for now. And it's not going to be officially announced for a few more weeks. But Median High was picked from the State lottery to send thirty students to England, France and Italy for twelve days at the end of October."

"Cold in Europe in October," I say, while feigning a shiver. He stares at me.

"Yes, well...," he pauses, literally to allow the bomb of my joke to explode in the silence. "I was wondering, this morning, which teachers would be best utilized traveling with the students, and well... I would like to formally invite you to be part of the trip to Europe... what do you think, Miss Decker?"

I want to say I'll think about it. That my request for a pay raise can't simply be won over by the promise of an overseas trip. But I don't. Because I know the adult places will be snapped up by other teachers as soon as the trip is officially announced. And I haven't had a vacation in I-dunno-how-long.

"Sure," I say nodding.

He places a hand to my shoulder which feels grossly uncomfortable.

"It might do you good to get away from your..." he pauses again and leans in further, his beard almost tickling my cheek, "personal problems."

Then he leaves my classroom, shutting the door tightly behind himself and drowning out the buzz of the students.

WENDY CAMPBELL

I grab her around the waist, leaning her heavy breasts over my right shoulder, and then begin to lift, using all of my strength. She groans twice, and screeches once. That's all she has the energy for. She's been heavy her whole life, has Momma. Same as me. But nobody ever had to pull her out of a wheelchair before and try to lay her to bed. When I have her squeezed so tight against me that I'm sure I won't drop her, I spin, and heave her onto the makeshift bed that me 'n' Sally prepared this mornin'. She groans again when she lands on her back, then slowly opens her eyes to look up at me.

"Thank you," she mouths.

I fake a smile at her, then look up at Sally. My younger sister ain't smiling, that's for sure. Course she ain't. Poor girl will prolly never smile again her whole life.

"Can you, uhm..." I call to Sally, "grab one of the small towels and dampen it with cool water for me?"

Sally stares at Mom, then races herself into our bathroom.

"You're home and comfortable now, Momma," I say as I pull the bed sheets over her, tucking 'em under her chin.

I remove the scarf from her head, slowly, to relieve her sweating, bald head. Then I press my palm to the sweat and lean forward so Momma can't see my face... just so I can take a moment to close my eyes and wish all of this wasn't real life.

"Here ya go," Sally says, appearing behind me, holding out a small gray towel that she has dampened so much the water is showering to the carpet. But I don't yell at her. Course I don't. Being yelled at is the last thing poor Sally needs right now.

I fold the towel up, then rest it to mom's sweating forehead before I shuffle my heavy frame so my ass can rest on the edge of the makeshift bed.

Me and Sally talk about fun times we remember, like Christmases and birthdays—conversations we know Momma would like us to talk about, even though she's too exhausted to join in. We discuss what we remember of Lisa and Jason's wedding. And we talk about that Christmas Sally found a Betty Spaghetty doll under our tree and almost screamed the house down.

"You best," Momma finally says, before stopping for breath, "get yo selves to school tomorrow. I be fine."

Then she closes her eyes. As she falls into a heavy sleep, I remain sitting with my big ass on the edge of her makeshift bed, just so I can stare at her heavy breasts, to make sure they keep risin' up, and down.

It's only my second day in school since tenth grade started two weeks ago. I don't even have a pen, let alone a note from Momma which Principal Klay is insisting I should have.

"It's no good you turning up whenever you feel like it," Principal Klay snarls at me.

"I'm sorry. I can't help it if I'm ill," I reply. "I've had a nasty cold. Probably flu. My Momma thinks it was flu, Principal Klay."

He raises an eyebrow.

"Just make sure you have a note from your mother confirming your absence. I want it handed into my office first thing tomorrow morning, okay?"

"'Kay," I say.

Then he strolls off while still eyeballin' me as if he knows I am lyin' to him. He heads to the back of the stage, while I rush into the assembly hall to find maself a seat. I stare around the room, wonderin' who I can ask a big favor of. I don't really speak to that many students. Maybe I can ask Kai. I know he ain't the coolest guy in the world. But at least he won't ask too many questions. I suck on my teeth, and am about to stroll toward Kai when she catches the corner of my eye. Or at least her bright orange hair does.

"Hey," I say, offering the new girl my widest smile.

"Hey," she mouths back to me, waving her hand.

I walk down a row of chairs and then up another before I sit my big ass next to her.

"I was ah..." I whisper as I scratch at the back of my neck, "wondering if you could... ah, sorry... do you mind stepping to the back of the assembly room?" I ask, only because Miss Decker and Mr. Charlton are sitting in the row ahead of us and I'm afraid they might hear what I have to say.

The Irish chick looks over her shoulder at the gray wall covered in posters of historical figures she prolly never even heard of, and then shrugs her shoulders.

"Sure," she says in her funny accent, making me respond, "To be shur to be shur," before Miss Decker snaps a stare at me. I bet Miss Decker thinks what I said was racist. Yeah, right, like the only black student in the whole school is the racist.

We shuffle our way out of our row of chairs then walk toward the gray wall, which she stands with her back to and her arms folded as I waddle to catch up to her.

"Girlfriend, I need a favor and I'm wonderin' if you can give it to me," I whisper. "You're new... obviously. And the teachers... well, they don't really know your handwritin', y'see. Think you could scribble a note pretending to be my momma, just saying I been sick over the past few days. Favor for a favor, maybe?"

She inches up on to her tiptoes to look over my shoulder while Principal Klay repeatedly slaps his hand off the top of the microphone to make sure it's working.

"Why can't your mom do it for you?" she asks.

"It's complicated."

Then she sort of stares into the distance. She could be so pretty, this girl. But she does nothing to bring out the beauty God has given her. She looks like a plain Jane to me, but she could so easily be beautiful. The right makeup; the right haircut. If she chopped her split-ended strawberry blonde hair into a sharp bob, she'd look really cute. More than cute. She'd look sexy.

"I don't really wanna get in trouble," she says, landing back on her heels and gazing at me, "but eh... favor for a favor, you say?"

"You bet, sista," I reply, leaning closer to her.

"It's just I need some inside info on what the boys are like in this school."

I laugh.

"I'll tell you what they would like," I say, picking up a fistful of her strawberry-blonde hair from her shoulder, "this cut into a sharp bob. You'd be hot as hell, girl."

"Oh," she says, taking the fistful of hair out of my hand and dropping it back on to her shoulder. Her face begins to turn almost as red as her hair. "It's not really advice I need on my hair, it's more... listen," she says, lowering her voice, "are there any other boys in this school who have the initials MM, who aren't Meric Miller?"

"Whatcha talkin' 'bout, sista?" I say.

She giggles awkwardly, then stares down at her shoes. Expensive shoes, too. But still ugly as hell. This chick has a lot to learn about how to look good.

"Well," she says. She looks *really* uncomfortable now; as if she wishes she hadn't come to the gray wall with me. "Tell me about Meric. I've been sitting beside him for two weeks in Miss Decker's class now and he hasn't so much as said a single word to me."

"Oh, Meric hasn't said a single word to anybody. He like that. He just keep himself to himself. Meric's always been that way."

She gets on to her tiptoes to look over my shoulder again, just as Principal Klay launches into his assembly.

"Why you asking about that boy?" I say. "I ain't ever hear nobody ask about that boy. And whatchu talking about MM initials? What's with that?"

She drops to her heels and stares down at her shoes again.

"I eh... I went to see a fortune teller the other day, and she told me I would meet and fall in love with a boy with two M's in his name. Next day, for my first period in this school, I sit right next to Meric Miller."

I turn to look over my shoulder in search of Meric, and see Miss Decker silently waving and pointing at us, signaling that me and Irish should sit down and pay attention to whatever it is Principal Klay is sayin'. I pretend I don't see her, and turn back to Irish.

"I've known Meric my whole life," I whisper to her, "and yet I don't know that boy at all. Only thing I remember about Meric is he pissed his sweatpants first year in elementary school. The smell of his urine stayed in that classroom for weeks. I remember that."

She makes a vomiting motion with her mouth, sticking out her tongue and holding her stomach. She's kinda cool. I think I might like this Irish chick.

"You prettier than you think, sista," I say. "I think you can do better than Meric Miller. None o' the other guys look good to you?"

I notice her flick her eyes to the back row, to where Beavis and Butthead are sitting.

"Oh, you prolly be better getting it on with Meric than any of those two beefcakes," I say.

"Really? Why?"

"Well... first, those two football jocks may be fifteen, but they haven't grown up since they were in kindergarten. Second, neither of 'em have two M's in their name. That's Brody Edwards. Other one is Stevie Jenkiss. Not an M to be found in them names."

Her face changes, and she tilts her head to stare at me.

"So you believe in fortune telling, too?" she asks.

"Oh, you betcha, sista," I say. Then she scratches her strawberry-blonde hair, at her left temple, before grinning at me. And I immediately know I'm gonna get on just fine with this girl. "I need a friend," I say. "You wanna be friends, Irish?"

CAOIMHE LARKIN

"Well, you're not gonna believe this," I say, grinning at her, "but I need a friend, too. So, yes."

She sucks on her lips.

"Bet you comin' from Ireland you've never had a black friend before." I nod. "Well, don't worry, see all them in there," she flicks her head back at the packed assembly room. "None of them have ever had a black friend either."

"Hey, you two," Miss Decker whisper shouts as she approaches us. "Assembly has already begun. Sit down and pay attention."

I hold my hand up in apology as I follow my newest friend, whose name I don't yet know, to the back row where we sit a few chairs away from the two square-headed boys.

"Yeah," she whispers into my ear, "I think Meric's the only boy with two M's." Then we both lean forward to look for Meric among the crowd, until I find him sitting in the far corner of the hall, his hair hanging over his face.

Then, suddenly, a cheer goes up. Like the way a pub ignites back home anytime Tipperary scores a goal.

"What the hell happened?" I ask as everyone breaks into applause.

"Principal Klay just said the school is sending thirty tenth graders to Europe this October," my new best friend says.

And when everybody has sat down again, and the assembly

room has fallen silent, I tune in to what Principal Klay is saying for the first time.

"The trip will largely be supplemented by the State thanks to Senator Edgar Owen, who ultimately chose our school out of the hundreds of schools throughout Kansas. However, it won't be totally free for those lucky enough to come. The full cost for each student is one thousand, eight-hundred dollars. The State of Kansas are sponsoring each student up to one thousand dollars, and I am proud to announce that the school will be able to supplement each student for a further four hundred dollars..." he pauses for an applause, almost bowing in anticipation of it, but it doesn't come, so he just continues. "Meaning the personal cost to any student wishing to take this once-in-a-lifetime trip is only four hundred dollars."

A mumbling echoes through the room; each student turning to the student next to him or her, plotting how they can possibly convince their parents to part with that amount of cash.

"You think you'll go on the trip?" I say, nudging my new friend.

"Hell no," she says, "I ain't got no passport. And I ain't got no four hundred bucks, either. If I did, I sure as hell wouldn't be wasting it on no trip to no Europe. What bout you? I bet your family all good for the money, right?"

"Oh, that trip doesn't interest me," I say. "I've only just come from Europe, haven't I?"

She snorts a laugh out of her nostrils, then leans closer to me.

"So when you gonna ask Meric out on a date?" she says.

I laugh. And when I stop she is still just staring at my face.

"Really?"

"Well if you're gonna leave it up to him, girl, I don't think you'll ever date again."

I stare over at Meric in between the bodies of the other students as they stand to applaud Principal Klay again. Meric remains seated, his head down, his heavy fringe covering his eyes.

"He's just... he's just not my type," I say loudly over the applause.

"How do you know?" she shouts back at me.

"Well... just look at him... he..."

"Look at him? All I see is a great head of black hair. I'm not sure I've ever seen Meric's face. And I've known him ten years. He might be a pretty boy under those bangs, you know?"

"But he just doesn't... he doesn't seem as if he's the type of guy I'd even get on with."

"Well... you don't know that for sure, 'cause Meric don't speak. Maybe Meric's full of genius. He could be the funniest guy in the world. Who knows? But if a psychic told you you gotta date the guy with the initials MM and then you join a new school and on the first day you sit next to Meric Miller then, girl, you gotta ask him out. Come on," she says, just after the applause dies and all of the bodies begin squeezing themselves out of the assembly room.

"Come on where?" I ask.

"Come and ask Meric out. Do it low-key... ask him if he'd like to have coffee after school or something."

LUCY DECKER

"Rough day?" Mia asks as she sits herself into her oversized armchair opposite me.

"Rough as the rest of them," I answer.

"Do you find it boring, teaching the same curriculum year after year?"

"Oh, it's not the teaching that has me tired," I say. "In fact, that's the only thing that keeps me going. No... it's the other thing... it's just exhausting me at this point."

"I'm so sorry, Luce," she says, "I really thought it was going to happen for you this time."

We sit in silence, not watching the episode of *Sally* showing on her television in the far corner of the room, even though we're staring at it. We've had this conversation so many times before. Mia must be sick of hearing me moaning about the fact that I can't get pregnant.

"Isn't it Zachary's birthday soon?" I eventually ask, breaking the silence.

"Yup. October twentieth," she says.

"What should I get him this year?"

"Oh... don't worry about it."

"No, don't be stupid. Of course I'll get him something. He's my brother-in-law."

She looks around herself, as if Zachary is going to walk into the living room, even though he hides away in his office almost every time I come over to visit my twin.

"Don't get him anything. Just throw a hundred dollars into a card. He's saving for a Vespa."

"A Vespa?"

Mia scoff-laughs.

"You know Zachary," she says, shrugging. Then she just leaves it there and we get back to not watching Sally Jessy Raphael even though we're both staring at the television again. "I was reading the other day..." Mia says, readjusting her seated position so she's face-to-face with me, "an article about pregnancies. Wanna know how old a female is at her most reproductive? Have a guess..."

"I dunno. Twenty-five?"

"Uh-huh," she says, shaking her head. "Way off. Fifteen."

"Fifteen?"

"Us humans, we've evolved too much," she says. "We're not supposed to live to eighty, you know. We really were only supposed to live thirty or forty years. And fifteen is the ripe age for pregnancy. It's when a female is at her most fertile. It's when males are most fertile, too."

"Great," I say, "maybe I should have sex with one of my students to get pregnant."

We both laugh, then turn to watch Sally staring down the camera lens and lecturing us once again about how great a country America is. Our televisions sure do like to tell us that.

"So, what's your next step, aside from underage sex with one of your students?" Mia asks.

"I've another appointment with my doctor next week. But at this point, I think IVF is my only hope. I've had eleven fails with these sperm donations."

"What's the cost of IVF?"

"Ten thousand," I say. "I've nearly four thousand saved... don't know how old I'm gonna be before that other six thousand comes along. I'm living on scraps trying to save."

Mia tuts.

"And work was a strong no on a salary increase?"

"It wasn't even a 'no'." I shrug. "They just waved me off without even listening."

"Assholes," Mia says. "Why on earth are teachers so badly paid? It don't make any sense. It's got to be up there with the most honorable of any careers you can choose. Educating the youth in society. Surely that deserves more than the average salary."

I shrug my shoulders again. It's an argument I've been involved in lots of times and yet I've never worked out an answer to it. It plainly doesn't make sense. Friends keep telling me I chose the wrong career. They're wrong. But only because I didn't actually *choose* it. I fell into it. I'm a History Major. I got a Ph.D. from the University of Edinburgh in Scotland. A Masters in Media History from Boston University. I was meant to be a... a... well, I'm not sure what I was meant to be. But I'm pretty sure I wasn't meant to be teaching American History at a High School in the middle of America. I thought I was being progressively liberal, and way ahead of my time by studying and traveling all through my twenties. I thought I'd be richer of mind for those experiences. But although Edinburgh was beautiful, if a little rainy, to live in, and although the six months I spent in Rome were idyllic and the year in Greece was beyond glorious, there are times when I'm alone in my tiny house in Lebanon that I begin to feel like I wasted my twenties. I didn't end up with the great career I could have had because the traveling and studying was proving too alluring for me. No love life blossomed from that allure either. And despite thinking I was being liberal and opening my mind up to the world, I've somehow ended up with a narrow life. A narrow career. And a very narrow salary. No husband. No kids. No one. I'm good with being a teacher. I am. And I'm good with living in Lebanon. It's where my life started. And it's where my twin sister and my folks live. Being in Lebanon makes me feel as if I've come full circle. But what I'm truly missing, all I truly yearn for, is to become a mother. I don't want a career change. I don't want a man. I just want a child. I have a calling to hold a baby. My baby. And time is ticking. I'll be forty-two soon. My biological clock ticked over while I was traveling the world on the student loans I am still, to this day, paying back.

I let out what must sound like an exhaustive sigh which makes Mia stick out her bottom lip. I feel terrible burdening her with all of this. Especially as everything worked out perfectly for her. A great husband. Two perfectly healthy and beautiful kids.

"Oh," I say, "I do have *some* good news, I guess. I'm heading back to Europe. For twelve days. It's for a school trip. The principal asked me to chaperone some of the tenth graders to London, Paris and then on to Rome."

"Oooh," Mia says, raising her eyebrows, "sounds like the perfect opportunity for you to have sex with one of your students then."

MERIC MILLER

My hand shakes as I pour the coins into hers.

"Thank you," I manage to mumble, which is unusual for me—
not because I don't like being polite, but because I'm too shy to talk
most of the time. Though I don't think the girl behind the counter
heard me 'cause she turned around to spill all my change into the
register just as I said it.

I take a deep breath before I lift the tray, and all I can see as I
walk toward them is me tripping and this tray smashing to the
ground just before my chin does.

"I've never seen teenagers sit around and drink coffee my
whole life," I hear her saying to Wendy in her really cool accent
just as I lose the panic in my stomach by reaching their table and
resting the tray down safely.

"Thanks Meric," Wendy says, picking up her oversized
cappuccino.

"Yeah, thanks Meric," Caoimhe says.

Then she clinks her mug off of my mug that's still steaming on
the tray before she turns to Wendy so they can knock their mugs
together.

I sit into the chair between them, hoping that I might actually
speak. I would sure like to speak. But here I am, finally sitting with
them, my mouth closed and my eyes staring down at the edge of
the table. It feels really awkward. Especially 'cause they're being

silent too, and staring at me... waiting for me to say something. I'm not sure if it's more awkward or less awkward 'cause Wendy is here. I was so shocked by Caoimhe asking me out for coffee that I said nothing at first, then she blushed in the silence and turned to Wendy to say. "Cause you're coming, too Wendy, right?" I didn't care that Wendy was coming. I thought having her here would make it feel less like a date for me and Caoimhe. But as I stare down at the edge of the table in this awkward silence, I'm starting to wish Wendy wasn't here and I was just staring into Caoimhe's pretty eyes instead. And then I laugh at the thought of me having the balls to stare into a pretty girl's eyes.

"Whatcha laughing at, dude?" Wendy says.

"Oh," I say, shaking my hair before lifting my gaze from the edge of the table to stare at the wall in between the two girls, "just... you know, sometimes you just think of something and it makes you laugh."

"Well, what were you thinking of that made you laugh, Meric?"

"Oh... I was.... ah...." I brush my hair down over my eyes.

"Leave him alone with all the questions," Caoimhe says, just before she takes a sip from her coffee. And as she does, I shift my eyes to take in her pretty face from behind my hair; even if, as I stare at it, she begins to wrinkle all the prettiness up.

"Uggh," she says, "why on earth do yis drink this all the time? It tastes like shit soup."

Me and Wendy both laugh. In fact Wendy laughs so hard that she folds herself on to me, and slaps at my arm. Ain't nobody ever done that before.

"See... she's a funny bitch, ain't you, Irish?" Wendy says.

"Yes she is," I manage to say, even surprising myself. "She is one funny bitch."

Then the laughing stops immediately and Wendy leans off me, to wave her finger from side to side just inches from my face.

"Nah-huh," she says. "We can call each other bitches, but you can't, brother."

I immediately look back down to the edge of the table.

"Don't mind her, Meric, she's just pulling your leg," Caoimhe says. And as she says it, she nudges my elbow with her elbow and my stomach immediately flips itself over.

"S'what do you do in your spare time?" she asks. I gulp, then reach for my mug, slowly picking it up before I take a sip from it while I lift my gaze again to stare at the wall in between the two of them.

"You're right," I say, placing my mug back down on to the tray that I still haven't moved from the table cause I wouldn't know where to put it. "This does taste like shit soup." It gets a laugh. But not as big a laugh as when Caoimhe first said it. Which I guess is how jokes work. So... I lightly cough into my hand, then look up at her through my hair. "I don't know, really. Not much to do round here. I like to um... I like to..." Come on Meric... think for God's sake... what *are* you interested in?

"Meric likes to write, right?" Wendy says, butting in and taking me out of my awkwardness.

"Oh yeah," I say. "I run the school newspaper. Well... it's called a newspaper, but it's more of a newsletter. One page. Well, one page printed front and back. It's called *The Median Times*."

"It's good," Wendy says. Then she takes another sip from her oversized mug.

"Really?" I say, turning to her. "You read it?"

She swallows her mouthful of cappuccino, then creases her lips downward.

"Sorry. No. I don't read it. But it's good that you have an interest in being a writer."

"So you wanna be a novelist when you get older or something like that?" Caoimhe asks.

God, I love her accent. My eyes light up. I can't believe I'm having an actual conversation with an actual girl.

"Well... not really a novelist. I'd like to work in news," I say.

"That'd be cool," Caoimhe replies. "Really cool. So... like, have a column in a newspaper or something like that?"

"Or be a TV reporter," I say. "Like Sarah-Jane Zdanski. She

grew up not far from here. And she's on TV all the time. She's awesome. I love her."

"Please," Wendy says, holding her mug of coffee with both hands just below her chin. "Which boy ain't in love with Sarah-Jane Zdanski?"

"No. I... I... I don't mean in that way," I say, stuttering. "It's not because of how she looks. It's... it's because of her reporting style. I think she's really good at it."

Wendy raises one of her eyebrows at me. Really high. As if she don't believe me.

"Hold on," Caoimhe butts in, "who the hell is Sarah-Jane Zdanski?"

BRODY EDWARDS

"Ya gonna do something or not, dude?" Stevie says.

"Hey," I say, slapping his shoulder, "you haven't exactly got your game in play either, dude. I haven't see you even talk to the Irish chick once yet."

"Well... you ain't spoken to Decker either."

"Yeah, I have," I say as we both stare at her standing with her back against the wall on the other side of the cafeteria. "I asked her that question in class today about FOX News."

"No, you doughnut," Stevie says, and we both immediately start giggling, "I mean you haven't said anything to her about... you know... you have to try have sex with her before the end of October. That's the dare."

"Yeah, and you gotta have sex with Irish."

"Oh, I will, don't worry about that. I'm just saying, my job is to try to convince some new chick to get my dick wet. But you have to convince a woman we've both known for two years to get yours wet. So you've got more work to do. You have to at least let her know you'd be up for it. Right now she sees you as just one of her students. You've gotta change her mind on that. You gotta start dropping little hints, 'til she starts to realize she can do you, dude."

"I guess you're right," I say, "Just a little hint here and there can't hurt, right? Then, who knows? Maybe in Europe, huh?"

"I'm gonna fuck Irish way before we go to Europe, dude. But if you wanna wait that long, be my guest.'"

"Fuck it," I say. Then I fist-bump Stevie and get to my feet, taking my tray from the bench and carrying it outstretched in front of me, my juice carton slipping from side to side. I stare at her as I walk to the trash can, then I empty the tray into it, spin the tray onto the rail really coolly and move in closer to her.

"Hey Miss Decker," I say. Then I wink. "That a new shirt?"

She looks down herself, then back up at me, her eyebrows raised.

"No. I'm pretty sure I wear this every week, Brody," she says.

"Well, it looks good on you. Really brings out your eyes," I say.

Then I just walk off, and as I do, I stare over at Stevie and hold my fist up.

LUCY DECKER

I pace the front of the classroom—my go-to stride when I want the energy in the room to lift. The striding helps keep their eyes moving, and that, in turn, ensures the cogs inside their brains begin to churn. It helps them tune in to what I'm saying, rather than daydream, which I'm pretty sure is the default setting for any teenager in any classroom. The key with teens is to talk *with* them, not *to* them. There's a gulf of a difference between those two approaches that most educators unfortunately never realize. It's also vital to use references that would interest teens, too. Teaching the phraseologies straight out of decades old textbooks is practically sleep medication for fifteen year olds. It definitely was for me when I was that age.

"When you think of it," I say as I continue to pace, back and forward on the worn carpet between the closed door of my classroom and my desk, "and do this when you go home, flick from network to network on your TVs. There are five twenty-four hour news channels. Five. Twenty-four hour. News. Channels. That means your TV is churning out over eight-hundred hours of news every week. Nationally. That's before we even begin to look at local news networks."

"That's literally the first thing I noticed when I moved over here. Why is there so much news on the telly?" Caoimhe says, without putting her hand up. Which is one of my pet peeves as a teacher. But because I love that she is showing so much interest in my class for somebody so new to it, I let it slide.

"That's always been my question, Caoimhe," I say, smiling back at her and nodding my head; a positive way to invite inclusion to a student. "Why is there a need for us folk to consume so much news? Wendy," I say, pointing to the first hand in the air.

"Because there is more news than ever before?" Wendy says.

"Is there, really?" I reply, shrugging.

"Money," Kai says, after shooting his hand up.

"Money?" I say. "Explain."

"Don't networks make money from all the commercials in between the newsy pieces?"

I nod my head slowly.

"They sure do," I say, impressed by Kai's input. He's normally very subdued, so I love it when he gets himself involved in discussions without me having to prompt him.

"And why is that a problem?" Caoimhe butts in.

I purse my lips at her.

"Caoimhe, if you don't mind following the rule of raising your hand before you make your point."

"Sorry," she says. And then she shoots her hand straight up.

"Yes, Caoimhe?" I say.

"Every channel, oh sorry, network you guys call them networks, right? But every other network that is not a news network has ads. So, what's the problem with news networks having them, too?"

"That is a great question. Caoimhe," I say, clapping my hands once and then pointing at her. "And it is a question we are going to dive into during our next class together. In the meantime, over the weekend, I would ask you all to start thinking about just that... why is advertizing during these twenty-four hour news networks potentially dangerous? Though what I would like you to do is to take a look at these twenty-four hour news networks while you are flicking through your TVs this weekend and ask yourselves this as you listen to what they're saying... why is it also dangerous for these news anchors to have an *opinion* on the news they are informing us of?"

"Why shouldn't they have an opinion?" Stevie says. Even Stevie puts his hand up before he mouths off.

"Well.. that's what we're going to study this term. The history of American Media. And I want you guys to understand how our media operates today... then we're going to go back in time, so you can see just how it has all evolved to the place we're in now... a place where America feels it needs over eight hundred hours of live news broadcast to the nation every week."

The bell rings — as it always does in my classes — right on cue, and as the shrill pierces the classroom, the students groan. I never show it, but I love it when they make that noise at the end of one of my lessons.

"Miss Decker." Brody jumps up, stretching his hand to the ceiling as the other students return to their backpacks to begin repacking them.

"Yes Brody?"

"Can I have one of the forms for the trip to Europe?"

I curl my finger at him, inviting him to my desk.

"Here ya go," I say. "Are your parents supplementing the four hundred dollars?"

"Dunno," he says, taking the form from me. "I'll have to beg my Mom. My Dad's still away..."

"Of course," I say. "Maybe your Mom will be happy to get rid of you for ten days so she can get some peace and quiet, huh?"

"Very funny, Miss Decker," he says.

"Okay, well, she just needs to complete this form," I tell him, "and then you need to return it with the four hundred dollars."

"Thank you, Miss Decker. Uh..." he says, turning away and then spinning back to me. "Miss, will we be studying Sarah-Jane Zdanski during this term?"

I laugh.

"What interests you about Sarah-Jane Zdanski, Brody? Her intellect? Her nose for news? Her blouse cut too low for day time TV?"

"Miiisss Deckerrr," he says, feigning shock by slapping his palm to his chest. "Sarah-Jane Zdanski ain't my type. I prefer brunettes. Women more mature than Sarah-Jane." Then he winks at me before spinning on his heels.

Cheeky little shit.

THREE

THEY WERE STILL SAT under the bright lights of the studio—
Sarah-Jane's pert ass perched on the edge of her twenty thousand
dollar leather chair, Howie leaning back on the cheap one next to
hers—long after they had finished going through their notes on
tonight's guests. Well, Howie had long since finished, but Sarah-
Jane still couldn't quite let the irritation of the first two sentences
she had to deliver to the camera leave the forefront of her mind.
She didn't feel they were appropriate. Though Howie tried to
convince her, calmly, that, from his wealth of experience in live
TV, he knew best. The rest of the script; what questions she should
ask each guest; what each guest was likely to answer in return; the
intros and outros to and from the seven commercial breaks, that
was all boxed away—literally underlined, circled and boxed in red
ink on the script that was staring up at Sarah-Jane as she began to
partake in small talk with Howie.

Phil was still standing in the shadows, Sarah-Jane's purse
resting by his feet, listening in with the bullish features of his jowly
face unmoving. He wasn't quite taking to Howie; assumed him to
be somewhat a weirdo. Especially so as he touched Sarah-Jane on
the knee too often. *Way* too often. Yet, despite that, Phil could
plainly see why the flamboyant, bespectacled executive producer
was regarded as one of the best in the business—just from how he

guided Sarah-Jane through her debut script, making her feel as at ease as she possibly could before the biggest night of her life.

Howie Laine had begun working in TV just over nineteen years prior—during the summer heatwave of 1978. He managed to land a job as a runner on *Happy Days*, when—because it was filmed nearby to the neighborhood he grew up in in Milwaukee — he begged, as a sixteen-year-old boy, one of the producers to let him help them out, only because he was desperate to duck behind the tape to experience, in real life, the magic television had to offer. Within a couple of months of working as a runner for no salary at all, he had proven so valuable that he was promoted to assistant researcher at seventy-eight dollars a week. Within two years, he was lead producer on his favorite-ever TV show—counting Henry Winkler and Ron Howard among his closest friends just as they were at the height of their fame, and earning more money than he had ever considered imaginable given his working-class roots. A director who worked on *Happy Days* found Howie so innovative in his vision for all things TV that he hired him to come work for him when he changed career lanes by diverting into the news division of MSNBC. Having helped — as lead producer — increase the network's audience by three hundred percent over a six-year run, Howie was headhunted by Walter Fellowes, just as the famed media mogul was forming his CSN News network. He's been Fellowes's go to executive-producer ever since, becoming the strongest voice on any show the mogul felt needed an injection of innovation. He was Fellowes's most obvious choice to executively produce *Zdanski* ever since the mogul first laid eyes on Sarah-Jane and knew instantly that he simply had to hire her and give her her own show. Fellowes even knew who the guests would be for that first show. And when he filled Howie in on the concept, they both agreed, without hesitation, that it would be a ratings smash.

"Did you work on Matt's show when he was here?" Sarah-Jane asked after Howie had told her he'd been, by now, at CSN for twelve years.

"You bet."

"What's he like... what's Matt Lauer really like?"

Howie looked around, squinting into the shadows either side of the studio, before leaning closer to Sarah-Jane so that he could whisper out of earshot of Phil—whom he'd only just realized was still standing in the darkness.

"Matt should be in the *Guinness Book of World Records* for two reasons," Howie whispered, holding two fingers aloft. "One, and I mean no disrespect to you or anyone else I've worked with, but Matt Lauer is by far the most natural TV host America has ever had the privilege of tuning in to see. He's simply the best. Nobody's ever made the art of broadcasting look so effortless."

Sarah-Jane's eyes widened, and she smiled, simply because she loved to hydrate on this flavor of juice.

"And... second?" she said, sitting even more forward on her expensive chair.

"Second reason he should be in the *Guinness Book of World Records...*" Howie leaned even closer, "is 'cause he's a contortionist without measure. I have never seen no other man have their own head so high up their own ass."

Sarah-Jane sucked in a gasp.

"Really?"

Howie double tapped his nose, and then flamboyantly flicked back his sleeve so he could glance at his Rolex watch.

"You..." he said, pressing a finger to the tip of Sarah-Jane's nose, "need to get a move on. You're due to have dinner with Walter in about half-an-hour... time to get you to wardrobe."

"Why the hell does he want me in wardrobe so early?"

Howie stood, hugging the notes he had been scribbling on during their meeting close to his chest, then shrugged one of his shoulders.

"Because he's Walter Fellowes."

After Howie left the bright lights of the studio, by pushing open the double doors to the side of the stage, Sarah-Jane took a step down and walked slowly toward Phil.

"Can you believe this?" she said, holding her hand to one of his biceps. "We've got our own show."

Phil huffed from his nose, then grabbed the hand Sarah-Jane

had placed to his bicep before twirling her around so she could face the bright lights her sausage-shaped desk and twenty thousand dollar chair were shining under.

"It's not *we*," he said. "The name on that neon sign up there... it's Zdanski."

Sarah-Jane spun back around, and tilted her head.

"You know what I mean. I may be front of camera and it might be my name all up in lights, but we're a team, buddy. We made this happen together." She slapped the bicep she had been placing her hand against just moments prior and then pursed her lips. "Anyway, I gotta get to wardrobe," she said. "Walter Fellowes, for some reason, wants to see me in my outfit before I have dinner with him."

"I heard," Phil said. Then he scratched at his patchy beard before they both walked toward the same double doors at the side of the stage Howie had left through a minute prior and found themselves back in amongst the dark maze of endless hallways.

It took them five minutes to find out where wardrobe was, and when they eventually found it, Sarah-Jane knocked on a door that looked more like it would lead her into a prison cell, rather than the wardrobe department of the third most popular news network in the country.

A woman — wise-looking, yet youthful — answered and immediately shrieked as she leaned in to hug her latest muse.

"It's so great to meet you," she said, kissing Sarah-Jane on both cheeks as if they were long-lost European acquaintances.

Isla Coyne had a rough-chopped blonde mullet and wore different colored glasses frames, depending on her clothing choices on any given day. On this day, her glasses frames were a rather characterless — by her standards, anyway — sky blue all over, similar in color to the denim overalls she was wearing underneath a long white cardigan that seemed to mop the floor of the wardrobe department as she glided along it. The pants of the overalls stopped half-way down her shins, as if the manufacturer had run out of denim, though that did allow her to show off her heavy Doc Marten boots that instantly looked, to Sarah-Jane as she stared at them, a nightmare to have to put on every morning.

"You look so cool," Sarah-Jane said.

Wardrobe was brightly lit with floor-to-ceiling mirrors all along one side and two rows of clothing racks on the other that were bending in the middle due to the weight of the garments hanging from them.

"Oh, are you ah..." Isla said when she had attempted to close the door, only for Phil to stop her by slapping his hand against it, "joining us?"

"Oh yeah. He's my producer. You can let him in," Sarah-Jane called out.

Phil didn't acknowledge Isla as he passed by her, clutching Sarah-Jane's purse to his chest.

"Well, hello producer Phil," Isla said as she shut the door.

And then there was a silence in wardrobe, only broken by the sound of Sarah-Jane swishing clothes hangers as she flicked through the garments on the rails.

Phil growled quietly in the back of his throat. He didn't care much for his title of producer, though he had acknowledged how grateful he was to Sarah-Jane for including him on this ride on a number of occasions up until this point. Phil had fallen into his career lane when, as a seventeen year old graduating high school in Cawker City, Kansas, he was faced with the dilemma of either picking a subject to study at community college, or face the stigma of unemployment. Because it sounded like the least academic option, Phil chose to study photography and, having earned himself a certificate in the subject two years later, he landed himself a job at the local PBS studios where he was earning less money than he would have been had he chosen the option of unemployment and received state benefits instead. At first, he would help with the live recording of news bulletins, standing behind a large camera and holding it on a presenter's face unmoving, until he was eventually promoted to the great outdoors; shadowing desperate reporters who went in search of breaking news just so they could land themselves a paycheck. He worked with a multitude of journalism graduates, each of whom thought him too quiet and too odd to befriend, until one day his station manager asked him to wait in his office while he trotted down to the lobby to welcome a new recruit. When that new recruit walked into the office Phil had been waiting in, he wasn't as struck by her beauty like most red-blooded men are when they first lay their eyes on her. He initially thought Sarah-Jane to be just another pretty blonde who would be joining PBS thinking she would find fifteen minutes of fame, only to leave — like the majority of pretty blondes do — within a matter of weeks, simply because they found it too frustrating to get themselves on air.

"So, where's my little black dress?" Sarah-Jane asked, smiling at Isla.

"Oh, it's in the back hanging up. You wanna see it again?"

"I have to put it on. Walter Fellowes has asked me to join him for dinner and I was told I had to visit wardrobe first."

Isla made a face, showing all of her teeth—even her crooked bottom row.

"It's not your dress Walter wants you to wear for dinner," she said. "It's this..."

Isla walked over to where Sarah-Jane stood by the bended racks, and grabbed a red-colored garment wrapped in clear plastic.

"It's just come back from the dry-cleaners, so don't worry about it."

She eased the garment out of the plastic while Sarah-Jane looked up at Phil, her eyebrows almost knitting together.

"A cheerleader's uniform?" she said. "Why the hell would I need to wear a cheerleader's uniform?"

Isla pushed the sky-blue glasses back on the bridge of her nose, then shrugged one of her shoulders.

"Because he's Walter Fellowes," she said.

Sarah-Jane glanced at Phil. He was standing with his fat hands stuffed inside the pockets of the double-breasted jacket she had bought for him the day prior, her purse resting by his sneakers. She had fought hard to ensure he would be part of her show; told the lawyers Walter Fellowes had sent out to negotiate her contract that

Philip Meredith simply had to come with her to New York, and be offered a role as a producer. She promised he wouldn't step on anyone's toes; that she just needed him with her, so she could bounce ideas off him. Walter's lawyers pretended to reluctantly nod their heads, agreeing to offer the cameraman slash producer an eighty-thousand dollar a year contract. Though that paled in comparison to the quarter-of-a-million deal Sarah-Jane was about to sign to greenlight *Zdanski*.

"Really?" she said, digging her knuckles into her temples.

Isla showed her crooked teeth again, then held the cheerleader's uniform closer to Sarah-Jane.

"Don't worry," she said, "I'll give you an overcoat to wear over it when you're going up in the elevator to Walter's office."

An extended sigh released through Sarah-Jane's nostrils and then she began to slowly unbutton her jacket, staring at herself in the mirror and noticing the worried expression creasing across her brow. By the time she was peeling off her blouse, revealing her pushed-together breasts packed tightly within the cups of a Wonderbra, Isla held her arm out, to use her long cardigan as a curtain.

"Oh, don't worry about Phil," Sarah-Jane said. "Nothing he hasn't seen before."

She shook herself out of her causal clothes while Isla let her cardigan go and then stood back, a note of confusion in her eyes. She didn't look at Phil while Sarah-Jane was undressing. But she could also tell, through her peripherals, that he wasn't staring at his boss's flawless physique as she slipped into near-nakedness, and figured there and then that he must be gay.

"So is wardrobe all good for tonight?" Sarah-Jane asked as she grabbed the cheerleader's uniform.

"Yeah, well, your little black number is hanging up in my office."

"Not just for me... what about the guests?"

"Oh," Isla said, "well the guests bring in their own clothes. They've each been told to bring in three outfits and I will choose one from those three for each of them to wear."

"Why three?" Sarah-Jane asked, as she stepped her feet into the uniform.

"Well, there are certain things that don't work on camera. Guests can't be wearing any branded items, for example; we can't have somebody wearing a top with Adidas emblazoned across it, of course. And then there are color clashes we don't want and certain designs that don't display well on camera."

"Such as thin black-and-white stripes."

"Exactly," Isla said. "Things like that look blurred or fuzzy. And so we assume that if they bring in three outfits, then they'll at least have one that doesn't blur on screen and that doesn't advertise a brand."

Sarah-Jane snapped the tight shoulders of the cheerleader's uniform on and then stepped toward the mirrored wall. Her reflection took her back to being sixteen years old at Esbon High School; the colors of the uniform were the exact same—mostly red with white trim and a big gold logo emblazoned across the chest.

"You look hot," Isla said.

"This is so wrong," Sarah-Jane whispered to her own reflection.

Isla didn't reply. Instead, she strolled to the back of the room and grabbed an oversized gray overcoat hanging from one of the racks.

"Here, wear this going up in the elevator."

Sarah-Jane's sigh fogged up the mirror, and by the time she had thrown on the overcoat and received another double-kiss from Isla, Phil had opened the door of wardrobe to allow his boss to re-enter the maze of dark hallways.

"He's a fucking pervert," Phil said out of the side of his mouth as they went in search of the golden double doors of the elevator.

Sarah-Jane didn't reply. But she shared Phil's suspicions, in much the same way anyone would after they'd been told that they must wear a cheerleader's uniform for a dinner date with their new boss.

"Are you gonna let him fuck you?" Phil whispered when they finally found the golden double doors and Sarah-Jane had pushed at the button. "Well, are you?" he asked again when he received no reply. "Is this what he does, hires beautiful women and then gives them their own show if they fuck him?"

"Phil!" Sarah-Jane snapped, just as the double doors slid open with a ping. She pressed a hand to her cameraman slash producer's chest. "I'm sorry. I didn't mean to raise my voice. Not at you."

Then she stepped inside, staring at herself in the walled mirror of the elevator and noting that she would probably look less suspicious if she had worn just the cheerleader's uniform rather than the oversized overcoat.

She spun around, to press her finger on button number 60, and as the golden doors slid toward each other, she stared through the narrowing gap at Phil standing in the dark hallway, her purse clutched tightly to his chest.

"I don't know," she mouthed back to him.

CAOIMHE LARKIN

He was awkward. As if it was the first date he'd ever been on.
Which I guess isn't as bad as it sounds. Cos I only had three dates
back in Ireland before I came here. Or two and a half, I guess is fair
to say, given that Carl Murphy didn't even realize we were having
a date when we went on a walk around the park that time. But it
wasn't Meric's inexperience or all of the awkward silences that was
the problem for me while we met in that coffee shop. It was the
things he said whenever he wasn't being silent that were the problem. We share no interests. He's into his school newspaper and
playing video games. I want a boyfriend who'll take me out to the
cinema on dates, or at least somebody who watches the same TV
shows as I do. "The news," is all Meric said he watches on telly.
The feckin news!

"So you don't watch *Beverly Hills 90210* or anything like
that?" I asked.

He snort-laughed. Then went all shy again, probably because a
tiny spray of snot flew out of his nose. It wasn't hard snot or
anything. It was just a spray. I didn't mind. Course I didn't. I
minded that he doesn't watch *Beverly Hills 90210*!

I think I'm gonna have to go back to Madam Aspectu again,
because I need more information on this MM boy. It can't be
Meric Miller, surely. Though every now and then I find myself
surprised at the coincidence of her telling me my boyfriend would

have MM in his name and then on my first day, in my very first lesson at my brand new school, I happened to sit right next to him.

It's been three days since we went on our "date" but he's said pretty much nothing to me since, even though I've sat beside him in Miss Decker's class for an hour twice. I think he grimaced a smile at me the morning after we met at the coffee shop, but by the time I looked up at him, his eyes were gazing back down at the edge of his desk from underneath his long fringe again.

"Okay, so did anybody take a look at the news networks over the weekend?" Miss Decker asks.

"I did," I shout. And then I cover my mouth with one hand and shoot the other straight into the air.

"Yes, Caoimhe," Miss Decker says, laughing at me. I think Meric laughs too. But I can't be sure 'cause I don't look at him. It sure did sound like a laugh. Or maybe it was a sigh.

"I did, Miss. And I thought about the two tasks you set us."

"And your findings were, Caoimhe?"

"I think there should be no ads on the news channels because news shouldn't be sponsored. And... oh yeah, and news reporters shouldn't be giving us their opinion on politics because that would mean the advertisers are agreeing with the news networks."

She opens her mouth a little. But says nothing. And while she's saying nothing, I'm pretty sure Meric looks up from under his fringe, too, while the rest of the class twist their necks to stare over their shoulders at me.

"Very impressive, Caoimhe," Miss Decker finally says, nodding.

"I don't get it," the brown-haired girl with the sharp bob on the far side of the room, whose name I haven't yet remembered, says.

"Well, Nicole," Miss Decker says. I note the name Nicole and repeat it three times inside my own head, just so I can tattoo it to my memory. "What Caoimhe is saying is predominantly what I will be aiming to teach you this term. All about the power these news networks hold, especially when they are funded by commercial sponsors."

"I watched the news networks with my dad over the weekend,"

I say, "and he pointed out to me how the hosts of the shows all give their opinion on what is happening in the news. He said it was the opposite in Ireland; that news hosts back home literally just tell us the news, but they can't give us their opinion. They aren't allowed to have an opinion."

"Well, he's a smart man your father," Miss Decker says. "Is he involved with media for his work?"

"Oh, no," I say, "He's a golfer. S'why we moved over here. He saw a job as a golfing instructor at Lebanon Golf Club posted on the internet and applied and well... he got offered the position and it was his dream come true... so, here we all are."

Miss Decker smiles at me again. I think she likes me. She's pretty cool for a teacher. She's interesting to listen to anyway. There's always a discussion to be had in her classes, always a debate. She makes me think. And she never says who's right or wrong in those debates or discussions. She just lets everybody have their say and then the bell normally rings right on cue and she lets us go to our next class. It's a kinda cool school, I guess. Sure beats the hell out of reading chapters from ancient textbooks with nuns who look just as old as those textbooks themselves.

The bell rings to let us know American History is over and math is about to begin. So it's no surprise that the students start groaning. They tend to do that at the end of this class. I might join in with the groaning tomorrow.

"Miss Decker, I have the money and the signed form for the Europe trip," Nicole cries out from the other side of the room.

"Give it here," Miss shouts back as we all begin to stuff our American History books into our bags.

"Are you going to go on the trip to Europe?" I whisper to Meric.

He lifts his gaze as he swings his bag over his shoulder, then shakes his heavy fringe from side-to-side.

"Move the fuck outta my way, weirdo," Stevie says, pushing Meric aside before sliding in to the chair next to me. "Kway-va, I've been thinking..."

"It's pronounced *Kwee-va*, Stevie," I say, my eyes squinting, wondering what the hell he wants. He hasn't so much as looked at me before, let alone wanted to talk to me.

"Just wondering what you get up to after school? Was hoping you'd like to hang out with me..."

What the hell? Isn't he supposed to be the popular one... the football star? What's he doing asking the little ginger Irish girl out?

"Hang out with you and...?"

"Well just me," he says, a big grin on his big face.

"As in, just the two of us? What would we do?" I ask.

I glance at Meric who has been left standing behind us, trying to fit his already curled-up notebook into his bag.

"Well... how about an ice cream at Daisy's Dairies?" He looks over his shoulder, catching Meric slowly zipping up his bag while still staring downward. "Move the fuck along, weirdo," he says, shoving him in the back.

Meric goes to walk on, but I stand up, blocking him.

"Are you asking me out on a date, Stevie?" I say.

The grin drops from his square face.

"Kinda... I guess..." He shrugs.

"Well I'm already dating somebody," I say. Then I swing my arm around Meric's neck and walk out of the classroom snuggled in to his shoulder. He smells kinda damp.

BRODY EDWARDS

"She sure likes getting involved in class," Stevie whispers to me.

"She's too intellectuable for you, dude," I whisper back.

"Bullshit," Stevie says. "I'm way outta her league. You gave me an easy dare, dude. All I have to do is make my move... and she'll be peeling her little Irish panties off in no time."

"You keep sayin' that, man," I whisper. "But you ain't made no move yet. And we made these dares two weeks ago."

"Alright, alright. Well..."

"Well, what?"

"Well I'm gonna make my move right after class."

I shrug at him, then tune back into what Decker is saying, 'cause even though me 'n' Stevie talk a lot through every class, we talk less through hers. Only because her classes can be interesting. Sometimes.

When I glance at my watch, I realize there's only one minute left. Then it's math. I hate math. What is the point of the bullshit they teach us in math class? I don't get it. It don't make no sense.

"Oh, no," the Irish chick says, answering Decker. "He's a golfer. S'why we moved over here. He saw a job as a golfing instructor at Lebanon Golf Club posted on the internet and applied and well... he got offered the position and it was his dream come true... so, here we all are."

"That accent is kinda sexy, ain't it?" Stevie says.

"You have a weird mind if you think that's sexy," I reply. "Look at her. She's a redhead. And she's got lots of freckles."

Then the bell rings and Stevie stands up to shove his notebook into his bag as if he's in a race.

"A dare's a dare," he says. "So I'm going in, dude. This should be easy."

I laugh as I spin around in my chair so I can watch Stevie in action. He pushes Meric out of the way with his hip, slides himself into the chair beside Irish and gives her one of those big grins of his. I try to strain my neck, to hear what he's saying to her, but between Decker shouting across to students about collecting money for the trip to Europe and the chatter of all the other students in the hallways changing periods, I can only try to lip read. Then Irish stands, spins around, and after saying something to Stevie, she wraps her arm around Meric. What. The. Actual. Fuck? My mouth snaps open as they stroll past my desk, her leaning into him as they join the chatter out in the hallway. I look back at Stevie, and notice his jaw is open further than mine. Then I double over into the biggest fit of laughing I think I've ever doubled into my whole life.

"What the fuck, dude?" Stevie says, walking up to me with his arms straight by his side, like a zombie.

"Boys!" Decker calls out. I lift my head, but I know it must be bright red from having it between my legs, laughing. "Haven't you got one more class to get going to? "Sorry, Miss Decker," I say, raising a hand while trying to stop laughing. Then I sling my bag over my shoulder. "Bye, Miss Decker." I wiggle my fingers and wink at her again.

As soon as I step outside, with Stevie behind me — still walking like a zombie — I double over into a fit of laughing again.

"She dissed you for Meric, dude," I say when I can catch my breath.

"She didn't diss me... that's bullshit, man. She said she was already dating Meric before I asked her out."

I slap Stevie on the back.

"Oh man, that is the funniest thing I've ever seen happen to you. The quarterback dissed for Meric the weirdo. Looks like your dare is pretty messed up now, dude. No chance of you screwing her before the end of October. I'm gonna win this."

"You're not far ahead, Brody," Stevie says as we turn onto the math hallway.

"I'm way ahead of you, dude," I say. "I've already been giving Decker the 'come fuck me' eyes. And from the signs I'm getting, I think I'm gonna be in there, even before we get to Europe."

"Bullshit," Stevie says.

"You are both late for class!" Charlton roars, poking his bald head out of the door. Charlton is a dick. I hate his classes.

"Sorry, Mr. Charlton," I say. "We were held up by Miss Decker."

LUCY DECKER

I relax into the chair facing Mia, slide a coffee across to her, and then giggle.

I know I giggle in class. A lot. But that's all rehearsed giggling, instructed by me, for me, within the scripts I have perfected in over eleven years of teaching the same lessons over and over again. I love my students. Well... most of them. But I never giggle with them the way I giggle with my twin. It's only in her company that I actually truly feel like myself. It's funny. I went in search of who I really am by traveling all throughout my twenties when I could have found the answer all along in the bed opposite mine in our family home. Lebanon is home. Being near Mia and her two boys is home. And as lonely as this existence feels to me, most of the time, it's probably as full a life as I am ever likely to have.

"Hear anything from the doctor?" she asks, before lifting the mug to her mouth.

"He says I can continue with the injections if I want to. But he was adamant my best chance is IVF. It's a guaranteed insertion to the egg, not a crapshoot like I've been attempting. Either that or I have actual sex, with an actual man, and not just with a turkey-baster."

"Ugggh, Lucy, stop using that phrase," Mia says, crinkling up her nose.

"Well, you know what I mean. I can't keep buying," I look

around the coffee shop, then lean across the table to whisper, "sperm from sperm banks and then go inserting it myself. It clearly doesn't work. I've accumulated eighteen months of proof that it doesn't work."

"So you need a man or a miracle?" she says.

"Finding a man *would* be miracle."

"It's not a miracle to meet a man, Lucy. I found one. All of our friends found one. You just don't have the—"

"I don't have the address, Mia. I don't have the zip code. I live in Lebanon, Kansas. It's hardly a blossoming orchard, growing Brad Pitts from every branch of every tree, is it?"

"He doesn't have to be Brad Pitt, Luce. Look at Zachary, he's no Brad Pitt. In fact, yours doesn't even have to be a Zachary, does he? He doesn't have to stay with you like my Zachary has stayed with me for fourteen years. He just needs to... y'know... have sex with you... get you pregnant."

I shake my head. She knows my position on this. Mia would. She told me she would, if she were in my situation, have sex with some random guy just to get pregnant. But I couldn't live with myself if I took that road.

"How much have you given to these sperm banks over the last eighteen months?"

"Not that much," I say. "It's only sixty dollars each time. Peanuts compared to what I'll have to pay going down the IVF road."

"And what's that? Ten K?"

"Yup," I say, before taking from my mug. "The doctor told me that in my situation, with what he called my 'receptive eggs', IVF would give me an eighty percent chance of getting pregnant. Only they remove my egg, inject the sperm and then... then it all goes back inside me."

She purses her lips at me, while gripping her coffee mug with both hands.

"I'm so sorry," she says.

"You don't need to be sorry for anything—"

"For not being able to give you any money toward—"

"Don't be ridiculous," I say. "This is not your burden to bear."

I shake my head sharply, to signal the end of this line of conversation. I don't want money from Mia. She shouldn't even think that way. It actually bothers me that she feels burdened by my inability to become a mom. As if my crying about it for the last eighteen months hasn't been enough for her, now she has to live with the guilt that she can't help me out financially. They do okay, Mia and Zachary. Enough to live in a lovely four-bedroom home on Chicago Avenue; enough to bring up and spoil two perfectly cute little boys. I love them all so much, I envy all they have. But I certainly don't expect them to help me. I would be a horrible person if I expected them to help me.

"So... eighty percent chance of a pregnancy if you can raise ten grand is pretty much what the doctor said?" she says. I nod. "It always costs big money, doesn't it? Anything they have a remedy for... it always has to cost thousands."

I laugh while sipping from my mug, and as I do, the bell chimes over the door, and in walks this bulk of a man, his figure eclipsing the shine of the sun as he stands in the doorframe wearing a khaki uniform, with stars and stripes stitched to the bicep, squinting at the chalkboard over the bar. Then he marches his desert boots inside.

"There's a new face," Mia says, leaning in to whisper to me. "Maybe you could ask him to get you pregnant. Though I bet it'd hurt riding him."

I slap at her elbow while she bends herself over to snicker into the table.

"Don't be dumb, Mia," I whisper. "I wouldn't subject my future son or daughter to the genes of a soldier."

"What? Why not?" she says, a little too loudly.

I shush her, by tapping her knee under the table and raising my eyebrows at her.

"A soldier's likely to be a Republican, isn't he? It's all about the stars 'n' stripes if you're a soldier."

"Wow," Mia mouths. "No wonder you're single." Then she sips from her mug.

"I'm messing with you. I'm messing with you," I say. Even though I'm not sure I am. What I am sure of — and Mia knows this — is that I just wouldn't have sex with some random guy to get pregnant. That's just not fair. It's not fair on the guy himself. Not fair on anyone. I don't think I could live as a mother knowing I had duped somebody into providing a son or a daughter for me. "Ya know what?" I say, distracting myself from even entertaining the thought, "talking about sex. I'm pretty sure one of my students is blatantly coming on to me."

MERIC MILLER

I fall back on to my bed, without breaking my fall, until my head slaps against the pillow. Then I clasp my hands across my chest and stare up to the ceiling, hoping the stains up there will somehow stop my head from spinning.

I couldn't believe it. Could. Not. Believe. It. Right when he was acting like the cock stain he can sometimes be, pushing me and shoving me out of the way, she stood up, wrapped her arm around me and walked me as if we were boyfriend and girlfriend all the way to math. Well, it wasn't *all* the way to math. Her arm slipped off on the way before she nudged at me and then walked toward Mr. Charlton's classroom on her own. But it was still so cool. Super cool. Ain't nothing like that ever happened to me before. Not even in my dreams. I've been trying to relive that moment in my head the whole afternoon. S'probably why my head's been spinning so much.

I spent my time in math not looking down at the desk, like I usually do, but staring at her hair because she was sitting two rows in front of me. I took in the different strands of orange and gold and I think I pretty much had a smile on my face the whole time I was doin' it. I certainly had a smile on my face when Stevie walked in late to that class. The cock stain. He didn't dare look at me. Him and Brody just sunk themselves into their seats on the other side of the room and kept their eyes straight ahead while Mr. Charlton went on and on about X and fucking Y.

I wasn't sure what was going to happen after math class. But I was at least expectin' her to stay around and talk to me. Afterall, she had only told me I was her boyfriend at the same time she announced it to Stevie at the end of American History class. But as soon as the bell went off when math was over, she shoveled her book into her bag, slung her bag over both shoulders and was gone in a flash. I watched her pacing down the sidewalk of the school from the classroom window of math while I was still trying to fit my notebook into my bag.

I tried walking a little faster to get home, to see if I could catch up with her. But she musta been much quicker than I was. Or maybe she'd taken a different route to the normal route she takes, cos I sure as hell didn't catch up with her. And I was walkin' really fast. Practically speed walking.

I turn on to my side and begin to rub at my stomach. It feels different; has felt different from the moment she wrapped her arm around me. I wonder if she'll do the same thing tomorrow as well. We could probably sit in the cafeteria at lunch time with our arms around each other. Or holding hands. I dunno. Maybe.

I raise an arm over my head and sniff, then do the same on the other side. I ain't sure I smell of anything, but I jump up off the bed anyway, head into our small bathroom and run the shower. Just in case I smell bad to her. It's actually been a long time since I've had a shower. Not 'cause I don't wanna wash. But because this shower is so shitty it only spits out water. I'm sick of sayin' to Momma that, "we shouldn't call this a shower, we should call it a spitter," but she ain't done nothing to try fix it. She don't really care. I don't think she washes that much either. Same as me, she prolly just wipes her armpits at the sink with a handful of water and a bit of soap.

After running the spitter, I sneak a peek at her by pushing at the living room door quietly and staring in through the crack. She's sittin' on the couch, swirling the phone line round her finger and flirting with whoever's on the other end of the line. It could be anyone. I wouldn't know. I used to keep count of the men, and boys, who came and went. But that stopped years ago.

I think about Caoimhe while the shower spits at me, but I don't jerk off. I don't see her that way. Not yet anyway. The sexiness will come in time, I'm sure. But right now, all of the feelings I have for her are in my stomach. Not my cock. I might jerk off later. But not thinking about her. I'll prolly do one to Sarah-Jane Zdanski. She looked super-hot today when she popped up on TV promoting some big secret interviews she's got coming up soon.

BRODY EDWARDS

"Smell my fingers."

"What the fuck, dude?" I say, slapping Stevie's hand away from my face.

"Ya know what that smell is?" he says.

"No," I say. Then, as he sits on the edge of my bed with a big grin on his face, the penny drops. "You didn't?"

"Yup," he says, holding two fingers up, "that is the sweet smell of Ireland, dude. Sweet Irish pus-say."

He stuffs his two fingers into his mouth, sucks on them, then loudly pops them back out from the side of his cheek

"You dirty dawg," I say, sitting down on the edge of my bed right next to him, "so when did this happen?"

"I saw her rushing out of school after math, so I was thinking *yo bitch, I ain't lettin' you get away with trying to embarrass me with Meric*, so... so I shouted after her. 'Yo, Irish,' I said. I wiggled my finger at her to come over to me, and you know how I roll, dude... two minutes later we were behind the shed at the back of the school with our tongues down each other's throats and my two fingers vibrating inside her like a washing machine. She was screeching, dude. Right into my ear. It was awesome."

"I was wondering where you went after math. Wow. Well, I guess you're ahead of me now. I'm still at winking stage with

Decker. You've already got your fingers dirty with the new chick, huh?"

"That's how I roll, dude."

Then we do our handshake.

"Hey," I say, "have you managed to convince your mom and dad to give you the money for Europe?"

"Yeah, dude. They'll do it. They've already signed the form. I think we're just waiting on my dad to get paid at the end of the month and we should be all good to go. It's gonna be one hell of a trip. I bet the French chicks will love nothing more than an American dude hitting on them. Be like winning the lottery for those chicks, won't it? Having two American football players in town."

I look at him, a little confused.

"Do they even know what American football is in France?"

"Sure they do, dude. They play American Football all over the world. Just cause it's called American Football doesn't mean it's only played in America."

"You sure?" I say.

He nods.

"Trust me, dude. We will not be hard up for pus-say when we go to Europe. We'll probably be swimming in it."

We do our handshake again, then I kneel down and wiggle myself under the small table in my bedroom to push the plug into the socket. Stevie snatches at the joystick as the TV flashes on and then shouts, "I'll go first today."

So I just sit back on the edge of my bed next to him and watch as he tries to take Mario through to level nineteen. We've been stuck on level eighteen since the end of August.

"Try bouncing on that mushroom, have we tried that before?" I say, and as I say it, my bedroom door swings open.

"Hey you two."

"Hey Mrs. Edwards," Stevie says, "Uhm... Miss Wallard."

"It's still Mrs. Edwards... they're not divorced," I say, snatching the joystick from him. "Yet."

"Stevie," Mom says before tutting. "I've been telling you since you were four years old to just call me Patricia."

Stevie's parents tell him that he should call his friends' folks Mr. and Mrs. whatever. I have to call them Mr. and Mrs. Jenkiss when I'm at their house. They're old-fashioned like that. And a bit up their own asses.

"Good day at school today?" Mom asks.

"The usual," I reply, while tapping away at the red button on my joystick.

"Want a snack before dinner... or?"

"I'm fine," I say.

"You, Stevie?"

"I'm fine Mrs. Edwar— Patricia," he says.

Then Mom shakes her head as she stares at the small TV, showing games meant for children much younger than us, before she tuts again while dragging the bedroom door back shut.

"I bet your Mom is dying for a ride," Stevie whispers. "How long has your old man been away... and they were split up well before that, too, right? Must be almost two years since she's had a cock inside her."

I slap him across the back of his head, hard; so hard I can feel the sting of it inside my palm.

"What the fuck, dude," he says. Then he jumps on top of me and we giggle all high-pitched like Michael Jackson while we wrestle on my bed.

"Man, I can't believe we're going off to Europe in tenth grade," I say after our wrestling has finished and I've sat up on the bed so I can flatten my hair back down. "This is gonna be the best vacation of our lives, dude."

Then I hear the tip-tap of heavy shoes — a sound I haven't heard in a long, long time — outside my bedroom window. It's Stevie who looks up first, kneeling on the bed and tweaking the blinds.

"Holy shit, dude," he says.

I already know what he's about to say, but I don't wait to hear it. I grab at the bedroom door, snatch it open and then race myself down the stairs as quickly as I can.

"Dad!" I say, grinning from ear to ear. Then I wrap my arms around his uniform and press my cheek right into his chest.

WENDY CAMPBELL

I press my hand to her forehead, and when she feels my palm stick to the beads of her sweat, she tries to smile up at me.

"Stay asleep, Momma," I say.

"I bin sleep all day," she whispers.

Chemotherapy is supposed to be the way to treat her illness, but she's had her one and only shot of it a week ago and all it's done is made her look and feel a hundred times worse. A thousand times worse. Her hair is falling out. Her eyes are all bulged. And she's tired. Always tired. She can barely keep those bulging eyes open no more. S'almost as if the doctors told us a few months ago that Momma has stomach cancer and so what he was going to do was have her attend a clinic to shoot her up with somethin' that'll make her feel even worse. Chemotherapy don't make no sense to me. Even when she went to the doctor the first time saying she had cramps in her stomach, she was fine, really. She was still herself. She could still live a life. Could still be our Momma. Could still stay awake for most o' the day. But ever since she had the chemotherapy, all she is is a heavy body, lying flat out all day long on a fold-down sofa in the middle of our living room. Every so often she'll smile up at us when she wakes. But that's about as good as it gets.

While my hand is still pressed against Momma's forehead, I turn to my little sister.

"So, what you want for dinner today, huh?"

She doesn't look up from the picture she is coloring in at the table, her tongue sticking out as she scribbles, then says, "Fries. And a hamburger."

So I heave my weight off Momma's makeshift bed, using the arm of our sofa to help me up, and head into our tiny kitchen where I push the button of the small twelve-inch TV to make it blink on.

As I'm pouring a large bag of fries into the deep-fat fryer, I hear the old guy with the gray side-part say, "And now over to Sarah-Jane Zdanski." I don't usually pay much attention to the news. But Miss Decker set us a task of checking in, so I stop pouring the fries and stare at Sarah-Jane. Good Lordy, she is beautiful. Her perfectly straight nose, her clear-blue eyes, the unblemished V of skin that points down to her breasts. Then I look down at myself, at the rolls of fat that are still obvious, even though I'm wearing three layers of clothing.

"We've got sensational exclusive interviews coming next week," she says, smiling her bright-white teeth into the camera. "But we're keeping that a secret just for now. But trust me this is something you will not wanna miss."

"Eat a frickin' burger, Sarah-Jane," I say to the TV. Then I pull down the oven door and toss three burger patties on to the tray before slamming it shut.

I turn to the TV again and notice that the news has turned into the commercials. It seems to do that every five minutes these days.

"Wendeeeeee," Sally shrieks. I turn and bundle my heavy frame into the living room, to see my little sister bent over Momma's makeshift bed. "Momma's foaming again."

CAOIMHE LARKIN

There was nobody inside when I pulled back the curtain. So, after biting at my fingernails, unsure what to do as I stood still for way too long, I eventually decided to just sit into one of the empty seats at the tiny round table. I can't believe she's late. I rushed out of school, as fast as I could, for this 'cause had to meet Dad exactly where I asked him to meet me — on the corner of Walnut Street, and *not* directly outside of the school. He was waiting for me because, firstly, he had to drive over to the golf course to drop off some paperwork, and secondly, because my appointment was at four p.m. and I needed to be here right on time. Dad let me drive from the golf course to Esbon again. I think I drove a little faster today. I'm getting used to it. I can't wait to start driving to school after my sixteenth birthday. It's going to be beyond the coolest thing I've ever done my whole life.

Meric must think I'm evil, though. I threw my arm around him, announced to American History class that we were now a couple then ran as fast as I could when the final school bell went off. I'll talk to him tomorrow, I guess. I don't know what I'm going to say to him... though I guess that's mostly why I'm here.

I look at my watch. Four minutes past four. I hate when people are late. Especially someone who can actually tell the future. Though, just as I pick up her crystal ball to squint right through it to see if I can see whatever it is she sees, she swipes open the curtain and stares at me.

"Forty dollars, young lady."

"Here y'go," I say, handing over the two twenty dollar bills my dad didn't hesitate giving to me last night.

"Please Dad," I begged him, "I need to see her again."

This moving to America doesn't seem so bad, certainly not when I can literally beg Dad for anything I want and he will give it to me.

"What's your name again, young lady?" Madam Apsectu asks.

I blink my eyes at her, wondering if she's joking or not. And when she doesn't react, other than to shuffle the two twenty dollar notes I gave her into a tiny black box that she then locks with a key and places under the table, I cough lightly, before answering.

"Caoimhe," I remind her. "Caoimhe Larkin."

"That's right. Irish girl. I shudda remembered you with that lovely red hair."

She leans down, clicks a red button on a small white box next to the table and a humming sound starts before steam begins to rise to the top of the tent.

"I'm eh... I'm here to find out more about my love life," I say. "Remember last time, you told me I would meet a boy with two M's in his name?"

"Oh," she says, offering me her first smile, "of course. Well, have you bumped into him yet?"

"Well, not so much bumped into him, but I think I sat right next to him for my first class in my new school."

"Ya see," she says, standing up and stretching her arms out wide. "I really need to start charging more than forty dollars, don't I?"

I look at her, confused, and then when she sits back down, I continue talking.

"Thing is," I say, "he's not usually my type and I'm not sure if I have the right boy. Maybe there's somebody else with two M's in their name and I was hoping you might... you might..." I point at her crystal ball before she nods her head and says, "Of course."

She picks up the ball, stares into it, then places it down and holds out her hands, inviting me to grip on to the tips of her fingers; same as I did a couple of weeks ago when I first came here.

"Well, your love life glow is strong," she says.

"Huh? What does that mean?"

"Well, it means that you have found love or you are close to finding love. Your love life glow is pulsating."

"Pulsating?"

"Kaylee, pulsating means—"

"It's *Kwee-Va*. Caoimhe."

"Sorry. Caoimhe. Pulsating means that love is strong within you and that you are in tune with your soulmate. I see him now. He is close by you." I look around myself. "No, no... not literally close by you right now. But close to your life. You are either about to meet him or...."

"Or what?" I say.

"Or you already have met him."

"Well, that's what I wanna find out," I say. "That's why I'm back here. I need to know if the boy with the two M's that I sit next to in class is the boy with the two M's that you told me I would meet and fall in love with."

"Hmmm."

"Hmmm.... what?" I say.

"Shhh, girl. Let me concentrate," she says. Then she lets go of my fingers, lifts her crystal ball closer to her face and stares through it.

"You said you see him right?" I say. "Tell me... is it the guy that I sit next to in class?" She hovers a hand over her crystal ball, but says nothing. "Why don't you just tell me what he looks like?"

She closes her eyes. Really tight. Then tilts her head backward as if she was looking up at the top of the tent, even though her eyes are closed.

"I remember," she says, sitting back upright. "He had black hair, long at the front; the bangs of his hair hangs over his eyes."

"Yes.... Yes!" I say, scooting back my chair. Then I hold my hand to my mouth as I stumble backward. "Holy fuckin' shit! That's him you're describing. That's really him. That's Meric."

JOHNNY EDWARDS

It's quiet. Peaceful. Quaint... All those words everybody associates with the middle of middle America. All the words I used to describe the middle of middle America whenever other soldiers would ask me where I'm from. I used to say, "I was born and raised in Lebanon, Kansas—the very center of the greatest country on this God-made earth." But given that I genuinely believe this is the greatest country on this God-made earth, right now I think I'd rather be back in Nasiriyah. The sound of another missile crashing into an Iraqi air base would sure beat the hell out of this silence. All's I've heard around here since I arrived back home yesterday is the odd hum of the odd car as it drives down the dirt road past my bedroom window. Then Lebanon falls totally silent again... for way too long. I'm beginning to think I hate quiet. That I hate peaceful. That I hate quaint.

I didn't know what to do as soon as I landed my ass back home. Me and Patricia ended things way before I was ordered back overseas. So, I just booked myself into the B&B at the far end of Lebanon and headed straight there from the airport, keeping my head down, hoping I wouldn't be noticed by any neighbors or family. Not until I was ready. I told myself I'd go see Patricia and the kids first thing this morning, but I think I've walked every street in Lebanon, except for the one my house happens to be on. I've been to the coffee shop twice, for two separate Americanos. I've been to the central monument three times. I've walked past the school twice, too. Though only after I knew it had closed for the day and I wouldn't be bumping into any of my kids. I don't know why I feel no fear whatsoever when I'm approaching an Iraqi Air Base driving a GBC180, yet when it comes to seeing my family, who I haven't seen for almost eighteen months, I seem to be shitting me some bricks.

I think what I fear most of all is the kids thinking I'm no hero; that I am in fact the opposite of a hero. A loser. A man who couldn't even hold his family together. They're too young to realize the truth; that me and Patricia just aren't meant to be together. It took us twenty years to realize that, so I'm not quite sure why I would ever expect two teenagers to be able to compute that in the space of the last year and a half. We got together too young, Patricia and I. That was simply our problem. Well... that and me joining the army. Being away for years at a time, and not being around much to raise the kids, sure does stretch a marriage. Though I have to say, aside from not being home so much, the army changed me in different ways. I take everything way too seriously now. No wonder Patricia fell out of love with me. I used to make her laugh when we were younger. The past five or six years all's I've made her do is sigh. She got sick of me. And I got sick of her getting sick of me. So, when she came to me a couple of years ago to tell me she thinks we'd both be happier apart, I instantly agreed. And I still agree. It's just... well, back then I had Iraq to go to. Now I got nowhere to go. I can't keep paying Mrs. Ferguson thirty-nine dollars a night to sleep in her frickin' bedroom with flower patterns plastered all around it, even if her breakfast is pretty much the perfect way to start a day.

"Thank you for your service, Sir," an elderly man says as he passes me on the street.

I stiffen my lips back at him and nod my head. It's my go-to reaction every time someone says that to me. I'm not sure what else I'm supposed to do... or even say. *You're welcome?* Sounds a bit pretentious, don't it? Though I have to say, wearing an army uniform could easily raise anybody's level of pretentiousness. It's like being a celebrity wearing one of these things. Everyone looks at you when you walk down the street, and everyone has something they would like to say. Two middle-aged women I saw yesterday when I came out of the coffee shop stopped and asked me if they could take a photo of us together.

"It's inspirational to know one of our own from little old Lebanon is leading the fight for our nation," one of them said.

That's when I stiffened my lips back at her and nodded my head. I couldn't think of what else to say.

You're welcome?

I find myself turning on to Oak Avenue, and just as I do, I pause, take in a large breath, and then, ever so slowly, let it blow out through my lips. It helps me to finally pluck up the courage to walk on. And on. This is actually the first time I've turned on to Oak in eighteen months. I guess now is as good a time as any. The kids have been home from school for a couple hours. Patricia will have gotten back from work. Dinner will have been eaten. I'm just so nervous... nervous that the kids won't greet me the way soldier's kids are supposed to greet their fathers when they arrive home from serving.

"Come on Johnny, just hug them, even if they don't hug you," I whisper to myself as I walk past the Schmitt's house. Once I've passed their house, I can see, just over the top of the fern tree that separates their home from ours, our front lawn. Nothing has changed at all. It all looks and sounds pretty much the same around here as it always has.

My stomach immediately flips itself over as soon as I step foot on our pathway and it causes me to take one step backward, then one step forward again before I pause and have to take in another one of those deep breaths.

"Come on Johnny, just hug them, even if they don't hug you," I whisper.

"Dad!" Brody calls out, pulling the front door almost off of its hinges and racing toward me. He wraps his arms around my waist, snuggles his cheek into my chest and when I look down I notice he is grinning from ear to ear. I feel relieved. *So* relieved that he is hugging me this tight.

"Look how big you're getting," I say, rubbing the sides of his shoulders. Then I lean him away from me a little, so I can stare into his face. It's like looking in a mirror back in 1980. A reincarnation of me. I just hope the reincarnation makes better decisions in life than the original.

"Missed you so much," he says. And I swear I feel the relief totally lift from my shoulders.

"I missed you too, Mr. Edwards," a familiar voice says. I look up to see Stevie — Brody's best friend — hanging out of our upstairs window, his arm waving.

"The team doing any better?" I ask.

"Training for the new season starts this weekend," Brody says. "Think you can come along and watch?"

"Sure will," I reply, tossing his hair. And as I do, I notice the door behind him slowly pushing open once again.

"Welcome back, soldier," Patricia says, leaning against the frame of the door, her arms folded the way she used to fold them when we would argue. "Figured out where you're gonna stay yet?"

KAI CHAYTON

I take the dress from the rack and then pace as quickly as I can — almost in a jog; my head covered by my hoodie; my face staring down at my muddied Converse sneakers — toward the changing rooms. I have never done anything like this before. I've thought about it. Lots of times. But I have never had the balls to do it. Not until today. Not until this dress caught my eye and I decided I simply *had* to try it on.

I sweep aside the curtain, to be greeted by a huge reflection of myself frowning in the mirror, before I take one giant step inside and sweep that curtain back closed behind me.

Then I breathe. A long, deep breath. The first breath I've taken since I removed this dress from the rack. I'm really drawn to patterns in summer dresses, but the pattern has to be subtle. I don't do loud in design. I hate loud. That's why the yellow roses on this yellow cotton dress caught my eye. They can only be seen if you really look at the dress; if you take the time to study the design. And I love this cut; the classic squared cleavage summer dress cut, with two pretty ribbon bows tied neatly on top of both shoulder straps.

I tilt my head back, just to listen out for any sound other than the regular hum of the shopping mall, and then when I feel the world outside this tiny changing room is as normal as it should be, I begin to unbutton my shirt.

This feels so naughty. But I'm getting more and more brave these days. I try on women's clothing almost every day now. When my parents and brother go out, I head straight into Momma's closet. And on days when they don't go out, I wait till everyone's sleeping. Then I'll try on whatever it is Momma left in the wash that day. Not her underwear or any of that stuff, of course. I'm not sick. Just her blouse or her dress or her skirt. Whatever she had worn that day. I do hate that the only women's clothes I ever get to wear belong to Momma, but that's the way it's got to be, I guess. I've always wanted to do this, though... go to a mall, try women's dresses on. I wish I lived in a world where I could put this dress on, walk out of this changing room and then further out through the whole mall without one other person snapping their necks to stare at me. It's depressing that I can't just be me; be the person I really am. Though I once read an article in a magazine that said nobody is truly who they want to be. But I at least have to try to be... right? Otherwise, what's the point in living?

I kick off my dirty Converse sneakers, then pull my jeans down before kicking them off too. When I stand back upright, taking in my long skinny body in the mirror, with only bright white socks, a bright white T-shirt and *The Simpsons*-themed blue and yellow boxer shorts on, I hold in another deep breath.

Then I reach down, pull the dress open and step my legs inside it. I hold my eyes closed while I slip my arms between the straps, snapping the yellow ribbons down to both shoulders.

"Okay, Kai... on three," I whisper to myself. "One... two..."

I open my eyes before saying "three" and gasp loudly; so loudly, I have to slap a hand to my mouth. Wow. This is perfect. Literally perfect. And I don't even have any makeup on. Imagine how good I'd look if I had a touch of sky-blue eyeshadow on my lids, just to contrast the bright yellow of this dress.

I feel so... so... comfortable. That's the word. I feel like me. I feel like the me I'm supposed to be. It's such a shame my whole life isn't lived inside this tiny box of a changing room; such a shame there's a whole scary world out there full of folks who would laugh at me if I walked out there looking like this.

"Wow," I whisper to myself again as I twirl in the dressing-room. I can't believe how good I look; can't believe how good I feel.

I have to buy this. I do. It's perfect. Perfect loud color. Perfect subtle design. Perfect fit. If I buy it, I could stuff it under my bed in like a shoe box or something. Momma or Poppa would never look there. Or maybe I could put it in the bottom of my socks drawer. Or in my sports bag. Nobody ever looks inside my sports bag. Not even me.

I notice, in the mirror, my smile is wider than normal, and I just know, *know*, that there is no way I am leaving here without this dress.

"Fuck it," I say.

Then I take my arms out of the straps, wiggle my way out of the dress and begin to pull my own boring clothes back on.

"Relax, Kai," I whisper. When I go to the cash register, the girl will just think I'm buying it for somebody else. I could say I'm buying a present for my sister or something. Or my girlfriend. Yes! Any normal guy can buy a normal dress for his normal girlfriend, right?

I fold the dress over my arm, then pull the curtain open a little and poke my head out. Coast clear. But I keep my head down, staring at my dirty Converse, as I walk toward the cash register on the far wall.

While I wait on the lady behind the counter to finish counting out some bills, I cover the dress with my other hand as much as I can, until she finally looks up at me and smiles, beckoning me to her.

"Hey," I say, unfolding the dress onto the counter. "It's ah... it's a gift for my girlfriend."

"It's beautiful, huh?" she says. Then she taps at some buttons on her cash register, refolds the dress, stuffs it into a bag and holds out her hand. "Thirty-nine dollars," she says.

I shove my hand into my pocket, take out two twenty dollar bills, uncrease them and then hand them over with a nervous smile.

"Thanks," I say, gripping the plastic bag she stuffed my dress into. And I'm off, racing out of the shop as she calls after me, telling me I forgot the receipt. I don't need no receipt. I won't be returning this dress.

I feel relief as soon as I step outside the store. I can't believe how easy that was. I walked into the women's wear section, picked up a dress, tried it on, went to the register, paid for it. And now here I am... walking out of the store with my first-ever item of women's clothing. Not Momma's. Mine.

"Kai. Kai. Hey."

I look down the bottom of the escalator I've just stepped onto, to see my cousin Halona grinning and waving at me. I grimace back at her while gripping the plastic bag with both hands as the escalator slowly takes me toward her.

"Hey," I say, releasing one hand from the bag to throw it over her shoulder. Then I kiss her on both cheeks—our regular family greeting.

"Buy anything nice?" she says, immediately. I stare straight back down at my dirty Converse again, saying nothing. "Kai," she says, "show me... what did you buy?"

LUCY DECKER

I drum my fingers against the calculator some more, then place it back down on the table before picking up my pen so I can scribble a number onto my notepad. I've been doing this for almost an hour now. It's torturous work.

"Fuuuck," I say after tapping at the calculator again. I scribble down the final figure, then lean back in the chair, interlocking my fingers behind my head and letting out a huge sigh filled with frustration.

I've just calculated it'll take me almost two years to get my hands on the ten grand I will need in order to undergo IVF.

"Shitty frickin' teacher's salary," I say.

I can just about afford to put two hundred and sixty dollars aside from the thirteen hundred dollars I receive each month from the school after tax is deducted. Twenty-three months of saving that amount will take me to the six grand I need on top of the four I've already put aside. The only reason I'd put that four grand aside in the first place was for him... or her... or whoever it is my baby is going to be. I wanted to have a little nest egg for the beginning of our lives together. It took me over two years to save that amount, after realizing then that I wasn't going to wait around for any man to get me pregnant; that I should — and could — do this all by myself.

I can't believe it takes ten grand for me to get pregnant when it seems as if every woman around me forms bumps at the sight of another man. I've bitten my bottom lip while congratulating my sister twice, as well as almost all of my friends from high school when they excitedly announced their pregnancy news. Even all of the female teachers at the school are mothers by now... well, except for Helen Gregg, but that's only 'cause she's just turned twenty-three. I'm always happy for them; *always* happy when somebody tells me they're expecting. But that happiness gets instantly eroded by a deep and nauseous feeling of sheer jealousy, and I always fear my fake smiles and congratulations seem transparent.

I grunt, then sit upright before picking up the calculator and launching it against the wall. I'm so weak that the calculator makes a quiet clang before landing on the floor unbroken, the face of it staring up at me and reminding me of the last figure I calculated. Twenty-three. The amount of frickin' months it'll take me to save the money I need to undergo IVF. I'll be almost forty-three by then, with my chances of getting pregnant dipping drastically month after month while I save.

"I can't wait another two years," I whisper to myself. Then I shake my head and pick up the TV remote control to try to distract myself. I stab at the standby button and wait to see what bullshit the networks are offering up as news today for my distraction.

FOX is still delving into the private life of Princess Diana four weeks after her death; interviewing a former butler of hers and trying to coax as much juice from the carton as they possibly can. I switch over to MSNBC. No surprises here. They're moaning again. They spend as much time moaning about the Republicans than they do talking up the party they're supposed to be seducing the nation into voting for. They're frickin' more obsessed with the Red Team than FOX News is. I switch to CNN, to see a middle-aged reporter standing outside the home of a family who have just lost their two-year-old son after he was mauled to death by the family bulldog.

"Thanks for the entertainment, guys," I say. Then I stab my finger at the remote control again and see Sarah-Jane Zdanski's face glowing on my screen. She's smiling her perfect teeth, teasing these damn exclusive interviews again—as if she hasn't mentioned them every ten minutes over the past few days. She's more interested in selling herself than selling any interview. It's all me, me, me with her. Though, if I looked like that... well, let's put it this way, I very much doubt I'd have to scrimp and save ten grand over the course of two years just to get pregnant. She has a line of men outside her door daily, I bet; a line that travels all the way down the block.

While she continues to tease her upcoming interviews, I decide I need another coffee in order to get through the evening without curling myself into a ball and crying. If the news can't distract me from my own reality, maybe a dose of caffeine will.

On my way to the kitchen, and purely out of habit, I lift up the phone and dial seven before balancing the receiver between my tilted head and my shoulder as I snatch at the kettle and begin filling it with water.

"Hello, Lucy," the robot barks as I turn off the tap. "You have....." Long pause. "One dating request."

FOUR

SARAH-JANE GLANCED up at the clock. Again.

It was fortunate that she had eaten a big lunch in the hotel with Phil before their limousine driver arrived to pick them up, otherwise her stomach would likely be growling by now. She'd been sitting in one of the squared armchairs in the overly-big, carpeted lobby just outside Walter Fellowes's office for over half an hour, only distracted by the ticking of the clock hanging high above the big brown door she sat facing.

The secretary had raised her eyebrows at Sarah-Jane when the elevator doors had pinged open and she'd stepped out wearing a gray overcoat.

"You're Sarah-Jane Zdanski," the secretary said, pointing. The secretary was bright-eyed, and wore her hair in a perfectly rounded 1960s-style beehive that was strapped down behind her thick bangs by a polka-dotted bow.

After Sarah-Jane nodded that the secretary had gotten her name right, she reminded her that she had a serious nut allergy and wanted assurance that those preparing the meal she was about to have with the network CEO were fully aware of that fact. The secretary nodded and said, 'yeah, yeah, yeah—don't worry,' as she was escorting Sarah-Jane to the squared armchair the network's newest anchor was *still* sitting in some thirty-five minutes later. She had already flicked through the magazine lying on the round glass table next to her. Twice. It was a copy of *Esquire*, with a photo of Walter Fellowes's jowly face sucking on a thick cigar splashed across the front page. On closer inspection, Sarah-Jane noted the magazine was dated September 1996—from over a year ago; and yet there was still a copy lying face up on each of the round glass tables next to the six squared armchairs spaced evenly around the overly large, carpeted lobby.

She was actually staring at the large brown door under the clock when that door eventually snatched opened and, as soon as it did, Sarah-Jane immediately sat more upright, flicking the loose flap of the overcoat she was wearing over her exposed knee.

The face that stared at Sarah-Jane when the door swept open was familiar. So, too, was the overcoat. In fact, it was an exact replica of the one she was wearing. Their eyes met, and as they did, Sarah-Jane flicked through the Filofax of faces from her high school and college days within her mind, dismissing each of them one by one.

The familiar face turned away, swishing her overcoat toward the double golden doors of the elevator to where she held a key card against a sensor, and then stood back to wait.

Sarah-Jane heard his disgusting throaty cough before she saw him.

"What's next, Barbara?" he croaked toward his secretary as he shuffled his short legs out of the big brown door, swiping the back of his hand across his mouth.

He looked like a toad; not just because his hairless, wrinkled head popped out from the top of his expensive suit as if he had no neck, but because he repeatedly licked at his dry lips.

Barbara pointed across the overly-large, carpeted lobby, and when Walter finally shuffled his old frame around, his beady eyes almost doubled in size.

"Ah, Sarah-Jane, that's right. I've got your company for dinner."

He swiped the back of his hand across his mouth again, as if he was salivating at the sight of his newest recruit, then held out that hand as he shuffled his short legs toward her.

She smiled, stood, curtsied, then placed her warm hand into his moist grip.

"Pleasure to see you again, Mr. Fellowes," she said, beaming a fake smile.

Walter waved her into the open brown door. Like the lobby she had been sitting in for almost forty minutes, Walter's office was overly large. Too large. There was simply no reason at all for it to be this big—taking up almost the entirety of the top floor of CSN tower. It appeared immaculately tidy and the many awards on the shelf that ran along the far side of the room glowed as if they had been newly polished. His oak desk was mammoth and fussy, yet it looked quite minimal when placed in the center of its current surroundings. And framed on the burgundy, velvet-papered walls, hung portraits painted of the mogul himself—all at different stages of his life. Though even in the watercolor painted of him in his more youthful days, Walter still looked old. He had lost his hair by his twenty-first birthday and the combover that he grew to hide that fact wasn't fooling anybody—certainly not the artist who painted this portrait. There was no disguising the fact that Walter Fellowes always looked much older than his years. When he was in his thirties, he looked as if he was in his fifties. And when he was in his fifties, he looked as if he was in his seventies. And now that he was on the eve of his seventies, he looked close to death's door. He moved ever so slowly. He talked ever so slowly. Yet there was still a hint of sparkle in the pupils of his beady little brown eyes as they stared at Sarah-Jane from under his hairless, wrinkled brow while she continued to feign interest at the portraits hanging on the wall.

When the awkwardness of him standing there, with his hands clasped, staring at her, became intolerable for Sarah-Jane, she lightly cleared her throat, then turned to face him.

"The uh..." she tightened the belt around the waist of her overcoat, "lady who just left your office... I think I know her face from somewhere. Is she from Kansas? Originally? I thought perhaps we went to school together..."

Walter licked his lips, then sniffled up his nose.

"That was Robyn Sweeney," he croaked.

Sarah-Jane squinted while the name bounced around her brain, until it eventually dropped into her memory box. Robyn Sweeney, she realized, was the weatherwoman on CSN's *Top o' the Morning* breakfast show.

"Does ah... does she have the same cheerleader's outfit on under her overcoat, too?" Sarah-Jane said, pushing out an uneasy laugh.

Walter cleared his throat as if he didn't care how disgusting it sounded.

"They're not always cheerleader's uniforms," he said, straight-faced. Then he shuffled his short legs to the far side of his large oak desk, where he sat in an office chair that looked similar to the twenty thousand dollar chair Sarah-Jane would be sitting in later that night as she probed her guests.

She didn't know where to look after he had answered her question so bluntly, so she swiveled to take in the portraits hanging on the wall again.

"Barbara," Walter barked in his croaky, husky, voice, while holding down a button on his square telephone set, "We're ready for dinner."

Then he released the button, pointed his whole hand to the chair on the opposite side of his desk, and swiped the back of his hand across his mouth again.

"I've had my fun for the day," he said, "so you may as well relax."

Sarah-Jane wasn't sure what he meant, but she hoped he was alluding to the fact that Robyn Sweeney had done enough to satisfy him sexually, and that her own services wouldn't be required. Not today, anyway.

Walter had made it known, albeit not explicitly, when he had initially met with Sarah-Jane to offer her her own show that he would be expecting favors in return. He didn't spell those favors out for her with specific words, but when he squeezed the air with both hands as if he were groping breasts and his dry lips turned into a grin, Sarah-Jane understood him to be alluding to sexual favors. Quite how far those favors were supposed to stretch, she still had no idea. But she was savvy enough to understand that this was how the system worked—not just in television, but in Hollywood, in Washington, on Wall Street... Men in high positions had been using their power to get what they wanted since the beginning of civilization. And what men wanted most of all were orgasms at the hands, or mouths, or indeed vaginas, of the prettiest women they could possibly lay their eyes on.

He gloated and seduced her in their first face-to-face meeting, while flashing his yellow teeth though an ugly grin, telling her just how skilful and effortless he found her live broadcasting to be.

"You stayed really calm," he croaked, "in a moment of mayhem, and that makes you a naturally gifted reporter. You'll fit into the CSN family without any issues at all. I'm certain of it. You're gonna be a smash hit."

"Gifted," or "calm," or "smash hit" or whatever superlatives Walter was throwing her way, Sarah-Jane was no fool. She knew she wasn't in a meeting with one of the country's most powerful media moguls just because she could stay calm under pressure, but more so because she could stay calm under pressure while also looking inarguably beautiful.

"Nervous?" he croaked.

Sarah-Jane scooted her chair closer and then leaned her forearms onto Walter's desk.

"Excited," she said.

"I told ya... you're gonna be a smash hit, kid. Howie tell you how many Americans will be tuning in to see you tonight?"

Sarah-Jane shook her head.

"He told me it was big, but he didn't tell me the projection, no."

"Thirty million."

Sarah-Jane heard her own lips pop open. But just as they did, the door rattled before the sound of shoes shuffled across the carpet behind her. She was in such a state of shock, that she didn't instinctively glance over her shoulder to see who was coming.

Then Barbara appeared, gripping two brown paper bags with

KFC logos splashed across them and a carrier carton that contained two extra-large buckets of Pepsi.

"Thanks Barbara," Walter croaked.

After Barbara had shuffled her way back down the carpet and eventually back out to her desk in the overly-large, carpeted lobby, Sarah-Jane swallowed, then leaned closer to the desk.

"Sorry... did you say *thirty* million?"

Walter ripped open one of the paper bags, before stretching his short arm toward the other one, so he could push it across the desk toward his dinner date.

"Can you believe it? America is already in love with you," he said. "They've seen your teaser commercials on TV these past few weeks. They've been looking at your billboard in Times Square today. America loves you. And they're obsessed with this story. Thirty million they are projecting. Thirty fucking million. It's gonna be the most watched show we've ever had here on CSN."

He plunged a hand into the ripped paper bag, snatched at a crispy chicken wing and began to gnaw his yellow teeth into it.

Sarah-Jane looked at the paper bag in front of her, then slid it away with a wave of her hand.

"But your seven p.m. slot usually gets around six million viewers, right? I assumed when Howie said it was gonna be a big number tonight that he meant eight million. At most."

Walter sucked on his fingers, his tongue swirling and slurping.

"What's wrong?" he said, pointing the bone of his chicken wing toward her brown paper bag. "You one of them? One of those freaks who don't eat no finger lickin' chicken?"

Sarah-Jane flicked her eyes toward the paper bag again then clenched her teeth.

"I appreciate the dinner," she said, "but ah... no. Fried chicken's not for me."

"Ah," he replied, before gnawing into another chicken wing, "one of those new-age vegie-tarians are we?"

"Something like that," Sarah-Jane replied.

Then she leaned back in the chair while Walter dipped fries, and the tips of his fingers, into a small, plastic tub of gravy before stuffing them into his mouth.

After brushing his hands together to rid them of excess crumbs and salt, he stood, loudly sipped from the extra-large bucket of *Pepsi* and then, while still chewing, walked around his oak desk.

"You look fantastic. It's a shame I had seen Robyn in her little maid's uniform before dinner and I'm all out of steam now." I like to make the new girls happy on their first day. Anyway," he said, before tonguing the gaps of his teeth in search of shards of fried chicken as he slowly approached his dinner date, "Lemme see you."

"Huh?" Sarah-Jane said.

Walter motioned upward with his hand, and so Sarah-Jane stood as her stomach began to wind itself into a knot.

"Come on, take off the coat," Walter said.

Sarah-Jane took a step away from the chair she had been sitting on, then unknotted the belt of her overcoat, before shrugging it from her shoulders. As Walter swiped the back of his hand across his mouth, she draped the coat over the chair, then interlocked her fingers while the mogul began circling her, still tonguing the gaps of his teeth.

"Of all the girls, over all of the years, you've got to be one of the prettiest," he croaked. "It's those eyes, what color are they... silver?"

"They change color," Sarah-Jane said, "depending on what I'm wearing."

"Mmm," he said, his breath glancing off the nub of her nose as he leaned in closer so he could stare at her eyes. Then he licked his lips, before running his hand across his mouth again. "I'm excited. *Very* excited." He stretched to his tiptoes, leaned in closer, and kissed Sarah-Jane on the lips before turning and shuffling his short legs away. "I'm excited because I can't wait to see you in action tonight. America's gonna fall in love with those eyes."

Sarah-Jane looked down, past the crest emblazoned onto her chest, past the pleats of the short skirt and past her bare, unblemished legs.

"I would hope, Mr. Fellowes, sir," she said, "that they won't just be tuning in to look at my eyes. We've got an incredible and important story—"

"Yes, yes," Walter said, perching his ass against his desk before picking up his bucket of Pepsi so he could sip and slurp from it again. "Yes, it's about the journalism and this story... boy oh boy... this story is something. But you delivering this story, you conducting these interviews? That's why thirty million Americans are gonna be tuning in tonight. You're not nervous, are you?"

Sarah-Jane gripped the back of the chair she had been sitting on.

"I'm not nervous, no. I don't get nervous. But I am feeling a little uneasy about one tiny detail," she said.

Walter coughed into the back of his hand, then swiped it across his mouth again.

"What's that?" he croaked.

"The opening two sentences... I just don't feel as if they are appropriate for—"

Walter held his hand up, causing Sarah-Jane to snap her lips shut.

"I hear you've been a drama queen about the first two sentences ever since you received the first script."

"Well it's just that it seems rather inappropriate—"

Walter held his hand up again.

"You will say those opening two lines, you hear me?"

Sarah-Jane shuffled her feet on the spot, then awkwardly brushed a loose strand of hair away from her beautiful face.

Sensing her discomfort, Walter turned, picked up his bucket of Pepsi and held it aloft.

"Lemme tell ya somethin'... and I don't ever want you to forget this. All you fresh-faces straight outta college, you think you're entering the news business when you come in here. This ain't the news business. This is the television business. And in the television business every story has extra juice to it," he said. "My job is to find the right flavor of juice. My executive producer's job is to find the ingredients for the flavor of juice I want. My director's job is to pour that juice into a nice carton... wanna know what your job is, as a broadcaster, Sarah-Jane?"

She flicked her eyes upward, to stare at his toad-like head poking out from the top of his designer suit, before shaking her head. Walter snarled at her, then crushed the bucket of Pepsi he was holding aloft until it collapsed in his grip and brown liquid began showering to the expensive carpet below.

"Your job," he croaked, "is to squeeze the juice."

MERIC MILLER

I'm always the first student at school on Fridays. Soon as I come through the double doors at the front, I head straight here—to this tiny office at the bottom of the back stairs. When Principal Klay asked me — because at one point I told him I like to watch the news on TV — to become the school's newspaper editor, he said I could have my own little office; told me he'd buy a brand new computer and printer for me, too. He almost kept his promise. The computer isn't exactly new and the printer is so big that it looks like some sort of futuristic coffin for a really, really fat person. But at least they both work. And they both help me get my weekly newsletter out every Friday morning.

I love it when the school is this quiet. I've often thought I'd love to come in at eight a.m. every morning and not just on Fridays. I would, too, if it meant I could go home an hour earlier. Heck, I'd do school at any hour of the day if there were no other students inside it with me. Or at least I would have preferred it that way... until she showed up. My stomach flips over as she comes to my mind again. Not that she has ever left it for too long since I first laid eyes on her. I actually wish I hadn't had a shower from our shitty little spitty shower last night because I think I washed all of her smell off me. I hope the next time I see her she'll just wrap her arm around me again and I'll get that smell back. But I'm not even sure if she'll even talk to me again, let alone wrap her arm around me. When I woke up in the middle of the night I was convinced she ran off from school yesterday to get away from me. But during my quiet walk to school in the dark this morning, I managed to convince myself she might have actually meant it when she told Stevie she was dating me now. I dunno. I'm confused. But I guess we kinda did go for a kinda date last week, even if Wendy was there, too. So... who knows? Maybe I do have a girlfriend. Which would be so super awesome. I knew going to the fortune teller would be a genius move. The thought just popped into my head when I was biking around the monument that afternoon and heard her talking to her family... Maybe you don't need to look like Stevie or Brody to get the nicest girls in school, after all. Maybe you just need to be a bit of a genius. Though the only person who knows that I'm a bit of a genius is me. My Mom sure has no idea how smart I am. None of my teachers do, either. That's 'cause I ain't smart like they expect me to be smart; all interested in why X should equal fuckin' Y or some shit like that. That's not smart. That's dumb. That's the dumbest damn thing I ever heard my whole life—adding up letters. No... I'm smart in a street-smart kinda way. And that's the best sorta smart there is. But I just keep my street-smart thoughts to myself. I don't like doin' much talking. I do my talking in print.

I can totally understand what Miss Decker is tryin' to teach us in American History even though I pretend I'm not listening to her. She's sayin' all the power lies in the hands of the folk who make the news. I know that. I have all the power in this school... except, well... I would have all the power if anybody ever read what I wrote. All's I know is I have a budget to print three hundred copies, front and back page, which is what I do every Friday morning — it's what I'm doing right now, if only this futuristic coffin would wake the hell up — and then I'll leave a few copies in each of the hallways around the school, as well as a large bundle at the front desk beside where the principal's assistant sits. Thing is, the large bundle at the front desk seems to stay large all through Friday, until the principal's assistant ends up trashing them before she goes home for the weekend. Some students read the copies I leave round the hallways, though, I'm sure. At least I know they're not left in the place I drop them in for long. Though, they are mostly used as throwing balls during class breaks between periods. There are always balled up copies of my newspaper found in almost every hallway of this school all through Friday. I just hope that whichever student squeezed the newspaper up into a ball before they threw it at another student's head at least read the headlines before they threw it.

The futuristic coffin double beeps and so I slam my hand down on to the desk.

"Damn it!" I say.

Out of ink. Again.

I press save on the computer, then head out of the tiny office and down the quiet hallway before turning left under the staircase. Principal Klay gave me a key to the storeroom. So, I let myself in and then begin to, as is a new habit of mine, whistle the theme tunes of the TV News Networks as I search the shelves for packs of colored ink cartridges. It's dark in here. It's dark all over this floor in the basement. After I grab a pack of cartridges, I turn on my heels, lock the storage room door and, when I look around me to notice there ain't nobody around, I continue whistling. My favorite is the MSNBC theme tune. But my favorite can change depending on what mood I'm in. Right now, I'm whistling the FOX News tune. I have been most of the morning. I don't really know why.

"Hey," she says.

"Shiiit," I say, holding my chest. "Nobody's ever... ever... ev—'" I stutter. And then I stop to allow my stomach to flip over. She looks so pretty perched on the edge of my desk.

"Sorry," she says. "I eh... was told I would find you down here before school started on a Friday morning. It sure is quiet round here at this time of the day, huh?"

I stand in the doorway, frozen, staring at the different strands of orange and gold in her hair. And when I realize that's all I'm doing, I nod.

"Ah...." I say. "So yeah... this is where I do it, where I write and print the school newspaper."

She looks around the tiny office, at all four of the blank white walls, then down at the futuristic coffin.

"I was hoping to talk to you about yesterday," she says, "about what happened after American History class."

"Oh," I say. And then my stomach flips itself over again. But heavier this time. As if it's daring me to vomit.

"Yeah, I mean... firstly, I'm sorry," she says, tilting her head to the side and looking as pretty as girls can look sometimes on the front pages of magazines.

"No, don't be..." I shake my hair.

"No. I am. I didn't mean to put you in the situation I ended up putting you in. And I just wanted to get away from Stevie. What a creep."

"Oh, yeah. Totally. He's such an ass," I say. And then my mind screams, *"Fuuuck!"* because suddenly it hits me that she only put her arm around me to piss Stevie off. It wasn't about me. It was never about me. It was only about her trying to look cool. In front of him.

"It's just... I mean... I don't really know how to say..."

She pauses. For way too long; long enough for her to look around all four white walls of this tiny office again.

"Just say it," I say to her as I scratch at the top of my hair, brushing my hair over my eyes so I can hide behind it.

"It's just... well, I've never done this before, but eh... I'm not quite sure what it is, or who it is, but something or somebody is telling me that you and me... that we should eh..."

My stomach flips again. I wanna burp. But I don't. Not in front of her. That would be disgusting.

"Huh?"

"That we should kinda, like, spend more time with each other."

"Spend more time with each other?"

"Yeah," she says, smiling so beautifully that I would love to do nothing more right now than to take three steps forward and kiss that smile. Even though I don't know how to kiss. I don't think I do anyway. Never tried it.

"Well, uh..." I scratch at my hair again then sweep it away from my eyes with my fingers, so her eyes can see mine.

"Or we could just be friends and... you know? After all, we do sit next to each other in American History and—"

"No... no... the first one, the 'see each other more' option," I say.

She smiles one of those beautiful smiles again. Then walks past me, nudging my shoulder with hers. By the time I turn around, she's out the door, her sneakers screeching against the freshly-cleaned hallway floors.

See each other more?

"Wait!" I say, spinning and grabbing onto the door frame. "When you put your arm around me yesterday you said we were dating. Are we... are we dating?"

She shrugs her shoulders, then holds her hands up.

"Well, in order for us to start dating, Meric, you'd probably need to ask me out on a date."

BRODY EDWARDS

It always amazes me that we laugh for the exact amount of time. Like, someone will be telling a story and when he finishes we'll all laugh, laugh, laugh, laugh... and then stop! Right at the exact same time.

"Guess what?" Jared says. It's his turn to talk now. "I found three full-on porno mags under the mattress of my old man's bed."

"You fuckin' kiddin', dude?" Stevie says.

"No man. Real ones, too. Not just chicks with their tits out. But, like, actual fucking, dude."

"Wow," Stevie says. "Can you get me one?"

"Th'fuck man. Why the hell would I steal a porn mag from my old man and give it to you?"

We all laugh, laugh, laugh... and then stop!

"What are the chicks like in it?" I ask, after pulling my T-shirt over my head. "They hot?"

"Yeah. Like professional models, dude. Gorgeous. Big tits, shaved puss. European, I think they are," Jared says.

"Hey, speaking of European chicks, what you guys think of that new Irish one with the funny name?" Lloyd asks.

"Ah, she ain't all that. Freckly. Isn't she? Not into freckles," Hawkins says.

"Nah, me neither," Stevie says.

"Stevie's already had his—"

"Shut up dude," Stevie says, shoving at my chest.

"Okay guys listen up," Coach Quill shouts, swinging the locker room door open. "Good session today. We know our plays. We've been through them all. If anyone doesn't know what their individual job is next Friday night, now is the time to let me know."

All of us stare back at him. No hands go up. And none of us open our mouths.

"Okay, well... now I know I can trust you to do your jobs."

He's such a great coach. But it's a pity we don't have the players to compete at State level. Me and Stevie carry this team. We'll get us as far as we can. But however far Median High gets, it'll all be down to us two. Us two and Coach Quill.

"You two," Quill says, turning to us as we're both grabbing our hoodies from the hook. He slaps us both on the shoulder, then squeezes us closer to him. "I'm relying on you guys, okay? You do what we practiced out there today and we'll get off to a winning start next Friday, I'm sure of it."

"You got it, Coach," Stevie says. Then they do their handshake thing. Then Coach Quill turns to me and we do our new handshake thing that we just made up earlier. And then me and Stevie do our handshake thing that we haven't changed in over two years. And after that, without saying another word, we yank our hoodies over our heads, hold our fists out to our teammates for bumps while we mumble a few "Catch you Monday, guys" before leaving the locker room.

"Hey, man," Stevie whispers to me as we're walking down the hallway, "just leave the Irish chick getting finger fucked by me between me and you, huh? Same with you and Decker, dude? It's our little dares that we've got goin' on that are just between me 'n' you, okay?"

"Sure thing, dude," I say. Then we do our handshake again.

"I don't want anyone thinking I was with some ugly chick, y'know how it is."

"I gotcha, dude. Won't say a word."

I pinch my fingers and swipe them across my lips, just as we are stepping outside.

"Hey, your Dad's there, dude," Stevie says, "I'mma run. You know me after a good practice—I like to jerk off soon as I get home."

"'Course, dude. I'll catch you later."

Then we do our handshake thing again before I walk across the parking lot to my old man. It's so great to have him back home. Well... not exactly home. But at Mrs. Ferguson's B&B.

"Quill put you guys through some tough drills out there today, huh?" Dad says, before play-punching me in the gut. "From what I see, you and Stevie sure could do with some help out there. You guys are wasted talents in that team. It's not the worst position to be in. Stand out players on a bad team can still get noticed."

"Yeah, that's what Stevie says," I say.

I love talking to my old man about football. In fact, it's probably the only thing we've ever spoken about. I genuinely don't remember ever talking to him about anything else. I'd love to ask him lotsa things. And when he was away for so long I told myself, when Dad's home I'm gonna talk to him more. But now I can't really remember what any of those conversations are supposed to be about. I guess I should ask him about Iraq. In fact, I don't even know why American soldiers are even in Iraq in the first place.

"Hey, Dad," I say as we begin walking. "Why don't we go out for a burger, huh? You hungry?"

"Ahhh," he rubs at the stubble on his chin. "I can't Brody, sorry. Not this evening. I've got a uh... got a dinner thing later."

He looks at his watch.

"A dinner thing? Whatchu mean a dinner thing?"

"Ah, it's nothing," he says, tussling my hair.

And there he is. Back home. Back to being my Dad... not answering any of my questions unless they're about football.

"So, tell me," he says. "How you think the Jayhawks will do this season?"

JOHNNY EDWARDS

I rub my palms up and down my jeans again.

Gee. Don't think I've ever sweated this much. Not even in Iraq. Not even approaching an air base in Iraq.

After I've dried my palms, I pick up the menu and turn it around in my hands. I already know what I'm going to order.

"Can I get you another drink, sir?" the waiter says to me.

"Uh. Not right now."

I check my watch. Seven minutes past eight. Then I stare at the door and begin to rub my sweaty palms against my jeans again when it slowly pushes open and my rubbing stops.

"Lucy," I say, standing up.

She smiles, then walks over to me, stretching her hand out. I rub my right hand against my jeans again, then place it inside hers, hoping it's not too wet.

"You must be John."

"Yeah," I say, taking a seat. "Or Johnny. E'rybody calls me Johnny. 'Cept my kids."

"Huh?" she says, removing the strap of her purse from her shoulder and placing it under the table. "What do they call you?"

I burst out laughing.

"Dad."

"Oh," she says, covering her face with her hand as she sits.

I take the time she's hiding behind her hand to rub my palms against my jeans again, then when I'm done, I slide the menu across the table.

"I haven't been here for a couple years, but they used to make the best hamburgers in all of Kansas... so I already know what I'm having."

She removes her hand from her face, smiles up at me while shaking her head, then she cracks open the menu.

I wouldn't say she's great looking. And I wouldn't say good looking, either. She's okay looking. Or average, is probably the best way of describing her. Average mousy brown hair, average face, average fashion taste. But I really don't care. When I promised myself in Iraq that I would start dating again when I finally got home, I kept having to remind myself that looks don't matter. I'm forty-three now. I have to be more grown up than just judging women on their appearance. I want somebody to talk to. Not somebody to look at. I learned that mistake from my first marriage.

"Didn't I, ah..." she says, looking up from the menu. "Sorry, I've just noticed the stars 'n' stripes on your collar... didn't I see you a couple days ago? Where you in Ladow's Coffee Shop? You walked in in your uniform."

"Yes! Right. I think I saw you, too. Was that you sitting in the corner, gossiping with a friend?"

"Yes! That's exactly what I was doing. Gossiping."

We both laugh. And then she looks back down at the menu as it goes all quiet again.

"A drink for the lady?" the waiter says, taking us out of our silence.

"Can I have a red wine, please? Any will do. One that's not too expensive."

I push out a laugh.

"And for you, sir?"

I tap on my pint glass.

"Another Bud, bud."

"So, you're a soldier?" she says as soon as the waiter goes to fetch us our drinks.

"Yeah. I've ah..." I lean forward toward the table, "spent the last eighteen months in Iraq."

"Ah, yes. The no-fly-zone operation."

"Oh," I say, raising my eyebrows. "You in the army too?"

"No," she says, snorting out a laugh. "I'm a teacher. I'm just interested is all..."

"Yeah, we're doing great work out there. It's a fantastic mission. We've got things totally under control."

"Oh, thank you," she says, and just as I'm about to say, "You're welcome," I notice the waiter has placed her glass of wine in front of her. She wasn't thanking me. She was thanking him. Then he passes me a large glass of beer from his tray, turns, and leaves us to it. "So ah... you think we'll pull out of Iraq soon?" she asks.

"Yeah," I reply. "Not much more to be done."

"That's good to hear," she says. And then I immediately know she's one of them; one of those opposed to us being overseas. A liberal. A Democrat. Though she doesn't really look like one of them. She sure doesn't look like she lives up her own ass.

"Well, looks like we've already found something in common," she says, closing the menu and smiling up at me. "I fancy the burger, too."

LUCY DECKER

It goes a little silent after I say that. Then he pauses, picks up his beer and takes a nervous sip. This isn't going so good. And we haven't even ordered yet.

"Well, looks like we've already found something in common," I say, to ease the awkwardness. "I fancy the burger, too."

It's a pity he's a soldier because he's kinda handsome. Not handsome to everyone, I wouldn't say. But he's got wide shoulders and looks as if he would be a great big spoon in bed every morning. That'd be nice; that'd be *really* nice. He's got one of those buzz haircuts that would just have to change if we were to ever get serious though, and his eyes are quite narrow. *Very* narrow, now that I look at them over the rim of his glass as he takes a sip from his beer. That could bug me. In fact it probably already is bugging me. But not much more than the fact that he's a soldier. I bet he's a Republican... there's probably zero chance we're gonna get along.

"Two burgers," I say, holding up a peace sign when I see the waiter approach us while folding over his notebook.

He nods, takes the menu from me, then turns on his heels to deliver our order to the kitchen.

I take a little sip from my wine and, as I do, it feels as if the whole restaurant has gone quiet, that it's not just our table.

"So teach—"

"So about the war—"

We both pause, having both talked over each other to fill the silence at the exact same time.

"No, no, you first."

"No you...."

"Well, listen, I guess we have two starting points. It's either war or teaching," he says, laughing. He's got a good laugh. Husky. It suits his bulky shoulders. "Rock, paper, scissors?" he says, raising an eyebrow. "If you win, I'll talk about the war. If I win, you tell me about teaching."

I giggle. A sincere giggle. Not a fake one, even though it probably sounds fake. Rock, paper, scissors... I like it. He's funny. Or fun, anyway. And I sure could do with some fun in my life.

"Let's do it," I say, holding a balled fist across the table.

When he does the same, and our knuckles touch, I finally feel at ease; as if I realize there aren't going to be any more awkward silences.

"Rock, paper, scissors, shoot..." he says.

We both laugh so loudly that the man sitting behind Johnny snaps a stern stare over his shoulder.

"War it is," Johnny says as I cover his rock with my paper. "Well... where do I start?" I shrug my shoulders then take a sip of wine through my smile. It's been a long time since I sipped wine through a smile. I normally sip it through a grimace. "Well..." he says, leaning his forearms on to the table. "It's different over there than everyone thinks it is. I mean, different in comparison to how they show it on the news and stuff."

"Isn't everything?" I say, with a laugh.

"Sorry?"

"Oh, don't mind me," I say, "I bet there's a lot of boredom, right?"

"Yeah," he says, nodding. "Nobody from the real world has ever said that to me... but yeah. You're absolutely right. It's pretty much twenty-four hour boredom. We are sitting around in heavy clothing under the sun for fifteen hours a day with not much to do other than patrol. And even when the sun goes down, we're still just sitting around in camp; same guys, same company, same stories. The guys are good fun though, so I shouldn't..."

"Lots of guy humor, I bet."

"You could say that. Us men don't ever grow up, do we?"

"Oh..." I say, shaking my head from side to side. "I teach teenage boys. I sure hope they grow up."

I take another sip of wine while he produces his husky laugh, then I follow up with my questioning.

"Will you have to go back to Iraq... or?"

"It's likely I won't," he shakes his head while sucking in a breath. "My squad seems to think America is done in the Middle East. Our specific mission — the squadron I'm in — is coming to an end."

"Cool," I say, nodding along; deciding whether or not I should inform him he couldn't be more wrong. If he thinks America is close to finishing their meddling in the Middle East then he doesn't know jack shit about America's meddling in the Middle East. "Well, let's hope everyone gets home soon, and gets home safe," I opt to say instead.

"God bless America," he says, holding his pint glass toward me.

"To humanity," I say, winking back at him, while I clink the top of my wine glass against the edge of his.

He laughs that husky laugh again. And I feel myself pulling at the collar of my blouse. Surely I can't be getting the hots for somebody who preaches at the altar of God. Let alone America.

"So... you don't believe in God?" he asks.

"I don't believe in any of 'em, no," I say, before taking another sip. "You?" I cringe while I await his answer.

"Yeah, nah... I don't know. Impossible to know, isn't it?"

"Exactly," I say. "That is what I always say. It is impossible for anyone to know."

"Yeah," he says, nodding.

"And that means anyone who is claiming to actually know is kinda well... they're making it up, aren't they?"

He snorts out a laugh.

"You cut deep right off the bat, huh?" he says.

The waiter arrives, laying down sky blue folded napkins and a knife and fork for each of us while we silently stare across the table at each other.

"What's the best thing about Switzerland?" Johnny then says, leaning more forward as soon as the waiter leaves us.

"What's the what?" I squint back at him.

"What's the best thing about Switzerland?"

"I don't know," I say, picking up my wine.

"Well, I don't know either," he says, "but their flag is a big plus."

I spray wine out of my mouth and on the table, spitting and dribbling it down my chin. I think I sprayed a little bit of him too, but that's his own fault; cracking a shit joke just as I'm taking a sip of wine. I reach over and brush his hand with my fingers.

"I'm so sorry," I say. He's laughing too hard to notice I'm touching him; his husky cackle on loop; his thick neck glowing red; his narrow eyes watering.

When we both recompose ourselves, he wipes at his eyes with his fingers, then holds his glass aloft.

"To humanity," he says.

When we clink, he winks one of his narrow eyes at me.

"So... you're a teacher, huh? Which school you teach at?"

"Median High."

"Oh," he says, "my son goes there."

KAI CHAYTON

Saturday night. Nine p.m. It's supposed to be the happiest time of the week, isn't it? I bet every young person I know is out there somewhere having fun. But here I am, all alone in my bedroom, tears racing down my face while my father watches some old movie on the TV downstairs.

I couldn't believe it when Halona grabbed the bag from me and took out the dress. She unfolded it there and then, at the bottom of the escalators, and said, "What the Holy Hell is this?"

I stuttered. Hesitated. And before I managed to get one full word out of my mouth, she already knew... Halona already knew...

Halona is great. And she's one of the closest people to me in my life. But she just doesn't understand. She can't understand. A boy wanting to dress in women's clothing doesn't make sense to her. Why would it? It barely makes sense to me.

I walk into momma's bedroom, take the small bench she sits on when she's sewing and then walk it back to my bedroom. I don't know why my hands aren't shaking. I should be petrified. Scared. Frightened. But I'm not. And that's how I know I'm doing the right thing. Once I'm gone, so, too, will the whole mess my life has turned into.

I pick up the rope, pull at the noose again, to make sure it's as tight as it can be, then I loop the loose end around the beams of my ceiling before I step up onto momma's small sewing bench. After taking in one large breath, I fit my head inside the loop of the noose and reach up to pull it as tight as it can possibly squeeze around my neck.

I stand still for a few moments, not really sure what to do with my hands. Then, I decide to place them behind my back, as if they were tied, before I begin to swing back and forward, rocking momma's small bench a little.

"Okay, Kai," I say to myself. "It's time."

Then I kick the bench from under my feet.

CAOIMHE LARKIN

As me and Dad are pulling up in the car I can see that he's already here; standing outside, silhouetted by the front window of the restaurant with his hands in his pockets and staring at us through his long fringe. When our car lights hit him, I realize he hasn't really dressed up. He's in the same T-shirt and jeans he normally wears to school. Maybe I've overdressed. Shit! I've *definitely* over-dressed.

"Okay, love," Dad says, "I'll pick you up at ten p.m. Not a minute later." He leans his cheek closer for me to kiss, which I do, before I push open the door.

"Thanks Dad."

As I'm walking toward Meric I decide I'll hug him, none of this shaking hands nonsense. One hug. That's it. No kisses on the cheek or anything like that. Just a one-handed hug, then I'll ask him how he is. It's that simple. Greeting people shouldn't be as compli-cated as I always seem to make it.

I smile at him, then he pushes his hand straight toward me, just as I lean in for the hug and his hand gets trapped between us and ends up dangling around by my vagina as I press him against me.

"Shit. Sorry," he mumbles as we release.

"No probs," I say. "I'm hungry... you?"

He shakes his fringe up and down before I turn around to pull open the restaurant door.

A waiter holds one finger up at us as he carries a tray to another table. So me and Meric just stand in the doorway next to the front desk, not saying anything to each other as we look around the restaurant. It seems nice. Nobody's ever brought me on a date to a restaurant before. Meric chose it. He says it's supposed to be the best restaurant in the whole of Lebanon. Though Dad did say to me that it may actually be the only restaurant in the whole of Lebanon. It's cute that Meric chose to bring me here for our first date. But what was really cute was how he actually asked me on the date... by sliding a note across our desk in the middle of American History class with "Saturday, 8:30 p.m?" scribbled on it.

"Isn't that Decker?" I say, turning to Meric.

He brushes his fringe aside with his fingers and squints.

"Yeah, think it is," he says.

"Now," the waiter interrupts, standing in front of us and blocking the view we had of our teacher and her boyfriend.

"Table for two..." I say.

"Do you have a reservation?"

I look to Meric.

"Uh..." He coughs. Nervously. "I booked a uh...table for two under the name Miller."

"Ah yes," the waiter says, pointing a finger at the paperwork in front of him, "Follow me." The waiter leads us to a table at the side of the bar and I take off my coat and drape it over the back of the chair before sitting into it. "Here are some menus, I'll be back for orders in a few minutes."

"Thank you," I say to the back of the waiter as he walks away. Then I look up at my date and try to smile at him. But he's just staring down at the edge of the table... same as he does in class all of the time. "Thanks for organizing the date," I say.

Meric looks up, nods, and says, "No problem," then stares back down at the edge of the table again.

"Didn't know Decker had a boyfriend," I say, pushing my chair closer to the table.

"Me neither."

He tries to crane his neck to look around the side of the bar.

"Whaddya think of her?" I ask.

"She's cool. Well... cool for a teacher," he says.

"Yeah. She is kinda cool. Her classes are cool, I guess."

I flip open the menu and begin reading through it.

"They do the best burgers ever here," Meric says, "look."

He nods his head to the left, and I stare over at the table across from us.

"Hell no. I couldn't eat that. The size of it," I whisper. My eyes actually widen as I take in the burger on the customer's plate. "That's about this size," I say, forming a football-sized shape with my hands." I stand up, and pinch at my stomach. "And my belly is only half that size. That burger, even all chewed up, couldn't fit inside me."

Meric giggles into his hand. Then, when he removes his hand, he properly smiles up at me; not just with his lips, but with his eyes, too. I've never seen him properly smile before. His teeth are a little crooked. But I shouldn't judge. I had to wear braces for two and a half years when I was in primary school.

"I think I'll have the Chicken Cesar Salad," I say, closing the menu.

And by the time I look back up at Meric, his giggling has stopped and he's staring at the edge of the table again. It's such a weird thing to do all of the time.

I chew on my bottom lip as I twist my bum from side to side on the chair, wondering what we should talk about.

"Eh... tell me about your family," I say to him.

I notice his eyes from under the strands of his hair flick upward, then he shuffles his chair in closer to the table and sighs.

"This won't take long," he says. "One mother. No father. No sister. No brother. You?"

"That's it?" I say.

"Well, I've had about twenty-two stepfathers, each for about a month at a time over the years... but..." He shrugs his shoulders up and then releases them back down slowly. "What about you? You from a dysfunctional family too?"

"I used to think I was," I say, leaning both elbows on the table, "until I moved here."

MERIC MILLER

"I'll get that," I say, sliding the check toward me as soon as the waiter places it in the middle of the table.

"Oh, no. You don't have to do that. I'm the kinda girl who likes to pay her way. My dad gave me some money to—"

"No, no. I want to," I say, taking the money out of my pocket and counting out six ten dollar bills. "I insist."

She smiles one of those magazine model smiles at me and I think I look cool as I count out the bills and toss them on top of the check. I've never done this before. Never taken anybody out to dinner. I had to steal the money from my Mom's oversized pink purse to be able to pay for it. She always has cash in there. Sometimes there's lots of it. Sometimes not so much. Luckily, there was a few hundred in there when I checked yesterday, so I hope she doesn't miss the ten ten-dollar bills I took. To hell with it. I'll just deny I took it anyway, even if she does start asking questions. I'll just tell her I was out riding around on my bike... like I always am.

I'm not sure how this date has gone, even though I feel happy. There were lots of awkward silences. *Lots* of them. From start to finish. Any time we did talk, it was usually because she asked questions. But I just feel like smiling because I've just brought a girl, a beautiful Irish girl, out on a date.

"Thank you so much," the waiter says, picking up the bills.

"Keep the change," I say. And then I look at Caoimhe to see if she is impressed that I left such a large tip. It's weird that I think this is how I can win her over when we've spent the last two hours sitting across from each other and I coulda won her over by actually talking or something. Instead, I just chomped on my burger, my hands dripping with grease and ketchup, while she ate her salad like a lady, using a knife and fork. I guess I don't really know how to win a girl over using just words. Words aren't really my thing. Unless they're in print.

The only question I thought of myself, and actually asked out loud, was about the trip to Europe. She says she's not going either. Great! Same as me. No way I could afford it. No way my momma would splurge four hundred dollars for me to have a good time, no matter how much cash she has in that oversized pink purse of hers sometimes.

"You know when I said I didn't have the money to afford to go to Europe?" I say as we're both putting on our coats.

"Uh-huh," she says.

'Well, I don't want you to think that I won't have money for us to... for us to... y'know do this again sometime. I'll find the money. If you want to go out on another date, I can definitely find the money."

She smiles at me again, then places a hand to my cheek. It feels warm. Really warm. So warm, I would love to tilt my head to the side so I can trap it between my cheek and my shoulder and fall asleep on it.

"Meric, stop stressing and calm down," she says. "Next time, it doesn't have to be at the best restaurant in town. A McDonald's will do."

My stomach flips itself over.

"So there *is* gonna be a next time?" I say. And as I say it I notice the waiter overhear me and cringe a little, his shoulders dipping, his teeth clenching.

"Sure," she says. I eyeball the waiter as we leave. The nerve of him cringing at me like that after I gave him a seven dollar tip. Fuckin' ass hole.

"Look," Caoimhe says, turning to me as soon as we step into

the cold, "my dad's already here. I'll eh... I'll see you in school on Monday, huh?" Then she slaps me on the side of the shoulder before running across the road to where her dad is parked.

I wait on the sidewalk and when their car eventually pulls away, I slap my hands together.

"Fuck yeah!" I say. "Meric, you're a genius."

WENDY CAMPBELL

I yawn. Again. A big yawn this time; much bigger than the hundred yawns I've already yawned this mornin'.

"Jeez, you really do look like a hippo," Brody says.

"Shut yo trap, you fuckin' jock strap," I retort as soon as I snap my jaws back together.

He sits in beside that other jock strap friend of his and they bump fists and giggle like ten year olds. Assholes.

"Hey," Caoimhe says, sliding in to the chair next to me. "Where were you Friday? I missed you. I've so much to tell ya."

"Ah... I was... well. Actually," I say, looking around myself. "Do you think you could write me another note, pretending to be my Momma again?"

"Another one? What's going on, Wendy? Everything okay?"

"Yeah," I say. And then I yawn again. And without even saying anything, Beavis and Butthead behind me start giggling. I choose to ignore them this time. "I just didn't feel like going to school on Friday, so I spent my day down by the center monument."

"The center monument? Doing what? There's nothing to do there."

"'Sactly. It's nice and quiet. Peaceful," I say. "And it gets me away from kids like these." I nod my head backward.

"Alright," Caoimhe says. Then she reaches into her bag, rips a page from one of her notebooks and begins scribbling a note for me in her fancy handwriting.

"You a lifesaver of a friend," I whisper.

"Not. A. Problem," she says, stabbing a period after her fake signature, before sliding the note toward me. "So, Wends," she says — nobody's ever called me Wends before. I think I like it — "whatcha do the weekend?"

I focus my eyes on the ceiling as if I'm trying to recall how I spent the weekend, when there's no need for me to reach into my memory at all. I spent all Friday in the hospital, sitting on one of those uncomfortable plastic chairs beside Momma's bed 'til the doctors eventually told us we had to go home. And on Saturday and Sunday, I did the exact same thing, only I was sitting in our armchair and not a plastic chair while Momma laid on the makeshift bed in our living room. They'd no more room for her in the hospital, they said. We'd heard it all before. What they mean to say is that Momma has no health insurance and black skin, so she don't belong there.

"I uh... did some shopping Saturday," I say, "then chilled out listening to some Mariah Carey CDs all Sunday. You?"

"Went on a date," she says, before sucking her lips so tightly together that they disappear into her face.

"Huh?"

I look behind me, and stare at Meric sitting in the back corner, staring down at the desk, just like he always does.

"How'd it go?" I say, swinging back around.

"Eh... I really don't know," she whispers. "There were a lot of awkward silences. In fact, most of the date was silent. But... I dunno. The psychic can't be wrong, can she? I mean she called it bang on. His initials. His hair. I mean... how could she have known all that?"

"Whatcha mean hair?" I say. Then I look back at Meric again. Good for him. Caoimhe's a great girl. He prolly needed this attention more than anyone. That boy might finally come out from those bangs he's been hiding behind his whole life.

"Get this," Caoimhe says, leaning in closer to me. "I went to

Madam Aspectu on Thursday night... this is why I was gutted you weren't in on Friday. She told me that the guy with the MM initials also has black hair that hangs over his eyes."

"What? That's craaazy," I say. And then I yawn again. Because I can't help it.

"Wendy, you sure you're okay?"

"I'm fine. Fine."

And as I'm saying it, Miss Decker walks into the classroom with a bright smile on her face.

"Okay, Caoimhe, into your regular seat," she says. Caoimhe squishes up her face at me before standing and eventually walking to the back of the class to sit next to her new boyfriend.

Decker hangs her bag onto the back of her chair, then shuffles around some paperwork on her desk before glancing round the room.

"Where's Kai?" she asks.

I look at the empty seat next to me, then turn to her and shrug.

"No idea, Miss," I say.

LUCY DECKER

I turn to the chalkboard and scribble.

"Okay, Nicole," I say, "explain to the class again why it may cause major issues if news anchors are given a platform to air their opinions during broadcasts?"

"Because news isn't meant to divide us," Nicole says. "It's meant to inform us. The men who own these networks shouldn't be able to impose their opinions on us."

I nod, enthusiastically, then scribble some more.

"So, what you're getting at, Miss Decker," Hawkins says, "is that news on these networks isn't really news, it's just entertainment?"

"Well... it's not what I think that matters," I say, turning back around to face my students. "This is all about making you guys think for yourselves. Should news just be straightforward news, or should it be entertainment?"

"Bit of both," Stevie says after shooting his hand up. "It's like real-life entertainment, isn't it?"

"Real-life TV, that's all we're gonna watch in the future," Brody says. Most of the class chuckles until I hold up my hand, shutting them up. "No, I'm serious," Brody continues. "I read about it in a magazine. You know like *The Real World* on MTV... well, that's... that's—"

"What magazine did you read it in, a porn magazine?"

Hawkins says. And then half the class laugh. I shake my head, not necessarily because of the chuckling again, but because that wasn't even remotely close to being funny.

"Brody's right, y'know," I say, slipping in to dampen the laughter. "Reality TV is going to be the real deal."

I nod and wink at Brody, and when he smiles back at me, I see his Dad.

That's weird. I never once looked at Johnny on Saturday night and saw Brody, even after he told me who his son was. But now, staring at the young boy in front of me that I've taught for two years now, all I see is that soldier who tried to charm me with terrible jokes over dinner on Saturday night. I've no idea if he'll ask me out again. We were supposed to call into our dating bot yesterday to rate the date between one and five. I gave it a three. I wonder if John rated it. And if he did, I wonder how much he ranked me out of five. I think a three is fair enough. He was nice. And kinda funny in his own way. And I was right. After I touched his hand early on during the date, it relaxed us both, and there wasn't one awkward silence after that. Not until he hesitated as I got into the cab at the end of the night, unsure whether or not he should kiss me. I got on my tiptoes and leaned in to peck him on the cheek, then said, "Thanks, I enjoyed that," before sliding into the back of the cab and slamming the door shut. I was being honest. I did enjoy it. It was fun. Funny. But we're just total opposites, Johnny and I. I seriously can't imagine us getting along. I'd say we likely disagree on almost every fundamental issue we could ever think of to discuss. And besides, I can't just start dating one of my student's dads. It's not right. It's not ethical.

"Okay, okay," I say, clapping my hands twice. "Before the bell rings, let me tell you that I am setting a mission we're all going to undertake in a few weeks' time. Sarah-Jane Zdanski has exclusive interviews coming up that she is teasing on her network... whatever it is, we're *all* gonna watch it. It's going to be the only homework I assign you over the next few weeks. The interviews are going to be on a Thursday night, and first thing on Friday morning what we're all going to do is openly discuss the interviews in this classroom.

And I want you to consider everything we have been discussing in these past few lessons."

"Who's she interviewing?" Caoimhe asks.

"We don't know… it's all a big tease at the moment," I say. "On top of that, I must also mention that there are a limited number of spaces left on the trip to Europe. So get your forms and money in as soon as you can." I hold my finger in the air, and on cue, the bell rings. "Off you go… enjoy math."

They groan before packing their backpacks and laboring their way out of my classroom. As I'm wiping down my chalkboard with a damp duster, I notice, in my peripheral vision, Principal Klay's heavy beard getting closer to me.

"Oh my Lord Jesus Christ," he says, blessing himself. He looks pale; much paler than the normal shade of pale he usually is.

"Are you okay, Principal Klay?" I say. "You look a little—"

"Kai Chayton," he says, before looking around and then leaning in closer to me, "tried to kill himself." I hold my hand to my mouth, as a heavy weight lands in my gut. "With a rope. He tried to hang himself in his own bedroom on Saturday night."

"Oh my…" I say. And it's all I manage to say, before I stumble my way backward so I can collapse into my chair.

"I never would have thought in a million years… I mean the boy is so quiet."

"*Sooo* quiet," I say. "And so… so nice. I've never once heard him say a bad word about anybody. But ah… you say *tried* to kill himself. He didn't manage. ..?"

"He's in Smith County Hospital. That's all I know."

I suck in a deep breath, trying to raise the heavy weight from the pit of my stomach.

"This is my fault — *our* fault — we need to understand these boys and girls—"

"You can't blame yourself, Lucy. Jeez. You've been working in teaching for over ten years. If you were to blame yourself for every depressed student you had no idea was depressed you'd be living one horrid life."

"Oh my..." is all I can manage to say again as I lower the center of my forehead to my desk.

"Well... at least the worst didn't happen," Principal Klay says, awkwardly patting me on the back. "And we all have something positive to look forward to with this trip to Europe. Has, ah... out of interest... has Kai given you a permission slip and the cash for Europe? Is he supposed to be going on the trip?"

"Nope," I mumble into the desk. "Actually," I then say, sitting more upright and pulling open the drawer of my desk. "I have eight permission slips right here from other students along with thirty-two hundred in cash. Can I give all this to you now?"

"No. No, you hold on to all that," Klay says. "If you can take care of all the money for the trip, that'd be a weight off for me. "

FIVE

WHEN THE DOUBLE gold doors slid back open on floor fifty-five, Sarah-Jane stepped out to find Phil sitting on an uncomfortable steel chair in the hallway, gazing down at the purse between his New Balance sneakers.

He had barely moved. After almost half an hour of leaning his shoulder against the wall of the hallway, staring at the double gold doors in anticipation of his boss strolling back out of them wearing a gray overcoat, he poked his head through the crack of the office door nearest to him, found himself a chair and then carried it back to the double gold doors where he placed it down, sat into it, and waited... and waited.

She had been just over an hour in Walter Fellowes's office, supposed to be eating, but not eating, on parade for the media mogul to gawk at. After she showed off her slim frame in the cheerleader's outfit Isla had given to her, she sat at Walter's desk and talked about, initially, her live broadcast in less than two-and-a-half hours before Walter stained the lush carpet beneath his feet with Pepsi while trying to give Sarah-Jane a metaphorical lecture. Not long afterward, with Sarah-Jane's eyebrows still knitting together due to the peculiarity of the meeting, Walter's secretary, Barbara, spat through the speakerphone on her boss's desk, to inform him his dinner hour was over.

Their eyes met and without asking the question Sarah-Jane

knew Phil would be desperate to ask, she answered it for him by slowly shaking her head.

Phil's shoulders seemed to sink an inch before he stood up, grabbing Sarah-Jane's purse and clutching it close to his chest.

"Oh, there you are," Howie Laine said, walking toward them and staring Sarah-Jane up and down. "Nice overcoat."

Phil growled in the back of his throat as silently as he could, though Sarah-Jane, standing next to him, could certainly hear it.

"I uh... I gotta go change and—"

"Yep," Howie said, "you go change and I'll see you in the control room for a quick run-through. Just over two hours till we're live."

He patted Sarah-Jane on the bicep, then awkwardly nodded at Phil before mincing away.

It took them both another twenty minutes to not only find wardrobe, where Sarah-Jane changed back into the clothes she had worn to the studio earlier that day, but to find out where the control room was within the maze of dark hallways.

When they finally pushed the control room door open, a row of seven male heads turned to face them. Two of them were dressed in suits, four of them — including Howie in his patterned, tight-fitting shirt and jeans — were dressed smart-casual, while one was dressed over-casual, wearing a Chicago Bulls jersey with the name Jordan and the number twenty-three emblazoned across the back.

"You've met Mikey McGrath, Sarah-Jane, yes?" Howie asked, pointing his hand toward the man in the red basketball jersey that was sucking on the end of a cigarette. It seemed a little grotesque to Sarah-Jane that Mikey was wearing the jersey over his bare skin, what with his arms so pasty white and matted with sweaty hair, but she moved closer to him nonetheless and held out her hand.

"Of course," she said, as Mikey placed his hand inside hers.

Then she immediately took a step backward, so she was in the much more comfortable presence of Phil. It was an awkward introduction. Not only did seven heads turn to face them as soon as they pushed through the control room door, but the room itself was eerily uninviting. There was no light, except for that provided by the twelve screens the seven men had been staring at from across an organized mess of buttons that seemed to sprawl out in front of them.

Sarah-Jane had briefly met Mikey at some point during the course of her day-long meeting at the network the week before. He was introduced to her as the director of her show before they shared an awkward back and forth about the Public Broadcasting Services she had worked for, to which Mikey seemed to dismiss as nowhere near impressive enough experience to warrant her getting her own show on CSN. He certainly didn't say as much with words, but Sarah-Jane got the distinct impression he considered her somewhat fortunate to find herself in the position she had found herself.

"I was thinkin'," Mikey said in his broad Chicago accent, "let's do a quick run-through, just so you're familiar with my voice."

Sarah-Jane nodded, then glanced at Phil when everything fell silent in the immediate aftermath. Phil was too distracted to notice, staring at the twelve screens that were showing different angles of Sarah-Jane's brand new studio.

"Oh," Sarah-Jane said, rounding her mouth when the seven heads continued to stare at her in the resulting silence, "you want me to go into the studio now?"

"Exactly," Mikey said.

"Here." Howie stood up and began fidgeting with his fingers. "This is your earpiece." He brushed Sarah-Jane's blonde locks to the side, then placed the piece into her ear before showing her to a door that led down two steps and directly into the shadows of the studio.

Phil wasn't sure where to go, so he remained standing at the back wall of the control room, clutching Sarah-Jane's purse to his chest as she appeared on the twelve screens across from him, fingering her ear.

She coughed, lightly—a cough that was picked up on the microphones above her head and played into the speakers of the control room.

"Can you hear me, Mikey?" she said, tapping at her ear.

"Loud and clear, and you can hear me?" the director said.

Sarah-Jane held her two thumbs up and then beamed her perfect white teeth directly into one of the cameras.

"Okay, in front of you, as I explained last week, there are four cameras, and one in the beam of the ceiling above your desk." Sarah-Jane looked upward. "This one will only be shown when we cut away for commercial breaks. The other four cameras will be used throughout the show at different points and I will be guiding you through which camera is beaming live to America. They are numbered from your left to right, as you can see..." Sarah-Jane squinted into the shadows, taking in each camera, noticing them numbered one to four. "Okay, and stare at camera one for me, and say something into it," Mikey instructed into her ear.

Sarah-Jane clasped her hands together, lightly cleared her throat and did what she does best. She presented.

"Hello, my name is Sarah-Jane Zdanski and welc—"

"Okay and camera two," Mikey said softly into her ear.

She pivoted, hearing the hissing mechanics of the cameras as they swished toward her.

"And welcome to the Zdanski show. Today we—"

"Camera three," Mikey said.

"Today we bring you astonishing—"

"And camera four."

"Astonishing interviews from—"

"Perfect. You look better on camera than you even do in real life," Mikey crackled into her ear. "So, camera direction is obviously very straightforward. Besides, you've been working at PBS for a number of years, so you have experience of how that works. The other directions I'll whisper into your ear during the interviews will be just as straightforward, I promise. Though you'll get to know my shorthand in time and we'll develop our own unique line of communication."

Phil stared at the screens, to see Sarah-Jane nodding in agreement. Then he noticed Howie stretching over the director's shoulder, to press at a red button on the control desk.

"You think she'll hold up tonight?"

Mikey pouted his lips and shrugged his shoulders. Then he re-pressed the button Howie had just pressed his finger to.

"You'll be fine, Sarah-Jane, right? You're not gonna be nervous are you?"

"Excited," she said, sticking her finger to the plastic piece in her ear.

Then Howie pressed the red button again.

"I haven't told her there's a projected thirty million tuning in tonight, so let's keep that to ourselves. She doesn't need to know."

Mikey nodded in agreement.

"Sure."

"She's got some experience at PBS, but she's never had a show of this magnitude, I'm just worried—"

"There's no need to be worried," Phil said, taking a step forward.

"Oh," Howie said, slapping his hands together. "He speaks. The producer speaks."

Phil growled at the back of his throat again.

"Sarah-Jane don't get nervous," he said. Then he stepped back, re-pressing his shoulders to the back wall of the control room while Howie swung from side to side in the chair he was sitting in next to Mikey.

Phil was surprised to hear there was an expected thirty million Americans due to tune in tonight. He and Sarah-Jane had spoken about the size of the audience back in their hotel suite over breakfast this morning. Well, she spoke. He listened. She gave him the impression she'd be delighted if more than the regular six million who tune into CSN at seven p.m. every Thursday night tuned in to see her debut show. But he knew that even if Sarah-Jane was privy to the projected thirty million view-ers, it still wouldn't affect her. She was as flawless as a reporter could be in front of the camera as far as Phil was concerned. He had worked with over forty reporters in his time at PBS before Sarah-Jane Zdanski came into his life. None of them could hold a candle to her. She was not only the greatest instinctive inquisitive mind he had come across, but she was the most natural and at-ease reporter in front of the camera he had worked with by a landslide.

They had spent three years together, driving around North Kansas in a white van with the Public Broadcasting Service logo peeling off the side of it. When they'd eventually stumble across a story, he would hold a heavy camera atop his left shoulder while she'd grip a microphone just below her chin, delivering news as wide-ranging as a cat caught up a tree on an avenue just outside Smith Center, to the kidnapping of little Theia Lancaster who was eventually found in her uncle's house some five days after being reported missing. It was a story that caught not only the interest of north Kansas, but the state as a whole. And Sarah-Jane was right on top of it from the very beginning. She had actually interviewed the uncle three days prior to his four-year-old niece being found under his bed, pleading straight down Phil's camera lens for her safe return. Sarah-Jane had thought at the time that her reporting of this story might endear her to some national news producers, but her phone never rang in that regard. In fact it would take over a year later for her phone to ring when the croaky voice of Walter Fellowes offered her her own show on CSN on the spot after he had been blown away, not just by how beautiful she was, but how calm she reported live when under so much pressure.

"Okay, so," Mikey said softly while every one of the seven heads in the control room stared at one of the twelve screens showing Sarah-Jane now sitting in her twenty thousand dollar chair, her surname flashing in neon blue behind her. "We are on air for ninety minutes tonight, from seven p.m. till eight-thirty. Within that ninety-minute time frame, there will be seven commercial breaks—each of them exactly three minutes in length. They are all marked with an asterisk on your script, Sarah-Jane, and the introductions to those commercials are all scripted too. Got it?"

"Uh-huh," Sarah-Jane replied, staring down at her notes.

"I should also tell you," Mikey said, "I will be placing a box of tissues under your desk before we go live."

"Oh..." Sarah-Jane pushed out a laugh as she scooted back to her chair to find the box, "thank you, but... I won't cry."

"They're not for you," Mikey said.

Then Sarah-Jane raised her eyebrows into camera one before she nodded.

"I see…"

'I want to see those tissues coming out tonight. The nation wants to see those tissues coming out tonight. It's your job to make these guests cry. Understood?"

Sarah-Jane stared down the lens of camera number one again, then she lightly cleared her throat.

"Understood," she said.

JOHNNY EDWARDS

I stare at the receiver in my hand as if the phone is going to decide for me. I'm genuinely not sure what I want to do. I'd like to see her again. But she kinda gave me the impression that we wouldn't work well together. She nearly had a seizure when I said, "God Bless America." And then she was all antsy about America being in Iraq in the first place. It'd probably be a waste of time for both of us if we went out on a second date. Yet, for some reason, I really want to find out if it will be a waste of time or not. There was something about her... I don't know what it was. Her personality? Her smile? Her laugh? I mean, she did laugh a lot. A helluva lot. Although maybe they were fake laughs. Shit. I bet she fake laughed all the way through that dinner, didn't she? That's what her sort do... liberals. They lie. They even lie to themselves.

I slam the receiver down, then sit on the edge of my bed again and stare around this cramped little room. Nah. We're not right for each other. She's one of them do-gooders; someone who thinks they know better than everybody else. She's not the one for me.

"Mr. Edwards," Mrs. Ferguson calls out, before knocking her frail knuckles against my door. "You have a visitor."

I walk to the door and open it to see Mrs. Ferguson beaming a grin at me. She thinks I'm some sort of hero 'cause I been at war. Poor thing. She'd be disappointed to know the most heroic thing I did over the past eighteen months was come back here... to

Lebanon. If it wasn't for my kids, God knows where I'd be right now. All I know is that I wouldn't be here. Not in Lebanon. Not when there's a whole world to live in.

"Hey, Dad," Brody says, appearing out from behind Mrs. Ferguson.

"Oh, hey kiddo, come on in."

"I can't stay for long, Dad. I've got a tournament to play with Stevie on Nintendo."

"A tournament?"

"Yeah, it's a big competition we play in the evenings. It's called *Madden 97*. After, y'know... Joe Madden."

"Wow," I say. "So you can play NFL on your computer games now?"

"Uh-huh," he says.

I tousle his hair as he enters my room before I shut the door closed, probably on Mrs. Ferguson's face.

It's great to see him again, to hang out with him, even if he is a big ol' dumbo like his old man used to be. He is a mirror of me at fifteen years old. Young. Dumb. Full of cum. I wonder if he jerks off as often as I used to at that age. Jeez. I think that's all I was doing back then.

"Find yourself a girlfriend yet?" I ask.

"Don't wanna be tied down, Dad," he says. "Just playing in loads of different positions on the field."

I tousle his hair again.

"I don't think that's how that phrase goes, Brody."

He sits on the edge of my bed.

"Is she a bit wacky?" he asks.

"Who?"

"That old lady who runs the B&B?"

"Mrs. Ferguson? Nah. Yes. Maybe. I guess. I think she has a little crush on your old man."

"Uggh," Brody says.

I sit down beside him and squeeze him close to me.

"Did you stop by for anything in particular?" I ask.

"Well... ah... kinda. Yeah. I... uhm..."

"Spit it out Brodester."

"I need money."

"Money?"

"Four hundred bucks. The school is bringing us on a trip to Europe in October and we need to pay four hundred. Mom says she doesn't have it.... that I should ask you now that you're home."

"Did she?" I say. "That's nice of her."

"Well... can I have it?"

I stand up, clasp my hands behind my back and walk toward the bedroom window so I can stare out on to the empty dirt road.

"Let me talk to your Mom first, see what she has to say."

"Well... I told you what she had to say. She says I should ask you."

"Where's the school taking you guys?"

"Paris, and some other places."

"Some other places? You're asking for money to go on a trip and you don't know where the trip is gonna take you?"

"Jeez, Dad. I'm only asking for a few hundred bucks. Not as if you've given me any money the past year and a half, is it? You haven't even been here. Forget about it," he says, standing up and striding his way to the door.

"Okay. Okay. I'll get it for you," I tell him, stopping him just as he grips the handle. "But I still wanna talk to your Mom first."

"Love you, Dad," he says, winking at me. "It's great to have you home."

Then he turns back around, pulls open the door and walks through it, leaving me alone. Again.

I look around the cramped little room, at the ugly flowery patterns on the bedcovers and on the curtains, and then I lie back down onto the bed because there's nothing much else to do.

"Boy am I fuckin' bored," I mutter to myself before blowing air out through my lips.

I hear a car humming down the dirt road. Then it disappears and I fall back into that horrible silence again.

I scoot myself forward on the bed, pick up the phone, and without giving myself a chance to hesitate, I begin dialing. I'll play it cool... just tell her I'm going to The Shamrock for a beer this evening and if she wants to join me... she's more than welcome. No pressure. Though try as I might to pretend to be playing it cool, my heart is beating heavy in my chest as the phone rings... and rings. Until, I hear a little click sound.

"Hi, you've reached the answering machine of Lucy Decker, please leave a message after the beep..."

KAI CHAYTON

My head still aches. So does my neck. In fact, it burns. Especially when I rub it. Which is what I'm doing now while Momma and Poppa are staring at me from the foot of my hospital bed. I'd much rather deal with this burn in my neck for the rest of my life than the pain of having to explain myself to them right now.

"You should have just come to us," Poppa says.

I nod quietly, while inside my head screams, *Yeah, right Poppa. And what would you have done if I came to you to tell you I want to be a girl, huh?*

"We would do anything to protect you, my dear. I am so... so..." Momma starts crying again, and as she does she grips my hand. For some reason I begin to feel grateful that I can even watch her cry. Cos if Poppa hadn't heard me kicking over her tiny sewing bench and ran upstairs to drag me down, she'd be crying even more than she is now. I don't know why I was being so selfish. I don't know why I didn't think about the pain I would create for everybody else. I just... I just wasn't thinking. I wasn't thinking about anything other than the pain and frustration I have been feeling. I couldn't bear the pain of not being allowed to be who I want to be.

"I.... I..." I stutter. And then I swallow. Which makes my neck pulsate in pain.

"Go on, dear. Tell us. Talk to us. Why did you want to... to..."

I stare up at Momma as she presses a handkerchief to her nose.

"Momma. I just wanted to not live anymore."

"Why?" she says, sobbing.

"I... I..."

"And why the hell were you wearing a dress when you did it?" Poppa says, placing his hands on his hips and pushing out his chest like he always does when he's barking out orders.

When all goes silent and I see his stare leave mine so he can look back out the window of this ward, I sit up properly in the bed for the first time since I came around.

"I'm not gay," I say.

"Huh?" he replies, spinning back and squinting at me.

"I knew you weren't gay," Momma says, spraying snot and tears onto me as she laugh-cries. "I knew he wasn't gay. I told you Nova."

Dad inches himself closer my bed, his eyes still squinting.

"Not gay?" he says, shaking his head slowly. "Well that doesn't make any sense. Why did you want to kill yourself in a dress?"

Fuck sake Poppa. I just want to be a girl. That's all. Not a boy. I was born with the wrong... the wrong parts. But I dunno how I am supposed to say those words to him. How the Holy Hell am I supposed to say those words to him?

"I... I..."

"Go on dear, now's the time to tell us. You can tell us anything you want. We'll understand, won't we Nova?."

Dad nods, then kinda shrugs his shoulders at Mom.

"I... I, uhm. Okay," I say, slapping my palms together and then nervously holding my eyes shut so I don't have to look at their faces as I finally reveal my secret. "The thing is, I've always felt as if I need—"

The ward door swings open and I stop talking. The three of us turn our heads to the pretty nurse who brought me my breakfast on a tray this morning.

"You have another visitor, Kai," she says, "if you're up for it?"

"Who?" I ask.

"Lucy Decker... says she's a teacher at your high school."

"Oh," I say, smiling a first proper smile since I woke up inside this nightmare. "Sure... send her in."

WENDY CAMPBELL

I press the wet flannel to the top of her head, while I beam a wide smile into her face.

"Y'okay, Momma?" I say softly, even though I know that's such a silly question to ask.

She takes a deep inhale, filling her tummy, then lets it out really slowly before trying to smile back at me.

"How was school today?" she whispers.

I look over my shoulder at Sally who is sitting inches from our blinking television in a world of her own where only she and the *Teenage Mutant Ninja Turtles* exist, and then I stare back at Momma's sweaty face.

"The usual," I say.

"What 'bout yesterday? Teachers ask where you were?"

"Momma," I say, "stop tryna talk. You tiring yourself out. And please don't worry 'bout school. Everything's fine."

"Okay," she says, blinking her eyes. "Well, if e'rything just fine, why don't you sing for me?"

I choke out a laugh. Momma is the only person in this big ol' world who would ever ask me to sing for them. When I was around Sally's age Momma entered me into a competition in Wichita 'cause she was sure that I was gonna be the next Whitney Houston. Turns out that she was wrong. Way wrong. The kinda wrong only a loving momma can be. There were thirteen children who entered that competition. Only ten got into the second round. I didn't. I looked pretty, I know that much. Momma had bought me a big puffy pink dress like the ones Little Bo Peep wore in my children's books. And I sure did sing the best I could up on that stage. But as I was singing I saw one of them judges kinda roll his eyes or somethin'. Me and Momma stayed quiet all the way home on the bus ride that day. And boy that bus ride went on and on and on. I thought it would never end. She never entered me in any singing competitions no more after that, but she sure does like to ask me to sing for her. Specially so since she got sick.

"What would you like me to sing, momma?" I ask as I continue dabbing at her forehead.

"Etta," she whispers.

I clear my throat, and as I begin dabbing under her eyes with the flannel, I begin the opening lines to the song Momma has already asked me to sing at her funeral. *At Last.*

Her eyes close while I sing and, as I always do when her eyes close, I stare down at her big breasts, just to make sure they continue rising up. And down.

Then, out of nowhere, our front door rattles and Momma's bulgin' eyes pop wide open.

I look at Sally, then back at Momma.

"Don't worry, Momma," I say, "I'll take care of it."

Nobody ever knocks on our door. Unless it's the mailman with a package so big it won't fit in our mailbox. I tiptoe to the window, and with one finger, I curl our curtains to one side and then breathe a sigh of relief.

"Don't worry, Momma," I say. "S'all okay."

I open the door and take a step out, in a way that doesn't allow her to see inside, then I offer my new best friend a great big fake smile.

"Hey," Caoimhe says. She looks pale. Paler then her normal pale. "I just heard this, you're not gonna believe it. You know Kai Chayton — ain't he the guy who sits next to you in American History?"

"Uh-huh," I say, folding my arms under my breasts.

"He tried to hang himself at the weekend."

"Say what?"

"Yeah... my mam told me. One of the neighbors called over with some hotpot stew or something as a welcome to the neighborhood thingy and she told her what happened. I was in, like, I dunno... in shock, I guess. I still am. I've never known anybody who tried to kill themselves before."

"Oh my deary Lord our God," I say, collapsing my back against our front door. "Kai tried to kill himself... why?"

Caoimhe shrugs.

"I thought you might know. I've never even spoken to the chap."

"Well, me neither," I say, soaking in the news. "Sweet Lordy, you never really do know who you're sitting beside in school, I guess. I mean, he's quiet, I know that much. But that's all I know. He is quite... quite... I dunno. I think he's gay. He walks a bit gay, dontcha think? And he has that long hair. Maybe he thought being gay was a sin and felt he had to... y'know..."

We both shake our heads.

"How d'you know where I lived anyway, girl?" I ask.

"Oh, the neighbor who brought over the hotpot... I asked her if she knew where the Campbell family lived and she pointed me here."

"Well, I guess e'rbody knows where the black family live," I say.

"So..." she looks around herself, up and down our street. It's probably the worst street in the whole of Lebanon. I bet she lives in one of those big old houses on Oak or something. "This is your home, huh?"

I turn to look at what she's looking at; the paint cracking on the wood panels of our house; the long grass on the lawn; the beat-up, old Volkswagen Beetle Momma bought but never really drove because she couldn't afford the gas, rusting in our driveway.

"Yep... this is it. I bet your house is way nicer, huh?"

"I think they're all nice houses round here," she says. "You wanna see the houses in Ireland. They're all on top of each other.

And only about quarter this size. Anyway..." she looks at me, her eyebrow arched. "You gonna invite me inside, or are we just gonna stand in your garden talking about Kai?"

"I uh...' I stare back at our faded-purple front door, then turn to face Caoimhe. "I can. But..."

"But, what?" she says, blinking her ginger eyelashes at me.

"Can you keep a secret?" I ask.

•

LUCY DECKER

I must be holding his hand for half an hour now. At least. In this day and age, with teachers getting fired for any physical contact with their students, I could probably lose my job for this. When, really, this is literally all I should be doing as a teacher. Looking after my students' well-being.

"I'm so sorry," I say. Again. As if I'm not smart enough to think of anything else to say.

"Miss Decker," Kai says, sitting more upright in the bed, "if you say sorry again, you're gonna drive me to suicide."

"Shhhh," Kai's mum says, "don't talk like that!"

I purse my lips at her and nod.

"Mrs. Chayton, you have my word that I will do everything to assist Kai in his recovery. Nobody, other than the school staff, will need to know what happened on Saturday night."

"You're a good woman," Mrs. Chayton says, rubbing my shoulder.

"So do you know why he did this?" Mr. Chayton asks, abruptly, having barely said a word to me since I got here.

He looks intimidating. Tall. Wide. Stern eyed. A heavy, deep voice. Poor man must be distraught. They must all be distraught. It's interesting that his first question is *why*? As soon as I heard the news, I thought it was pretty obvious why Kai wanted to end it all. Poor kid feels a massive burden about his sexuality, I bet. He's so

obviously gay. Has been sashaying around the hallways of our
school like a catwalk model ever since I've known him. But given
his traditional heritage, I bet it's all but impossible for Kai to come
out. Native Americans are staunch in their traditionalisms. I guess
if Mr. Chayton really wants to know the truthful answer to his
question, then he need only look in the mirror. Because I'm pretty
darn certain Kai wanted to end his life because he knew your reaction to his sexuality would be torturous for him to handle.

"I don't," I say, shaking my head at Mr. Chayton after pausing
for way too long. "But rest assured, I — and indeed the rest of the
staff at Median High — will be doing our utmost to ensure something like this never happens again. We love you Kai," I say,
stroking the top of the hand he still has placed inside mine. "And
you need to know that. You need to know you are loved. We love
you no matter what."

Mrs. Chayton places her hand on my shoulder again.

"That's what we keep saying to him," she says. "He has so
many people in his life who love him."

I lean down and kiss Kai on the forehead, something I would
no doubt be fired for if any of those do-gooder school board idiots
saw me do this. Then I stand back upright to re-fix the strap of my
handbag onto my shoulder.

"I've outstayed my welcome. I'll phone tomorrow. And you can
let me know when you are ready to return to school. We'll tell the
students you had a little illness of some kind."

I shrug, and as I do, Kai smiles a genuine smile at me, and in
this moment I am finally certain that he will be okay. I'll have a
strong word with him when he returns to my class; let him know
that he is as worthy of being who he truly wants to be as anybody
else in this world is.

"Have, ah... have you given me money for the trip to Europe?"

Kai stares down the length of his bed and his nose stiffens.

"What trip to Europe?" his mother asks.

"Oh," I say, "maybe I have spoken out of turn. But our school
won the state lottery. We're being subsidized for a trip to Europe
on the thirtieth of October. Each student only has to pay four

hundred dollars. Twelve days, we'll be away for, traveling to London, Paris, Rome..."

"Oooh, that sounds nice," Mrs. Chayton says. "Perhaps it would do you the world of good to go. We'll pay the four hundred, won't we Nova?"

She glances at her husband who huffs, puffs and then sits back in to the blue plastic chair beside Kai's bed, lifting the steeple his fingers are forming towards his chin.

"We'll see," he says.

And then the ward falls silent. Awkwardly silent.

I bend down to kiss Kai on the forehead again before leaving, and then find myself making my way around the maze of brightly lit hallways of the hospital. My head begins to spin. I lean over, resting my hands on my knees, and suck in a deep, deep breath. The guilt feels nauseating. A student of mine attempting to take his own life. It's not the first time it's happened to me, either. This kinda thing happening makes me feel inadequate; as if I'm a failure as a teacher.

I listen to the local radio station blast out tacky boy band songs while I drive back to Lebanon, attempting to sing along, just so I can try, in some way, to lift my mood. But it's not working. I've been feeling so down lately. Pathetically so. I think my self-pity is the reason I didn't call Johnny back after he left a voicemail on my phone earlier. He's nice. And he made me laugh on our date. A lot. But I don't need the extra burden of dating somebody right now. I have too much going on. My priority is to get pregnant, not to get into a relationship. It's not right for me to burden anybody else with my complications.

I eyeball myself in the rearview mirror after turning off the button of my car radio, putting an end to NSync butchering an awfully repetitive pop chorus, and notice that my eyes look heavy. Really heavy. As if I've been crying, even though I haven't. Then, I flick the turn signal, drive down the entirety of the 281 twenty miles over the legal limit, before reversing into an empty parking space. I open my purse, take out a tissue, dampen it with my tongue and then dab it all over my aging face.

"Fuck it," I say to myself. "Let's do this."

I toss the tissue on the passenger seat, snatch open my car door, hook my handbag over my shoulder and dash straight across the quiet street. When I push open the door, the stale smell of beer mixes with the woman who is sitting by the door's bitter perfume and I almost turn back around and race back to my car. But it's too late. He's already seen me. And his eyes have lit up.

"Hey," he shouts down the entire length of the bar.

Everybody turns to face me, and so I offer an awkward smile to all eight folks in attendance at The Shamrock as I make my way toward him. He embraces me with an overly friendly hug, and as he does, I lean in and whisper in his ear, "Boy, could I do with a fucking drink."

MERIC MILLER

I really should bring a bottle of water out with me when I go on long rides to nowhere. I could click it to the underside of the crossbar like I see cyclists do when they're in races on the TV.

I stop pedaling, lean my bike against the wall at the side of a gray-bricked building, and then put my hands on my hips so I can suck in a deep breath. As I'm looking around, I notice, across the street, a small grocery store. Damn it! I prolly shudda reached into Momma's oversized pink purse before I came out for a ride, just for some loose change... enough to buy myself a drink. I shove my hands into the pockets of my jeans, just to check, even though I know I don't have a cent in there. I'm a frickin' idiot. I should know better. This is literally all I do when I'm not at school. Ride. Though maybe now, for the first time in my life, I might have other things to do. I can't believe I have a girlfriend. At least I think I have. I dunno. The date on the weekend went okay, I guess, even if there were lots of awkward silences. But she was just as silent as I was, I guess, and... well... I dunno. She didn't say much to me at school today, though. In fact, she didn't say anything but nod and smile at me as we passed each other in the hallway. But we didn't have American History today, so we didn't get a chance to sit next to each other. We've American History on Thursdays and then again on Fridays. We can speak then. I prolly shudda asked her for her phone number when we were on our date, just so I could call her up and we could talk. But if we didn't have much to say in that lovely restaurant for an hour and a half then a phone call might be pretty meaningless, I guess. It'd prolly be just the two of us standing in our kitchens with our phones pressed to our ears, listening to each other breathing. But listening to her breathing would even sound good to me.

I push open the door to the grocery store and when I glance at the woman behind the counter I see that she's reading a newspaper. So, I take a look around the different aisles, until I come to the fridge. I lick my lips as I stare at the drinks, and then turn to the woman behind the counter again. She glances up at me, then back down at her newspaper. I edge open one of the fridges, and snatch a cold bottle of purple Gatorade, then pull at my sleeve so that there's enough room for it to slide up into.

"Hey," I shout out to the woman behind the counter. "You sell any alcohol?"

She closes her newspaper, slides down her glasses on the bridge of her nose and stares up over them at me.

"You're too young to buy alcohol, boy," she says.

So I just shrug.

"I'll go home and get my ID then, I guess," I say.

I leave her store with my arm down by my side so she doesn't see the bulge in my sleeve. And as soon as I'm outside, I race across the street, and grab at my bike.

"You!" I stare back across the street, and see the woman by the door of the grocery store, waving both hands at me. Damn it! I jump on to my bike and begin to pedal as quickly as I can; so quick that the fuckin chain snaps from the cog and hangs low to the sidewalk. "I wanna speak with you," she says, pacing across the street toward me. I don't know what to do with my arm, so I just hide it behind my back and smile up at her as she approaches.

"Yeah?" I say.

"I know your face."

I squint at her.

"What?" I say, shrugging.

"You're that boy. That silly boy."

I look up and down the street hoping nobody else comes along; certainly not the cops. I don't wanna get in trouble. Momma would go nuts if the police brought me home for stealin' from a store.

"I... I... I was just thirsty, is all. I've ridden my bike all the way from Lebanon and—"

"Don't you know who I am, boy?" she says.

She's starting to creep me out now.

"No. Should I?" I say, shaking my hair.

She looks up and down the empty street just as I did, and then stares back at me.

"I'm Madam Aspectu in the evenings, boy."

"Huh?"

"Remember, you came to me to lie to a girl so she'd fall in love with you?"

"You're not Madam Aspectu!"

I stare into her face, my mind spinning like it can do sometimes. She just looks up and down the street again, sucking on her lips.

"Ahhh... pull the curtain over and come right in," she says, her voice all crazy high-pitched. "Ma crystal ball is bubbling just for you."

Holy shit! She looks so different. No makeup. Different hair. Her eyes aren't big and black no more.

"But you... you...'

'I wear a wig," she says, "and contact lenses when I'm being a medium in the evenings."

"What? And... and you work in the grocery store in the day?"

"Listen, boy," she says, taking a step closer to me. "You owe me. That sweet little red-haired girl came back to me and was asking more questions. I told her that the boy with the two M's also had long hair that hung over his eyes." She reaches a bony finger toward my face and brushes my bangs aside. "I know she is going to come see me again. Do you want me to tell her I got everything wrong, boy?"

"No. Jeez. No. Don't do that!" I say. "Here, here, you can have the Gatorade back."

I slip the bottle from my sleeve and hold it to her. She tilts her head, looks at it, then back at me, before snatching the bottle.

"Did you just take this from the store, boy?"

"I was thirsty," I say. "And I had no money."

She leans closer, so close I can feel her breathing on my face.

"Listen to me clearly, boy. If you want me to keep up the lies with your little girlfriend, you're gonna have to pay me."

"Pay you? But I don't... I mean... I have no—"

"One hundred dollars."

"One hund... I mean, where am I supposed to get one hundurd dollars from?"

"I don't care, boy. All I know is that if you don't bring me one hundred dollars by this weekend, the next time the little red-haired girl pays me a visit I'mma tell her I got it all wrong; that she's supposed to fall in love with a boy whose name begins with B, perhaps."

"No. No. I'll get you the money. I'll get you the one hundurd dollars. I will. But... but..."

"But what, boy?"

"What will you tell Caoimhe if I do get you the one hundurd?"

She looks up and down the empty road again.

"Whatever you want me to tell her."

My stomach rolls itself over.

"Okay. Okay," I say, sweeping my hair back down over my eyes. "Tell her this. Tell her that the boy with the two M's might be quiet, but that's not a bad thing. Tell her what she must do to find love is to get him out of his shell. Once she does, she'll fall in love with him. And I'll fall in love with her. And we'll.... you know, we'll be together and... and.... but she needs to give him time, okay, tell her she *has* to give him time, won't you?"

"Whatever you want, boy. I'll say exactly that. But it'll cost you one hundred dollars."

"Yes. Perfect," I say. "Of course. I'll get you the one hundurd. I'll take it to the tent you do your readings in this weekend."

"Good boy," she says. Then she twists the cap off of the bottle, takes a large swig of purple Gatorade, burps loudly into my face, and then slaps the bottle to the ground.

"Tastes like piss," she says.

CAOIMHE LARKIN

It's a good thing the roads round here are flat, because I've been running nonstop for about a mile now. If I had to run a mile back in Tipperary, up and down all the little hills and across the cobblestones, I certainly would've had to stop by now. Probably with a twisted ankle.

When I finally reach our pathway, I skid into it, sprint to the door and begin slapping my hands against it.

"Jeez, are you okay?" Mam says to me, when she pulls the door open.

I hunch over and take in a few sharp breaths.

"Mam, Wendy, in school, y'know the black girl I was telling you about? Well her... her..." I bend over, panting some more, "her mam is dying. Literally dying right now on a bed in the living room of their house. It's not even a bed. It's a fold-down mattress."

"What?" Mam says, pushing the door wide open.

I step inside and as soon as I do, the tears immediately begin to stream down my cheeks.

"She is dying in front of her two daughters. One of them is only eleven. Same age as Aine."

"What do you mean dying? Has she had an accident? Did you ring the paramedics?"

"Not an accident, no. She has cancer. Stomach cancer."

Mam's face looks the same way mine must've looked when

Wendy invited me into her home. I couldn't believe it at first. I genuinely thought Mrs. Campbell was a dead body when I stepped inside their tiny living room. Her eyes were closed. Her face was pale; pale for a black woman. And three feet away sat little Sally, watching cartoons as she shoveled spoonfuls of cereal into her mouth.

"What's wrong with her, Wendy?" I whispered.

Wendy blew out her cheeks.

"Take a seat."

So I did.

"Why isn't she in a hospital or something like that?" Mam asks, just as Dad jogs down the stairs to find us both stunned in the hallway.

"That's the thing," I say. "The hospital said Mrs. Campbell didn't have enough money to take a bed in there... so they sent her home."

"What?!"

Dad looks even more confused than Mam. And that makes me more confused than I've ever been. Because Dad is never confused.

"Wendy told me," I say, "that her Momma could afford one round of chemotherapy, which she had a couple weeks ago. But that was it. She was just sent home to die after that in front of her daughters."

Dad squeezes my shoulders, because he can hear in my voice that I'm about to cry again. And so, I wrap my arms around his waist and squeeze him as tight as I can. I'm so lucky. So, so lucky. And there I was, complaining all summer and acting like a diva because I didn't want to move to America with my perfectly still intact and perfectly healthy family. America is so weird. I asked Wendy where her dad was. She told me her and her mam left her father when she was barely two years old. Said her mam was sick of all of his cheating and stuff. His name was Tyrel Nelson, she told me. They all used to live in a place called Black Pearl in New Orleans. When Wendy's mam had enough of her husband's cheating, she packed their bags and moved up to Kansas where she got a job as a waitress. Her younger sister, Sally, doesn't share the same dad. She was only born after they had moved to Kansas... but Wendy isn't sure who Sally's father is because she doesn't remember her mam ever having a boyfriend. I've never known anything like it. I asked Meric about his parents, too, on our date at the weekend — just to fill an awkward silence — and he said his dad up and left, then divorced his mam when Meric was only two years old as well. He's only seen him on two occasions since. Twice... in the past twelve years! What is it with America? Why are there so many split-up families? I don't know one family back home in Ireland who are split up. Not one. Divorce was actually illegal in Ireland until last year. It should still be illegal. It should be illegal here, too. It should be illegal all over the world.

I sob, a proper big sob, into Dad's chest as he squeezes me tighter.

"Wow," I hear Mam say. "What a welcome to America, huh? Teenage boys in her class trying to kill themselves and now we have cancer patients dying at home in front of their own kids."

"Let me eh..." Dad says. And then he stops to think, while still squeezing me tight. "Let me call the paramedics to your friend's home and we'll see what we can do from there."

"No," I say, leaning away from him. "You can't. Wendy made me promise we wouldn't get anyone involved. She's scared, Dad. Really scared. She says her and her little sister will be taken away when her Mam dies. And that they'll probably be separated from each other."

Dad releases me from our hug, sighs, then washes his hand over his face before, through my tears, I watch him and Mam hold each other's stares.

"We gotta do something," Mam says.

JOHNNY EDWARDS

"You two okay?" the bartender asks, interrupting us as we were ribbing each other, by twitching his outstretched finger between our two glasses.

"One for the road?" I ask her.

"No, no. I really must get going. It's a school night and I—"

"One more won't hurt," I say, placing my hand on her knee before moving it as quickly as I can away. Shit. That mighta been too forward.

She pretends not to notice though, and instead glances at the near empty glass of wine standing tall on the bar in front of her, before looking back up at me and sucking on her own lips.

"I've already had three glasses. I can't—"

"One more. Go on. We're having fun. Or, at least, *I'm* having fun."

She sighs, with a smile.

"Go for it," she says nodding at the bartender, "one more for the road."

I turn away to try to hide my smile. I'm enjoying her company. And I'm pretty sure she's enjoying mine. Or at least she's not as down as she was when she first walked in here. She whispered in my ear when I hugged her to welcome her to The Shamrock, "*Boy do I need a fucking drink.*" Then she sat down, huffed and, almost in tears, told me that she had come here straight from the hospital. She says she can't tell me exactly what happened, but it's got something to do with one of her students. She was down. No doubt about it. But she's been giggling for the past couple of hours, even if we haven't quite agreed on one single talking point that has been brought up since she sat down.

"Crazy, us saying we don't really have anything in common, yet you don't wanna leave," I say, before snickering.

"Ahhh..." she replies, shaking her head, "you really are arrogant."

"Me?" I say, pointing my thumb at myself, "you're the damned liberal."

She purses her lips at me, trying to look disappointed but finding it difficult given that she's grinning at the same time.

The bartender places a glass of red in front of Lucy, then a Bud on the beer mat in front of me.

"This one's on me," he says, waving his hand at us, "for your service, sir." I glance down at the stars and stripes on my collar. "And you ma'am," the bartender says to Lucy, "if I'm not mistaken, you're a teacher at Median High School, right?"

"Yeah," she says, "did I teach you?"

"Not me, ma'am. My younger sister, Jennifer Hirsch."

"Ahh... how is Jennifer?" Lucy asks, leaning into the bar genuinely intrigued to find out how her former student has been living her life. More proof she really cares for her students, even if they have long since left the school. I wonder what Brody makes of Miss Decker? He's probably as infatuated with her as his old man is.

"She's great. She's in the city — in Wichita — working in design for a tech company."

"Awesome," Lucy says. "It was always obvious Jennifer would make something of herself."

"Well... I don't wanna disturb you guys. Just wanted to buy you both a drink... you are both two fine members of society."

Then he walks away backward, his hands clasped together and his head slightly bowing at us.

"Wow, that was nice," Lucy says, turning to me.

"Oh," I say, batting my hand at her. "I get that all the time." And then I laugh.

"Well I sure as hell don't," Lucy says.

She picks up her glass of red, swirls it and then takes a sip while smiling.

"So... what were we talking about?" she says.

"Clinton," I remind her.

"Ah yes," she says. "And what was it you were trying to say to me again, with your tinfoil hat on?"

I laugh another husky man-laugh.

"I am not a conspiracy theorist," I say. "I just don't know how you can look at that man and tell me he's squeaky clean. It's as clear as day, it's in his eyes. That man is as slippery as they come."

"Jesus, Johnny," she says, using the Lord's name in vain, which is probably my biggest pet peeve. But given that we're both smirking and smiling and grinning at each other, I don't say a word. "The man is probably the most scrutinized man on the planet. He's just won the White House. Twice. If there was a scandal to be had, it'd be out there already."

"We'll see," I say shrugging my shoulders at her. "The two of them — him and Hilary — they just... they just..."

"They just, what?"

"They just creep me out, is all. Wouldn't trust them as far as I could throw 'em."

"But you wudda trusted George Bush for another term instead?" she says, creasing her brow smugly at me before taking a sip from her wine as if she's just won the discussion.

"See... this is the trouble with you Democrats," I say. "You always assume you're smarter than the rest of us."

"Well, statistically we are," she says.

"See!" I point at her. "This is a prime example of that arrogance I was talking about last Saturday. Democrats are so arrogant."

"Ha," she replies, "says the Republican with his finger pointed in a woman's face."

"Well... I mean..." I snatch my hand away. "I'm sorry about that — I was—"

"Relax," she says, laughing and then leaning in to touch my wrist. "I'm only pulling your leg, Johnny."

We both allow our shoulders to sink back down, and I take a large sip of beer while the silence settles between us.

"Are Americans the only folk in the world who talk politics on dates?" I ask, placing my beer back down.

I see the smile drop from her face. Darn it! I bet that's 'cause I said the word "date." She doesn't think this is a date, does she?

"Probably," she says. "It's the two-party system in America that divides us, isn't it? You're either on the red team or the blue team in America. Bipartisanship goes out the window, doesn't it? Bipartisanship doesn't exist in our country. Whereas in Europe, there are a multitude of political parties their people can vote for, so the population isn't divided on such a sharp knife edge. Not like we are. We are divided literally down the middle. Wanna know what the average percentile difference is in our Presidential races?"

'Go on,' I say, intrigued. She may be arrogant. But she's right. She's definitely smarter than me on this subject.

"Fifty-three percent to forty-seven percent. No matter what way it goes... sometimes the Republican wins by a few points, sometimes it's the Dems. But no matter what, the nation is split pretty much down the middle. Always."

"Wow," I say, leaning on the bar. "I never realized it was always that close. So you think we should have more political parties than just two? But, wait a sec, would that not just divide the nation into more groups?"

"Well... kinda, yeah. I guess," she says, shrugging. "But at least the division wouldn't be so razor sharp. The difference between four groups wouldn't always be on a knife edge like we are with two, right? But that's not the main reason for the division in America anyway."

"What is?" I say before taking another sip of beer.

"The media," she says. "They thrive on this division. Their

main objective in this country is to divide the population of the United States right down the middle. Every single news anchor's job in this country is to scare us, and then divide us. S'what they're paid to do."

SIX

"DO you think we're doing what's best for America?" Sarah-Jane asked as she continued to pace around the small, oval coffee table in the middle of her tight dressing room, with one hand held against her forehead.

Phil took his eyes from his roaming boss, then, using two of his chubby fingers, hooked aside the cuff of his left sleeve.

"You're asking this ninety minutes before going live?"

"It's just.... ugggh!" Sarah-Jane stopped pacing, then held both hands to her face so she could mumble into them. "I hate those opening two lines. It's not what this should be about. I'm just worried all we're doing is dividing the American people. We should be reporting this as a human story, not..." She shook her head, then looked up at Phil's bullish features. "There are thirty million projected to tune in tonight."

Phil scratched at his patchy beard.

"Somebody told you?"

"Walter."

"Hmmm," Phil said. "Listen..." he took a step closer to his boss, and reached a hand to cup her elbow. 'The producers didn't wanna tell you how big the audience is projected to be, 'cause they thought you'd start getting panicky and... and well, pacing around your dressing room worrying about what America is gonna think. I promised them you wouldn't panic; that you never panic."

Sarah-Jane curled her lips at Phil, though he didn't mirror her half-smile like most people would, simply because Philip Meredith never smiled.

"Thanks Phil," she said, cupping the hand that was cupping her elbow.

As they stood staring into each other's eyes, a knock rattled against the door of the dressing room, and while Sarah-Jane moved to answer it, Phil glanced down at the coffee table, noticing all of the newspapers fanned out on the top of it were still leading with photographs of Princess Diana—even though her death had occurred many weeks prior. In that moment, as he stared at the Princess's heavy blue eyes, he realized that these newspapers would most likely carry the image of his boss on their front pages the next day.

"Ninety minutes till live," the pock-faced boy who had greeted her in the lobby three hours earlier said. "Time to get you to hair and makeup.'"

Sarah-Jane glanced over her shoulder at Phil, to catch him picking up her purse. Then they both left the dressing room she had inherited that was clearly too small to pace furiously in.

They were led down one floor via the back stairwell and then through a narrow maze of dimly-lit hallways that mirrored upstairs before the pock-faced young man whose name Sarah-Jane couldn't recall, abruptly stopped outside one of the doors and knocked on it. When that door opened, a flood of light hit them.

"Oh hellu," a thick Scottish accent called out. Sarah-Jane adjusted her eyes to the light, to see a beautiful, older, brunette woman smiling kind eyes at her.

"Hey," Sarah-Jane said.

The brunette nodded once.

"Ya nervous?"

"Sorry?"

"Nervous fo' tonight?"

"Excited," Sarah-Jane said.

Then the brunette led Sarah-Jane to a large chair in front of a mirror framed by two dozen naked light bulbs—all of them sizzling and humming with white light.

"I'm Mollie," the brunette said. "And I'll be doon ya hair 'n' makeup."

"You look beautiful," Sarah-Jane said to Mollie's reflection as she sat back.

"Ach aye," Mollie said, "I think me 'n' you gonnae get on just fine."

They did get on just fine—talking as if they had been best friends since high school with such haste that Phil realized early on his presence wasn't required. So, he slid himself into the waiting lounge chair next to the hair and makeup front door where he picked up a newspaper with Princess Diana's pale face on the front page, crossed his legs, and began thumbing through the pages.

Sarah-Jane and Mollie discussed the level of the anchor's nerves versus her excitement, then they talked about how naturally pretty she was before the conversation turned to the people Sarah-Jane would be interviewing in just eighty minutes time.

"Will you be doing their hair and makeup, too?" Sarah-Jane asked.

"Light makeup. Just enough to make sure their skin is no' shinin' through the screen. A wee bit o' powder. And if they have any spots or blemishes I normally cover 'em up. Sometimes guests turn up and their hair is a right mess, so I might give it a little goon over. Though tonight who knows who's gonnae show up, eh? These guys are hardly used to bin on television, are they?"

Sarah-Jane agreed by producing a little grunt in the back of her throat, simply because she couldn't nod her head, nor audibly communicate with Mollie while the makeup artist was busy applying, with the subtlest of strokes, lipstick to her latest muse.

"Just make sure, is all I'll tell ya," Mollie said with her nose an inch from Sarah-Jane's, "that you don't become one of the overcoat girls."

Sarah-Jane sat immediately upright, causing Mollie to tut and then swivel around to grab a wet wipe.

As she mopped up the streak of scarlet lipstick stretched across

Sarah-Jane's cheek, the anchor, deadpan, asked, "what's an over-coat girl?"

"I shuddnae say," Mollie said, "but once or twice a day some o' the girls are asked to wear somethin' sexy up to Walter Fellowes's office—and Isla in wardrobe, she gis 'em a gray overcoat to wear over it as they're goon up the lift."

"Something sexy? For what?" Sarah-Jane asked, squinting into the mirror.

"Well, that's what we'd all love tae know," Mollie said as she re-screwed the square lid onto her lipstick.

Sarah-Jane pretended her neck was itchy so that she could turn around sharply to take Phil in while she scratched at it. He was peering up over the pages of the newspaper at her, then he let his eyes drop back down.

"So, what's Walter Fellowes really like?" she elected to ask next, as she turned back around to the mirror.

Mollie sucked on her own teeth, then pulled open a drawer below the glowing mirror.

"He's a'right, I guess. But ya ne'er see him down here, no' really. He's a'ways up there in his big office and sure he just comes straight doon the lift to the parking lot underneath and gets driven home. I rarely see 'im. Have you met with 'im?" she asks into the mirror.

"Twice," Sarah-Jane said. "First time when he offered me the job and second, when, well... I just met with him for dinner just now."

Mollie nodded and then creased her kind eyes at Sarah-Jane's reflection while a silence swept its way through the overly-lit room. It was most unusual for hair and makeup to fall silent, given that Mollie McRae rarely took a breath from talking. She, stereotypical to her profession, loved to gossip, and often opened up to the new female employees as soon as she met them about the gray overcoat scandal, just so she could at least try to save them from falling into the trap. She rarely did save them, in truth, with stories of female employees looking sheepish in the gray overcoats she had warned them never to wear pushing their fingers on a button next to double golden doors of the elevator still being told on a regular basis.

"Have you ever worn a gray overcoat?" Sarah-Jane asked as Mollie took a hair brush and a spray bottle from the drawer.

"Was asked to once," Mollie replied. "By Walter's secretary, Barbara. Have ya met her?"

"Yes," Sarah-Jane said. "She seemed really nice."

"She's a fookin' enabler, she is."

"A what?"

"She does all his scoutin' for him. Helps get all the prettiest girls up tae his office."

Sarah-Jane widened her eyes, and in that moment would have loved to have glanced back at Phil once again, only she felt a magnetic pull to hold Mollie's stare through the mirror.

"And so, what did you do when you were asked to go to his office?" she asked.

"I told Barbara to go and shi'e."

"Go and shy?"

"Shi'e."

"Shy?"

"Shite," Mollie said, annunciating the T as forcefully as she could, kicking it off her top palate.

"Oh," Sarah-Jane said as Mollie began squirting water to the back of her hair. "And what happened after you told Barbara to go and shite?"

"Dunno," Mollie said. "She musta moved on to find another wee girl for Walter that day."

Sarah-Jane furrowed her brow. She wasn't sure what to make of Mollie's revelation; having assumed that if you didn't succumb to Walter Fellowes's advances, then surely you were bound to lose your job.

"And you're working at CSN how long?" Sarah-Jane asked.

"Eight years."

"And he's never asked you up to his office again?"

Mollie shook her head, then placed her spray bottle down on

the counter beside the mirror and began brushing through Sarah-Jane's wet locks.

"That's what I'm sayin'... start as ya mean to go on with 'im. If he asks you to wear something up tae his office, just tell him to go and shi'e."

Sarah-Jane coughed and laughed at the same time.

"I sure will," she said. Then she pretended her neck was itchy again and turned to face Phil while she scratched at it. Phil kept his eyes on the newspaper. "Wait!" she said, turning back to the mirror. "What are you doing with my hair? I'm just gonna go with a simple tied-back ponytail tonight."

"We're doing the Farrah Fawcett-style retro blowout, similar to what you had in the teaser advertisements," Mollie said.

"No. I've thought about this. I want a simple ponytail. I don't want to look all flashy. Just tie it back tight from the front and give me a simple ponytail."

Mollie swiveled Sarah-Jane's chair around, then took one step back and folded her arms.

"Exec Producer's already had a word with me."

"Howie? Howie wants me to wear my hair blown back and fancy?"

"Makes sense, I guess. Audience is tunin' in to see the woman in the teaser advertisements, so may as well make you look as familiar as possible, aye?"

"Tonight isn't about glamour," Sarah-Jane said, and as she said it, Phil folded the newspaper over before slapping it down on the lounge chair next to him.

"I mean, we can call Howie and ask—"

"I want a simple ponytail!" Sarah-Jane said, interrupting Mollie.

"It's just that Howie is ma boss, and—"

"She wants a ponytail," Phil said. Then he stood and folded his arms, just as a knock rattled against the door.

"Don't worry," Sarah-Jane said to Mollie as Phil moved to answer it. "I'll let Howie know I was adamant you did my hair in a ponytail. He can't tell me how to do my hair.. he can ah... what's the phrase, he can go and shy."

Mollie puffed out a laugh while Phil inched the door open to find a man whose face took a moment to register in his memory.

"Sorry," Phil said, "Sarah-Jane isn't meeting with any of the guests before going live."

"Oh please, sir," the man said. "She knows me a little. I've spoken to her before. Can I just have a quick word. I won't keep her."

Sarah-Jane squinted at Mollie through the mirror, then spun around in her chair.

"What's going on, Phil?" she said.

"One of the guests is here. Says he wants a quick word."

"Which guest is it?" she asked.

Phil turned back to the crack in the door.

"What's your name again?"

"It's ah, Patrick," the guest said, before shifting his feet awkwardly. "Patrick Klay."

BRODY EDWARDS

I collapse face-first to the grass and begin to breathe in and out as quickly as I can.

"Good session today. Keep it up," Coach Quill says, stooping down to slap me on the ass before he jogs off to the locker rooms.

I'm shattered. I feel as if I could sleep here for the night. So, I close my eyes, and just as I do, another body collapses beside me.

"Fuck me, that was torture," Stevie groans.

"Sure was. But we'll be a better team for it," I say. "I think we might win a couple games this year."

"If we can do those changeovers in games the way we did 'em today, we could win more than a couple. You were handling the ball well out there today, dude."

"Your Mom was handling balls well out there today," I say.

And then he slaps me on the ass. Really hard.

"Speaking of handling balls, when you gonna start turning the heat up on Decker? It's all starting to go very cold."

"Tomorrow," I say.

"Really?"

"Yep. I'm gonna start coming on to her tomorrow, and before you know it, she'll have her panties down by her ankles and she'll be taking in a mouthful of my—"

A cough frightens me. And when I turn over on the grass, I see Dad staring down at the two of us.

"What were you saying?"

"Nothing, Dad. Promise," I say, sitting up. And as I do, Stevie sits up beside me and begins plucking blades of grass from the field.

"Nothing, Mr. Edwards. Honestly," he says.

"Sounds to me like you were talking about girls. If I ever hear that you've treated a girl badly, Brody, I swear I'll... I'll..."

"We weren't talking about girls, promise, Mr. Edwards," Stevie says. He's so good at lying. Lies come to him as naturally as the truth does. "We were talking about the changeovers in our game next week."

Dad stares at him, unsure, then eyeballs me. But I just look down at the white line in the grass and say nothing.

"Well listen," Dad says, reaching into the back pocket of his trousers. "Here's the four hundred dollars for your trip to Europe."

"Yes!" Stevie says, and then he jumps on top of me and we both wiggle around on the grass celebrating as if we've just won the Superbowl.

"Dad, you're the best," I say after my wrestling match is over and I get to my feet to hug him.

"You're only getting this amount because I think the trip will be good for you. It'll help open your mind. But I want no fooling around on that trip from either of you, you hear me?"

"We'll be on our best behavior, Mr. Edwards," Stevie says. And then he slaps me on the back. "C'mon, man, let's go get changed."

I hug Dad again, then me and Stevie head for the locker room.

"We gonna do some fuckin' damage in Europe, baby!" I say when we're out of earshot of Dad. "Can you imagine the European pus-say? I can't wait!"

"Well that can wait," Stevie says, just as we step inside the locker rooms. Then he leans in to me. "Cos don't forget, you've still got a lot of work to do on Decker before we go on this trip. You being straight sayin' you're gonna make a move on her tomorrow?"

"You betcha," I say.

LUCY DECKER

I dig the knuckles of both index fingers into my temples while Mia slides a large glass of water in front of me.

"So what did you do all day in school if you were dying with a hangover?" she asks as she sits into the chair opposite me.

"I just assigned all the kids a writing task on Walter Fellowes while I sat at my desk staring at my watch. Three-thirty couldn't come quick enough."

"And you call yourself a great teacher?" she smirks.

I laugh, then pick up the glass of water and take a large swig from it.

"I *am* a great teacher. This is only the second time I've ever had a hangover in class in eleven years. And the first time I had a hang-over, I blame you."

My twin hugs her mug of coffee while she cackles from the back of her throat, remembering that she arranged her bachelorette party on a Sunday night.

"Well it's good to see you having fun. So, tell me... how did the date go?"

"It wasn't a date," I tell her. "I just felt I needed a drink, especially after the day I'd had."

"Go on," she says.

"Well... it's terrible news. One of my students tried to commit suicide over the weekend. Tried to hang himself in his bedroom.

He's gay, Mia. And so afraid to come out. His parents, they're just so old-school."

"Oh my fuckin' Jesus," Mia says, her jaw dropping as she places her mug back down to the table. "This isn't the first time this has happened to a student of yours, huh?"

"Nope. But at least this time the student wasn't successful."

We both sit there in silence, her picking back up her mug, me swirling my glass of water as if it was another glass of wine. Then last night hits me again, and I shiver. It was fun. Jonny is great company. And I've laughed my ass off both times we've been out together. But my life is so screwed up right now that I really shouldn't have gone to The Shamrock last night. I've probably led him on by showing up. I was just... I was just so desperate not to go back to my place and be alone with my own thoughts.

"So how is the kid?" Mia asks.

"A slight neck burn, but that's the least of his worries. He's now faced with the task of having to come out to his parents."

Mia shakes her head.

"In this day and age, huh? 1997 and so many people still find it impossible to just be who they want to be."

I shrug. And then... without warning, tears start spilling from my eyes and a sob leaps from the back of my throat.

"Oh, sis," Mia says, walking around her kitchen island to comfort me by rubbing circular patterns into my back.

"I'm so s-sorry," I say, my shoulders shaking. "It's just all too much for me to handle right now."

"There, there," Mia, says, continuing to rub my back as if I'm a big baby, "you're going through a lot."

"I'm alone. I can't get pregnant. My students are trying to kill themselves."

"Please," Mia whispers into my ear. "This is not your fault. None of those things you've mentioned are your fault."

But I don't answer her, or debate her, even though I want to. Because I'm sobbing. Hard.

Then, during the loudest of my sobs, a key turns in the door and in walks Zachary, whistling his way toward us.

I swipe my sleeve over my face.

"Please don't tell Zachary any of this," I whisper.

Mia shakes her head.

"What's up, ladies?" Zachary says, kissing my twin on the lips and then staring at me.

"Y'okay Luce?" he asks.

"Fine. Fine. Ohhh..." I say. And then I get off the stool I've been sitting on to grab my purse. "For your big day tomorrow."

I hand him his card and he holds out his arm for me to step under so he can embrace me in a one-handed hug.

"You're so sweet," he says.

"Can't believe you're almost fifty," I say.

"Fuck you," he says back to me. And then he releases me.

"Where are the kids, babe?" Zachary asks Mia.

"Up in their rooms playing."

Zachary drops the envelope I handed to him on the kitchen island, then runs up the stairs to see his pride and joy.

"He's such a good dad," I say. "Shit brother-in-law, but a great dad."

Mia laughs and then she, just as her husband did, holds out her arms so I can be engulfed in another tight squeeze. I must look like I need hugs.

"You're being way too Lucy," she says. "Listen, forget about saving up the ten K. It's gonna take you over... how long did you say it would take you again?"

"Another two years," I groan on her shoulder.

"Yeah.. forget about that. Why don't you just do what most other women would do in your situation. Just have sex with somebody, Lucy. Just let somebody fuck you and then... I mean you wouldn't have to tell them. Just get pregnant and raise the baby yourself. Your plan of taking two years to save up ten grand is just nonsense. Just screw somebody. That'll take ten minutes. You could be pregnant by next week!"

WENDY CAMPBELL

I sit beside Sally on the couch and wrap my arm around her shoulders, so I can squeeze her into me.

"What's this one called?" I ask.

She shrugs, then stuffs her mouth with the sandwich I made her while she soaks in the cartoon she doesn't know the name of. Then, as we both watch one of the characters getting squashed by a falling piano, she begins to giggle. And her giggling makes me giggle. Which is weird. Us two giggling while Momma is dying by our feet on a makeshift bed. I stare down at Momma's heavy breasts, to see them moving up and down, then I squeeze my little sister tighter to me.

"Hey," she moans, "I'm eating!"

Then the door rattles with a heavy knock.

"Shit," I whisper to myself.

"Who that?" Sally asks.

I stare down at Momma again, to see her bulging eyes blinking back to life.

"Don't worry Momma," I whisper, "I'm on it."

I walk over to our window and pull the curtain back an inch to see two strangers — a man and a woman — standing at our door, both of them with their hands on their hips. Then the man, who has his back to me, glances over his shoulder and I'm sure he sees me letting the curtain go and jumping backward.

Shit!

"Who is it?" Sally asks.

"Shhhh... I dunno," I say.

Then the window receives a rattle of the man's knuckles. And it frightens me.

"Hello," a voice calls out. "I saw you in there. We'd just like a quick word."

I try to remain calm because Sally is staring at her older sister; a sister who promised her she'd never let anybody hurt her.

"Momma," I whisper, "what'll I do?"

She blinks her eyes, then her head tilts to one side, as if she just wants to fall back asleep again so she doesn't have to deal with any of this.

"Hello," the woman's voice calls out this time. An odd accent.

After taking a few steady breaths, I decide to walk to the door so I can inch it open.

"Oh, hi there," her friendly face says, smiling at me. "You must be Wendy."

I look over my shoulder at Momma, then back out through the crack in the door.

"Who's askin'?" I say.

"Our names are Brendan and Mary Larkin. We're Caoimhe's parents."

"Oh," I say, relieved. "But I told Caoimhe not to say anything to nobody."

"We're only here to help," Caoimhe's father says, "to see what we can do."

I look back over my shoulder at Momma again, to see her eyes closed, her breasts moving up and down. Sally looks up at me, her eyes wide, her body frozen with fear.

"It's okay, Sally." Then I turn around and open the door fully, inviting them both inside.

CAOIMHE LARKIN

Meric smiles awkwardly at me. Again. It's so weird to be only able to see the bottom half of somebody's face when they're talking to you. I wish he'd cut that thick fringe off. If me and him were to officially become boyfriend and girlfriend, I sure as hell would be begging him to cut it.

"Here y'go," he says, handing me one of his newspapers, hot off the printer.

"Coooool," I exaggerate, faking my interest. I mean, that may be a little unfair. It's just I'm not that into newspapers at the best of times even when they have lots of celebrities in them, let alone some crappy one-sheet school newsletter.

"See... so I print all the school updates on the front page, latest goings on and whatever. And then..." he flips the page over... "on the back we do some news about the school football team and drama classes... stuff like that."

"You should be very proud of yourself," I say, handing the page back to him without reading anything but the headlines.

"Oh, take that one with you. You can read it at lunchtime."

"Eh... okay," I say.

And so I fold the sheet up and place it carefully inside my schoolbag, sandwiching it between two of my copy books.

"Tell you what?" Meric says, sitting beside me. "Why don't I interview you for next week's newspaper? I can write it from the angle of a new girl at school, all the way from Ireland, and you can give me some quotes about what you think of Lebanon."

"Oh, hell no," I say. And as soon as I say it, I see disappointment in his face... well, the bottom half of his face, anyway. "Sorry Meric, the last thing I would want is to have my picture splashed on the front of the school newspaper. I don't want to be noticed like that. I'm not one for attention."

"But... but..."

"But, what?" I say.

He just shakes his fringe and mouths, "Never mind" before turning back to the printer so he can organize all of the freshly printed newspapers that are now spitting out on to the tray.

"Tell you what could be a good news story," I say. "You know Kai... he's in our American History class?"

"Yeah, course," Meric says, brushing his fringe away with his fingers.

"Well, you know he tried to kill himself at the weekend?"

"What?"

"Yeah... I mean, it's so sad."

"I should do a story on Kai."

"No... no. Not on Kai," I say. "He wouldn't want that. Meric, I don't think people want the attention you think they want all the time. I'm just suggesting that you could do a story on mental health. On depression. Something like that."

"Oh," Meric says. Then he just shrugs his shoulders and sits back into his chair while we both suffer in another bout of overly long and awkward silence.

I think about poor Wendy while we're quiet. Mam and Dad popped round to see them yesterday; said they were gonna take care of things and try to help them out. Dad didn't say much to me when they got home — because he was still trying to figure it all out — but I think they're gonna start contacting hospitals to try to get Mrs. Campbell a bed somewhere. I actually feel bad that this past week has made me feel really lucky; lucky to have two parents living at home with me. And two parents who happen to be healthy. I should have known that already. I shouldn't have had to move all the way to America to realize all the good things I have.

"Hey," I say, turning to Meric, "what's your dad situation again?"

"Oh," he says. "I've no idea who he is. Mom says he was a really good guy and really handsome, but..." Then he shrugs his shoulders.

"You haven't tried to look for him?"

Meric sticks out his bottom lip and ever so slowly shakes his fringe from side to side again.

"Nope."

"But what about if—"

"Don't wanna talk about it," he says.

"Oh... I'm sorry."

Shit. I'm always running my mouth off. Dad says I ask too many questions. Though Mam normally argues against that, and says nobody can ever ask too many questions. I hope I didn't offend Meric that time. So, I sit forward a little in my chair and try to stare up into his face, from underneath the heavy strands of his fringe, to see if I can catch his eyes.

"Eh.. so you got anything exciting happening this weekend?" I ask, trying to change the subject.

"Nah... not really. Prolly just go on a few bike rides around town. You?"

"Me, what?"

"You got anything interesting going on?"

I tilt my head, something I always do when I'm trying to think. And it makes me remember that daddy surprised me with a little something last night when he got back from the Campbell's house, only because he knew I was feeling down and thought that it would pick me back up.

"Actually," I say, "I've got a psychic reading on Saturday. I guess that's something to look forward to."

KAI CHAYTON

Halona grips my hand as she pushes through the door and as she does, a bell chimes above our heads. Then a man with a scruffy beard pokes his head around a huge computer screen before exhaling a cloud of smoke.

"How can I help you guys?" he says.

"We'd uh..." Halona says, looking around the dank and low-lit room, "we'd like to use the internet for about an hour."

"No problem dude and dudette," the man says before taking in a lungful of smoke from his cigarette. "Nine dollars for one hour. Try computer number six down the back."

He points us to the back corner of the low-lit room as he exhales another cloud and I follow Halona in the direction he is pointing, the two us still gripping each other's fingers.

She's been such an angel to me over these past two days. It was her who calmed Poppa down. Although I'm not sure if "calm" is the right word to describe Poppa right now. He's still coming to terms with it all. He'll probably be coming to terms with it the rest of his whole life. Two days ago, his worst fear was me telling him I'm gay. Today I bet he wishes that was all I had to say to him.

I sat Momma and Poppa down, with Halona by my side, and told them *everything*. Momma didn't cry like I thought she would. Instead, she sat herself in between me and Halona and squeezed us both close.

"This is just a phase," she said. "You'll grow out of it."

Then she kissed me on the head before telling me she was gonna give me the four hundred dollars so I could go on the school trip to Europe; probably thinking that me breathing in European air will somehow make me forget who I am. Poppa was pacing the floorboards of our living room, huffing out of his nose like an angry bull. In fact, I don't think he has stopped huffing like an angry bull ever since. But at least he didn't shout and roar like I told Halona he would.

"You know how to work this kinda thing?" Halona asks.

I snicker, then shrug my shoulders as she moves the mouse from side to side.

"Scuse me, sir," Halona shouts back to the smoker.

"What's up, guys?" he says, strolling toward us, puffing out a large smoke cloud.

"How do we search for things on the internet?"

"Ah," he says, leaning over us and moving the mouse himself. Then he hovers his fingers over the keyboard, with the cigarette pinched between his lips, and pauses for a couple of seconds, before he begins to type quicker than I've ever seen anybody type before. "We go on this website page called *AskJeeves* and then you can type anything you want in this search bar here." He points his finger at the screen. "'So uh... what is it you guys wanna search for?"

I look at Halona and her eyes eventually meet mine.

"Oh, it's okay, we can take it from here," she says, waving him off.

The smoker holds his palms up to us as if we've just offended him, then backs away.

"Whatever dude and dudette," he says.

Halona and I watch him sit back down behind his huge computer screen, and when he is fully out of sight, she turns around and hovers her fingers over the keyboard.

"I'm so grateful for you being here with me," I whisper to her, leaning my cheek onto her shoulder.

Then she begins to type.

How does a boy become a girl?

MERIC MILLER

It's so exciting that she has a psychic reading tomorrow night. If I can get my hands on a hundurd dollars, then that crazy psycho psychic bitch who works outta the grocery store will finally make Caoimhe fall in love with me.

I'm so giddy about this. Even though I was feeling the opposite of giddy just a few minutes ago because Caoimhe didn't seem to be showing any interest in my newspaper. I asked her if she wanted to be in it, but she shook her head really fast and said, "No." I don't understand that. Why wouldn't somebody want to be in a newspaper? Instead, she came up with some stoopid idea about me writing an article on men's depression or somethin' crazy like that. That's not what I do. I just report on what changes are being made at the school; updates to the school rosters; changes in the lunch menus; latest updates on the school football team. I mean, it's sad that Kai wanted to kill himself. But it's not the first time something like this has happened around here. When we were in middle school, I heard about a boy who killed himself at Median High. It was actually all over the local newspapers back then. I even remember Sarah-Jane Zdanski talking about it on the TV.

"Any idea where I can get my hands on a quick hundurd bucks?" I ask Caoimhe, just as she's throwing her bag over her shoulder and getting ready to leave.

"A hundred? Jeez," she says. "Think you'll need to get a part-time job, Meric."

Then she hits me on the side of my shoulder and spins around.

"I better go, bell is gonna ring in one minute."

"Okay, cool," I reply. Even though I don't think it's cool. I was hoping she might wanna help me deliver these newspapers around the school hallways.

Instead, she floats out of my tiny office without saying goodbye before I pick up the three hundred newsletters and follow after her —her walking about twenty feet in front of me, and in total silence, until the bell screeches.

I leave a bundle of newspapers on the main corridor and then spread some out at the bottom of the stairs as I usually do before leaving the biggest box on the edge of the desk in the reception area near the principal's assistant. She glances up at me every time I leave the newsletters on her desk, then back down at her computer screen without ever saying a word. After dropping off the last of the newspapers and with the hallways now packed with students, I decide to stand under the stairs that lead to the science rooms, just to see if any students pick up a newspaper. It's a good main head-line today... all about the tenth graders' trip to Europe. Even though I'm not going, it was still cool to write about it. I got a quote from Principal Klay, too. He said more news is gonna come out about the trip soon and that he couldn't tell me everything just yet. But I'm hoping it's a story a lot of the students will want to read about once they see the headline.

I watch as two seniors pick up a paper each, and as they climb the stairs and out of sight, I begin to follow them. The boy in the yellow T-shirt balls up the paper then throws it at a kid walking in the opposite direction. The one in the red shirt waits a while and I stare at him wondering if he's gonna read the front page. But then he balls his newspaper up too and throws it back at the student in the yellow T-shirt.

Assholes!

I turn around and walk back down the stairs where I watch student after student walk by the bundle of papers I had dropped on the bottom step without even noticing them. Then I sniffle, swipe my sleeve across my nose and make my way to class, hoping Momma has a hundurd bucks in her oversized pink purse when I get home this evening.

LUCY DECKER

"C'mon, in you come, take your seat," I say to Meric as he, as per usual, arrives slightly late for class. He told me he'd be late on Fridays because he has to print off his little school newspapers and deliver them around the hallways. I used to read his newspaper, when he first started writing them. But I just don't have the time anymore.

"Okay class," I say, "There are only two more weeks until we go to Europe."

A wave of *"whoooos"* echoes through the classroom and it offers me my first genuine smile of the day. I've been so low. So very low. Lower than I've ever felt before.

Trying to get pregnant has taken a toll on me before, but not like this. Maybe I'm just being overly self-absorbed because I've finally realized I'm going to have to lay out ten grand to get pregnant. But I know there has to be more to my depression than just feeling wounded because I can't get pregnant. On top of that stress, one of my students tried to kill himself last weekend. Kai hasn't been in all week. But I phoned his mother last night and she says they've talked everything through and are coming to terms with what their son has revealed. I'm glad he has finally come out to his folks. The worst of it is over for him now. At least I hope it is. Still, knowing Kai had finally taken such a brave step didn't stop me from spending all last night crying into a large glass of red. I even muted the TV, just so I could cry in silence. Added to all of that is the whole mess with Johnny looping around my head. I need to nip that in the bud pretty soon. I shouldn't have gone to The Shamrock to meet him during the week. I was only leading him on. My life is too complicated right now for me to be dating somebody; certainly somebody who has opposite views on the world to the ones I have.

"Miss Decker, what lessons will we be learning in Europe?" Nicole asks after shooting her hand in the air.

"Well, you won't be doing any lessons per se, but what you will be doing is broadening your mind."

"Huh?" Brody says.

"Put your hand in the air if you wanna talk, Brody," I say.

And for some reason, instead of mouthing "I'm sorry," like one usually would, he winks at me. A bizarre slow, sultry wink.

"I mean, it'll broaden your mind in terms of richness. We all learn when we take steps outside the zones we are used to living inside. It'll be interesting to notice all of the cultures France and Italy and England have to offer that are so different to ours. We are such an insular nation that we Americans don't expand our minds enough. Well, you guys are going to have an amazing opportunity to open your minds in two weeks' time."

Hawkins shoots up his hand and I nod at him.

"What do you mean by insular?"

"Well," I say, sighing, because I'm really not in the mood of teaching today. I shoulda just let them continue their assignment on Walter Fellowes so I could sit at my desk wallowing in my own self-pity again. "For example, if you watch TV you will only see shows about America, right? Our news even... we are only concerned about news that occurs *inside* America. We don't know much about what goes on outside our own country. In fact, here's an interesting question... wanna take a guess at how many American people even have a passport to travel outside the country?"

I point at Stevie.

"Half. Fifty percent?"

"Nope," I say.

"Forty percent?" Hawkins says.

"Nope. Lower."

"Twenty-five percent?" Nicole offers.

And when I shake my head and point downward, the class erupts into a chorus of *"Whaaats?"*

"Sixteen percent," I tell them. Audible gasps hiss through the room. "I told you we are an insular nation. Thankfully, though, the passport numbers are rising and our younger people — which is you guys," I say, pointing around the room, "are getting your passports readily. So hopefully this sixteen percent continues to rise. But that's quite something... huh?"

All heads around the classroom nod, which is always a great sign to me. I know they're engaged. I know I'm doing a great job. Even if I do feel like shit.

"But anyway, moving on with the class. The big Sarah-Jane Zdanski interviews are taking place next Thursday night so I want to prepare you for what we might see."

"Do we know who she is interviewing yet?" Caoimhe says, after putting her hand up.

"It's still a big secret," I say. "It's not likely to be a big deal, and those of you hoping it's Jason Priestly or the Backstreet Boys will end up disappointed. But it's not the people she is interviewing that I want you to study. It's Sarah-Jane herself. I want you to study what she says, how she says it."

When the school bell chimes, right on time, I dismiss the class with a wave of my hand. And when I sit back down in my chair, I bend forward and rest my forehead on my desk. That period exhausted me. Though I guess it stopped me from feeling sorry for myself for forty-minutes.

"Hey, Miss Decker."

I look up to see Brody grinning at me, a bundle of bills in his fist.

"Ahhh... you're coming with us to Europe?"

"I am. My Dad coughed up. So... strap yourself in," he says.

I look at him funny. And he swivels his head to stare around the room; pausing until the last student — Meric, as usual — leaves my classroom.

"Miss Decker," Brody says, turning back to me, "I think you and me have something going on between us. What do you think of us maybe... I dunno... getting to know each other better when we're in Europe?"

I look him up and down; taking in his cheesy grin; his broad shoulders; his stupid-ass Nike Air Jordan sneakers with the laces open. Brody is a perfect stereotype of a fifteen-year-old high school football player. Young. Dumb. Full of cum. I've taught a hundred of these guys over the years.

"Why wait till Europe?" I say, winking at him. "Come back. See me after school today."

His eyes widen, and when he goes to say something he is interrupted by the voice of Principal Klay heading our way.

"I... I... Okay, Miss Decker. You mean come here, to... to your classroom? After school?" he asks.

"You bet," I say.

And then he backs away, almost bumping into Klay as he rushes out to the hallway.

"Good morning, Miss Decker," Klay calls out, approaching my desk. "Ah. More money for the trip to Europe, I see. Places must be almost all taken by now, huh?"

I open my drawer, brush away the notes and flick through the acceptance sheets.

"I've ten now, including this one from Brody Edwards."

"Ah yes. I've heard his father returned from Iraq two weeks ago. Perhaps he gave him the money for the trip."

"Probably," I say, shrugging.

"Ahhh," Klay says, rubbing his hands together. "I see you have Sarah-Jane Zdanski's name written on your chalkboard. Doing some media lessons are we?"

"We are indeed."

"Goodie," he says. "You talking about her secret interviews next week?"

"We were actually," I reply. "I'm going to have the tenth graders study the interviews as homework."

He chuckles, a light chuckle that turns up in volume as if he's begging for me to ask what he's chuckling about. Then he taps at his nose with his index finger before bending down to get nearer my face; his beard almost brushing against my cheek.

"I'm not supposed to say," he whispers, "But ah... I know who she's interviewing."

Then he taps his nose again.

"Huh?"

He leans closer to me, awkwardly close... so close I can feel his warm breath inside my ear as he whispers.

"I'm one of the people she's interviewing next week," he says.

"Huh?"

He winks at me, then spins on his heels and disappears into the crowded hallway.

WENDY CAMPBELL

The walls and the floors and the beds and the curtains might look cold around here — 'cause they all pale — but it feels kinda warm, I guess. I'm so happy; much happier than I've been feeling these past months. Or grateful. Yeah... that's the word. That's actually how I'm feeling. Grateful more than anything. Caoimhe is so lucky to have parents like Mr. and Mrs. Larkin. They're superheroes; superheroes to me and Sally and Momma anyway. Ain't nobody ever done so much for us our whole lives.

Momma looks more awake than she has done in weeks. I never thought I'd see her sitting upright again. And there's a twinkle back in her eyes that I thought had died long before she had. I wink at her as Mr. Larkin talks to the doctor in the doorway, and then I reach out my hand so she can grasp it.

"You gonna be just fine," I whisper, so I don't disturb Mr. Larkin and the doctor talking.

Then, as soon as they say their goodbyes, I stand up and bear-hug Mr. Larkin, a bit like football players do when they score a touchdown.

"Thank you so much, sir. I mean... I don't... I can't..."

"You don't have to thank me, Wendy," he says, patting me on the back while I squeeze him. "Thank the nurses and staff here who will care for your mother."

"They wouldn't be taking care of me if it wasn't for you,"

Momma says. It's so good to hear her voice again. Her full voice. She's not whispering. Not trying to talk in between wheezes of breaths. "And we *do* need to thank you. You and your lovely wife. Ain't nobody ever done anything so nice for me befo'."

Mr. Larkin crinkles the corners of his Irish eyes and then let's me go before walking over to Momma so he can place his hand on top of hers.

"It's just human decency," he says.

Then he lets go and as he turns, he taps me on the shoulder.

"Wendy, can I have a quick word outside?" he says.

I nod, then look at Momma to offer her a wide smile before blowing her a little kiss.

Mr. Larkin walks out to the all-white, brightly lit hallway, and as soon as I waddle to catch up to him, he turns to me and crosses his arms.

"Wendy, I know your mother looks as if she has picked up, but truth be known, that is solely down to the drugs the doctors have given her this afternoon. Unfortunately, her current state is not sustainable. You know what sustainable means, don't you, Wendy?"

"Sure," I say, nodding.

"I've spoken to the lead oncologist and he says... well he says... he says..."

Mr. Larkin scratches his chin and I feel my bottom lip beginning to tremble. It does this when I know there's bad news comin'.

"What is it Mr. Larkin?" I ask, before sniffling.

"Well, your mother's cancer is particularly aggressive and well... she doesn't have much time left, Wendy."

I look down at my shoes, then back up at Mr. Larkin because I know the tears will just spill outta ma eyes if I stay lookin' down.

"I know," I say. And soon as I say it, the tears begin to fall anyway.

"Do you understand what a hospice is?" he asks. I try to bite down on my bottom lip, so that it stops trembling, and then I shake my head. "It's not a hospital, it's not somewhere for patients to seek treatment and get better. Hospices are well... they are places people come to die, Wendy."

He holds my shoulder, but that doesn't help. In fact, it just makes me cry even more. I sob; sobs that make my whole body and not just my bottom lip tremble. Mr. Larkin pulls me to him. Oh boy, I wish I had a Poppa to hug like this my whole life. Caoimhe is so lucky.

As I am squeezing her Poppa under one of the all-white, bright lights in the hallway, I hear Caoimhe and her Momma walking toward us.

"How did you get on?" Mr. Larkin whispers over my shoulder.

"Good," Mrs. Larkin replies. "Wendy... we have decided that while your mother is in the hospice that we will take Sally into our home." I release my squeeze on Mr. Larkin and turn to face my new best friend and her angel of a Momma. "She's in school right now and we will continue to ensure she goes to school every day... well, as much as possible. You, too. We'd like you to continue going to school as often as you can. We're trying to get more and more answers for you both for what'll happen when... when..."

"She understands," Mr. Larkin says as he squeezes my shoulder.

Then Mrs. Larkin does what Mr. Larkin did earlier and hugs me as tight as she can.

Only this time it doesn't make me cry more. In fact it makes me smile through my tears.

"You guys are angels," I say.

. And then Caoimhe joins in on the hug and we all stand there under the bright lights, resting our chins on each other's shoulders, rubbing circular patterns into each other's backs.

"How long is it until Momma passes?" I ask, as I sniffle my tears.

The pause is long before Mr. Larkin finally answers.

"The doctors think it may be just a matter of days," he says.

BRODY EDWARDS

I hold my finger against Stevie's doorbell, and when Mrs. Jenkiss finally answers, by snatching the door open and staring at me as if I have two heads, I immediately hold up my hand.

"Sorry," I say. "I'm just itching to see Stevie. He in?"

She continues to dry her hands with a kitchen towel, before nodding her head toward the stairs. When she does, I run up them, two at a time, and push my way into Stevie's bedroom before closing the door tight behind me and standing with my back to it.

"Duuude," I whisper.

"'What the fuck man?" he mouths back.

"I did Decker."

"You what?"

"We did it. The whole thing."

"You fucked Decker?" he loudly whispers.

"Shhhh... shhh, man. Yeah. I fucked Decker."

Stevie coughs and sneezes into his elbow before getting to his feet.

"Really?"

"Really."

"What was it like, man? Ya know... I obviously know what it's like to fuck, but what's it like to fuck somebody so much older?"

"She was totally experienced, dude. She knew what she was

doing. She bent herself over the desk, man, told me to just get right up inside her and to keep pumping. So I did."

We do our handshake thing, and with huge smiles plastered across both our faces, then we sit down and reach for the Nintendo controllers.

"Imagine, dude," he says, "if you and me can fuck all the hottest chicks in school as well as one of the teachers, imagine the damage we are gonna do in London and Paris and wherever else it is we're going...."

"European pus-say," I say, cupping my mouth and pretending to shout.

"European pus-say," Stevie says, doing the exact same thing.

Then I press at the red button and we begin our game.

MERIC MILLER

There weren't many bills in Momma's oversized pink purse when I looked through it while she slept. Three ten dollar bills and a few loose quarters. I couldn't take that. She'd definitely notice it missing 'cause it's such a low amount. So here I am, biking round Esbon, wondering how the hell I'm gonna get my hands on a hundurd bucks so I can take it to that crazy-ass psycho psychic bitch before Caoimhe's reading tomorrow night.

I decide to wait across the street from the bank that Madam Aspectu's tent is set up behind. She's in there already. Cos when I rode round the back earlier and somebody pulled back the curtain, I saw her with her wig on, sitting at the table, smoke rising behind her.

A man stops at the cash machine, sticks his card into the slot and waits. So, I wait too. And as I do, I measure him up inside my head and realize he's prolly only the same height as me, but he's not worth robbing. He could beat me up. Easily. Would prolly even call the cops. Then I'd end up arrested and in a shit load of trouble. So, I stare through my hair up and down the street to see if anybody much weaker than him might come by to pick up some money from the cash machine.

I'm nervous. But I'm also kinda excited. Because if Madam Aspectu tells Caoimhe that she's already found the right guy, then I'm officially gonna have a girlfriend. And a really pretty

Irish one, too. This is prolly the most exciting thing that's ever happened in my life. Either this or the time Mom bought me this bike for my birthday five years ago. She says I was old enough for a big gift that year 'cause I had finally reached double digits. I'm also excited 'cause Caoimhe came down to my newspaper office yesterday, even if she didn't say much while she was down there. But she still looked pretty. And she still took the time to come see me. I was pretty weirded out by the fact that she didn't really wanna read my newspaper, though. She looked at it, *definitely* looked at it, then nodded her head, before she tried to hand it back to me. I told her to hold on to it, and she stuffed it into her bag. But I bet she didn't read it. She prolly threw it in the trash can as soon as she got outside. What weirded me out even more was that, when I asked her to be in the newspaper next week, she shook her head and said, "No way." She had no interest. Why would somebody have no interest in being in a newspaper? That doesn't make any sense. Maybe when she gets to know me better and we officially become boyfriend and girlfriend she'll agree to be in it. I'll write a great article about her. Take a picture of her beautiful smile and put it on the front page.

As I'm daydreaming about her orange-and-gold hair, two old ladies approach the cash machine. Perfect. They take forever pushing the buttons to get their cash out, prolly 'cause they're both in their seventies or maybe even their eighties. When I finally see them leaving to walk t'wards the town, I throw my leg over my bike and begin to slowly pedal after them. The woman with the hat on folds the bills she got from the machine into her wallet, then places her wallet into her side coat pocket.

When they turn onto a quiet street that leads to the town, I pick up my pace. I try not to make any noise, but the squeaking wheels on my bike don't really care. I skid the bike to the ground behind them, then grab her, the one with the hat, around the neck, while I reach inside her pocket with my other hand.

"I'm so sorry," I say. "I never do anything like this, but I need this money... I just need it."

They both gasp and the one with the hat begins to shake while I still have a hold of her.

I let go, then open the wallet, to see that she has lots of bills inside it. Then I remove five twenties before throwing the purse back at her.

"Sorry, this is all I need. I'm sorry. I'm sorry," I say as I pick my bike back up and begin to pedal away as fast as I can.

After a few minutes of riding around the dirt roads, I find myself at the back of the bank again. I look up and down the quiet street, drop my bike to the grass, then jog toward the curtains.

"I've got the hundurd bucks," I say, sweeping the curtain aside.

"Ahhh... thought I'd see you today, boy. Your little Irish girl has a booking with me tomorrow night."

She snatches the bills from my hand, then stares up at me with her black eyes. She's such a freak. But she's a freak who's going to help a pretty girl fall in love with me.

"So... you want me to tell her she has already found the right one, that right, boy?"

"Yep," I say, nodding. "And tell her she has to give him time... that it's her job to bring him out of his shell, okay?"

"You got it, boy," she says. Then she opens up a small box that she took from under her table and tosses the bills inside it before slapping the lid back closed. "You ah... you told me when you first came to me and gave seven dollars and two candy wrappers that your name is Miller, boy, that right?"

"Uh-huh," I say.

"From Lebanon?"

"Uh-huh. How'd you know where I'm from?" I ask her.

"Says so here in ma crystal ball."

"What?"

"Says your Momma's name begins with an A, that right?"

"Abigail. Yeah. *Really?*"

I take one step forward so I can stare into the ball on her table. But I don't know what I'm supposed to be looking for; all's I can see is a funny reflection of my own nose.

"Ma ball is saying you should visit Bloom Avenue in Smith Center."

"What? Bloom Avenue in Smith Center?"

"Yep."

"Why?"

"That's all, boy..." she says, tapping her long fingernail against the small chalkboard on her table. "Reading is over. It's forty dollars if you want more. I just gave you a little free sample 'cause you gave me the hundred bucks."

"Bloom Avenue in Smith Center? But... what the hell does that mean?"

"Ma ball just said that's where you should visit."

She shrugs, then holds out her hand.

"I don't got no more money," I say.

"Well, in that case I can't tell no more details, boy."

I scratch my head.

"Well... you know what to say to Caoimhe, right?" I say, pointing at her.

"Don't worry, boy. When that girl leaves here tomorrow night, I'll make sure she is going to fall head over heels in love with you."

I brush my hair away from my eyes and smile at Aspectu. Then I turn around, sweeping her curtain open before jogging across the grass.

"What the hell does she mean by Bloom Avenue?" I say to myself as I throw my leg over my bike.

CAOIMHE LARKIN

We hold hands, as if we're madly in love, while we continue to walk a long — very long — dirt road that leads us out of my new hometown. Kai lives out a fair bit; about two kilometers north of Lebanon; further up north than the center monument.

"You sure you're comfortable doing this?" I ask Wendy.

"Of course. It's what he needs, isn't it? In fact the reason he prolly tried to kill himself is 'cause nobody ever visited his house before. Shit. I don't think I ever saw Kai even talking to another person at school cept that pretty little cousin of his. Kai has no friends. We can be his friends now."

I grip her fingers even tighter, because I've never heard anybody talk like this before. I'm beginning to feel as if I'll never have a better friend than Wendy Campbell. I mean, Debra and Elaine back home were cool best friends and all. And I still love them to bits. But Wendy is somethin' else. This girl was literally told yesterday that her Mam only has days left to live, and yet here she is thinking about somebody else already.

"I love America," I say to her.

"You love America, girl? You sure?"

"It's just... I mean, where in the world would I ever meet a girl like you, Wendy? Where else would I meet somebody like Kai? I don't even know him yet... but already... he's... he's... I dunno. It's like he's already had an impact on my life. I've never known anything like the madness I've lived through these past few weeks. I just love how different everybody is. A Black girl. A Native American guy. I've got classes with two dumb jocks who are like real-life versions of Beavis and Butthead. Teachers who are funny and cool. America is... well, it's like every single person is unique, isn't it? In Ireland everybody's the same. We're all white. We're all Catholics. We all go to the local pub every weekend for a sing-along. S'like we're all clones of each other. Sure, even when Irish folk go on holiday, all we do is find other Irish people so we can all go to an Irish pub together where we can sing Irish songs. Ballymun in the sun, me Dad used to call those holidays. I guess he's right. I love Ireland and all... it's just, I'm finally starting to feel excited about living in America... about living here in Lebanon. I'm falling in love with it. I'm falling in love with the people round here. Especially you."

She lets go of my hand and turns to face me.

"Your eyes are getting all wet, girl," she says, patting at my cheeks with the cuffs of her sleeve. And then she turns back around and we continue to walk up the thin dirt road we seem to have been walking up for ages now.

"I hated it at first," I say. And when she turns to look at me again, I just continue, "being here. Really hated it. I mean, I knew I was in the middle of America, but it seemed to me as if I was in the middle of nowhere. But it's not the middle of nowhere. It's the middle of everywhere. Does that make sense? I think I've done more growing up in these past few weeks than I ever remember doing in all my fifteen years before."

"Sixteen soon," Wendy says.

"Yep. Sweet sixteen," I say.

"Your Poppa take you lookin' for cars yet?"

"We're doing that next weekend," I tell her.

And then she screeches a high-pitched scream from the back of her throat and lets go of my hand so she can clap both of hers together really quietly.

"Girl, when you have a car we can drive to Smith Center all the time. We can even go to Wichita. That's the nearest big city."

"Wichita? How far is that away?"

"Three hours."

"Three hours?" I say, almost as high-pitched as Wendy's screech was. "That's like driving the whole length of Ireland."

When Wendy stops giggling, she stretches her finger to point through the bare branches of the trees, to a chimney in the distance puffing out clouds of smoke.

"That's Kai's house there," she says.

And then she re-grabs my hand and we continue up the narrow dirt road toward the smoke.

"I'm nervous about this," I say. "Are you?"

LUCY DECKER

I fold up another tissue and dab my eyes before swiping it across my nose. Then I toss it onto the carpet — on top of the heap of tissues already forming a mound down there — as I lay my head back down on the sofa cushion.

I've felt down before. Depressed before. But I've never cried uncontrollably because the pain of the depression was physically hurting me like it is now. The worst thing is that I know the depression has gotten this painful because I'm mostly feeling sorry for myself. I'm all me, me, me. I've been wrestling with the fact that I am the arrogant leftie Johnny told me I am. He's absolutely right. Us liberals are arrogant fuckers. Of all the things going wrong in the world right now, all I seem to be able to think about is myself. I'm feeling sorry for myself because I can't get pregnant; I'm feeling sorry for myself because I can't afford the money it would take to get pregnant; I'm feeling sorry for myself because I didn't realize a student of mine who sits in front of me two days a week has been having suicidal thoughts; I'm feeling sorry for myself because all I do is teach when my life promised so much more when I was younger. It's all me, me, me. Suffocatingly and depressingly so. I'm also feeling bad about how I handled Brody yesterday. That was out of order. In all my years of teaching I have never done that to a student. My face was purple with rage. I could actually feel the veins throbbing in my neck as I roared and screamed at him. My spit actually sprayed his face as he sat there blinking at me, in total shock that I could rant and rave as much as I did. He just flipped a switch in me that was begging to be flicked. I've had students flirt with me before. But none have blatantly come on to me like Brody did yesterday. My impatience, coupled with my depression, just finally erupted. I let him have it. Both barrels. I scolded him like I've never scolded any student in all my years of teaching.

"If you ever say anything like that to me again, young man," I spat, "I will be calling your mother up here and telling her exactly what you have been saying to me."

He looked like a lost puppy, sitting all stiff while I sprayed his face. Then I just pointed to my door and he got the message that it was time for him to leave. After I calmed down, I immediately started feeling sorry for myself that I ranted and raved so much. Brody's only a kid. I shouldn't have got so angry. I shouldn't have taken all of my rage out on him.

"Ugggh," I say, balling my fists as the anger erupts within me again. I hate being this fucking sad. In fact, sad is the wrong word to describe me right now. I'm pathetic. Pa. Thet. Ic. Especially when I have so much I should be looking forward to. Who wouldn't want to be heading to Europe to see three of the most fabulous cities this world has to offer in just two weeks' time?

Maybe being in Europe will offer me the ideal opportunity to do something I swore I'd never do. Mia is right. I should just screw somebody; let them do me the way every man wants to do a woman and then hopefully I'll get lucky and my egg will hatch. I could do with a good fuck anyway. I don't know how long it's been. Too many months to count. Too many months that I should no longer be counting in months, but in years. Well... one year and then some months, I guess. A fuck would actually be quite nice. I imagine myself being taken by a faceless French man; me bent over a bed and him slapping his hips against my stretchmarked ass. And then the thoughts of an orgasm suddenly makes the weight of my depression lift a little and I think about taking out my vibrator that may or may not have working batteries inside it because I genuinely can't remember the last time I used it.

"Fuck it," I say to myself. Then I heave myself up from the sofa and head down my narrow hallway so I can go look under my bed for my pink vibrator. I'm down on my hands on knees, patting the dark carpet under the bed when the doorbell rings, startling me.

"Shit," I whisper, slapping my hand off the carpet. Then I tut before making my way to the door and snatching it open.

"Hey," Zachary says, grinning at me. What the hell is he doing here? He has *never* knocked on this door before. He leans against the doorframe and grins up at me. "I uh... I hear you're trying to get pregnant," he says.

KAI CHAYTON

I stare at the gorgeous yellow dress I bought two weeks ago as it hangs in my closet. It feels so weird that I almost hung myself while I was wearing it. I don't know what I was thinking. I've tried to think my hanging through lots and lots and lots over the past few days, but I can't seem to get my head into the same space it must have been in that day. I mean, I'm still down. Still hurt. Still an absolute mess of a human being. But I feel like such a weight has lifted from my shoulders ever since I told Momma and Poppa that I wanted to be a girl. In fact the weight has lifted so much that there's no way I'd wanna kill myself now. I see a full life ahead. A full life of me being who I am meant to be.

I think I'm gonna keep my same name. Momma and Poppa would appreciate it and nobody would have to get used to calling me anything different. Kai is a unisex name, anyway. But aside from that, everything else is gonna change. Especially this closet. Which is why I have it open right now and am staring at the shitty black and navy blue T-shirts I've worn ever since I can remember.

Momma said she's gonna have to take time to get used to everything. But Poppa... well, he hasn't really spoken to me since I came out to him. The only noise he has made around the house is to breathe in and out really loudly through his nose. I feel sorry for him. I do. I know he's hurt by this. Deeply hurt. But he'll come to terms with it. He'll have to.

"Kai," his voice shouts up the stairs just as I was thinking about him.

"Yes Poppa?" I say, my heart picking up speed. Maybe he wants to talk.

"You've got friends at the door."

"Friends?" I say.

What the hell does that mean? I try to take a peek out my bedroom window, but the angle isn't quite right. So, I leave my bedroom, with my brow wrinkling, and walk down the stairs until they come into sight.

"Oh... hey, guys," I say.

Wendy smiles back at me while the new Irish girl waves awkwardly. Then Poppa huffs loudly through his nostrils as I squeeze past him.

"We just thought we'd come by to see if you wanted to go for a walk?" Wendy says.

"A walk?" I say. "With you two?"

"Uh-huh," Wendy says, nodding.

I spin on my heels and race myself back up the stairs where I snatch at my coat before sprinting back down.

"Momma, Poppa, I'm going out," I shout.

Then I slam the door closed behind me and breathe in fresh Lebanon air for the first time in a very long time.

LUCY DECKER

I point my hand to the armchair across from the sofa and as I do a wave of panic washes through me, because I realize that from where he is about to sit he'll be able to see the mound of wet tissues I have been tossing on the carpet all night.

He clears his throat as I try to back-kick the tissues under the sofa while I sit into it, but I already know it's too late. There's no way he can't see them.

"I told Mia not to bother you with my troubles... she shouldn't have said anything—"

"I wanted to drop by to thank you for the birthday card," he says, interrupting me.

Okay. This is *definitely* weird. Zachary has barely thanked me for birthday cards before, let alone dropped by my place to do so. In fact he has never dropped by here on his own. I recall he briefly helped when I first moved into this place, by carting some of the heavy boxes from the car to my kitchen countertops, but aside from that, I don't recall Zachary ever being in my home.

"It's the least I can do," I say. "I just wish I had more imagination than just throwing two fifty-dollar bills inside your card."

He clears his throat again. Awkwardly.

"You uh... gotta glass of water?"

"Sure," I say. I get up from the sofa, back-kicking more tissues before I walk over to my tiny kitchen where I begin to pour him a small glass of lukewarm water from the tap. It's the best I can offer. In fact, it's all I can offer. I'm not sure when I've last been to the store.

"It's just... when I opened your card it got me thinking about you," he says, following me over to the kitchen where he drums his fingers noisily against the countertop. "And then I asked Mia why you haven't been yourself lately."

"I haven't been myself lately?" I say, turning to him, my brow furrowing.

He nods his head back to the sofa, to indicate the wet tissue mound I tried, but clearly failed, to hide.

"Mia opened up, told me all about your struggles to get pregnant. I had no idea."

I grin at him while shaking my head, hoping he gets the message that this is not a conversation I wish to have with my brother-in-law.

"Well... just one of those things, isn't it?" I say, gripping the glass of lukewarm water I just filled for him.

"I've booked you in for your IVF treatment," he says.

"What?"

"Here's a number for a clinic in Smith Center. They said you have to call them as soon as you can to make an appointment. As soon as your... uh... eggs are... uh..."

"*What?*" My brow furrows even further, and I'm pretty certain I'm about to cry, right here in the middle of my kitchen, standing in front of a brother-in-law I've never really felt comfortable in the company of.

He shuffles closer to me, and takes the lukewarm glass of water from my grip.

"Lucy, you have given me a hundred bucks inside a card for every single one of my birthdays since I started dating Mia... wanna know what I've given you for your birthday all these years?"

"Well, Mia always buys me a lovely gift from you all—"

"Exactly," he says, before taking a sip from his glass, making a face, and then placing it back down on the countertop. "Mia gets you a gift from each of us. Yet you always buy each of us a gift for our birthdays. That's one gift, once a year from us. You give me and Mia and the two kids a gift for each of our birthdays. That's not fair."

"Well, it is... there's only one of me," I say, my head shaking, my mind whirring.

"We want more than one of you. I want a niece or a nephew... or ... whatever it is you want, that's what I want. It's what we all want. Take your IVF appointment as a gift for all of the birthdays I have missed in the past, and all of the birthdays I will miss in the future."

"*What?*"

"I've paid for your IVF session from my savings."

"*What?*"

He smiles at me, then reaches into his back pocket.

"All you gotta do is call this number, make an appointment for when your eggs are next... whatever the science is. All you gotta do is call this number."

I take one large step closer, so I can wrap my arms around him and I squeeze as tight as I can.

"I can't take your money, Zachary," I whisper.

"Yes you can. I'm giving you a lifetime of birthday presents from me, all at once."

I swipe my sleeve across my face as I rest my chin on top of his shoulder.

"But you were saving for your Vespa," I say.

"I don't want a fuckin Vespa,' he whispers. "I'd rather have a niece or a nephew."

BRODY EDWARDS

It's boring as hell around here. Mom kicked us out of my bedroom 'cause we were playing video games for too long. So, me and Stevie have just been walking round Lebanon not knowing what to do but talk about who we will probably jerk off thinking about when we go to bed tonight.

"So did Decker have, like, a big bush?" he asks, before coughing into his elbow.

"Yeah," I say, 'it was like a newborn baby's head of hair, all sweaty and hairy and ugggh."

He makes a face. And so do I.

"I wonder if all older women have big hairy bushes like that. You think SJZ has a big hairy bush?"

We both turn to each other, then shake our heads at the same time.

"Nah!"

"We're not far from the monument. You wanna take a walk around it?" he says.

I shrug, and then, without really answering him, we take the left down the narrow dirt road that leads to the central monument. It's unusual we walk this way, but it's also unusual that we're not either at football practice or playing games on one of our Nintendos.

We hear the voices before we see them. Wendy is so loud when she talks.

"Oh hey, you two," the Irish chick shouts over, waving at us.

"Don't say anything about me finger fucking her," Stevie whispers as we walk toward them.

"I won't... and you don't tell them about me and Decker doing it on her desk," I say.

"Holy shit, Kai!" Stevie says as Kai pokes his head out from behind the monument. We both sprint toward him.

"What the heck, man, I heard you tried to kill yourself," I say. And as I do, Stevie elbows me in the ribs. "Oh... uh... sorry. Sorry. I'm not sure what I'm supposed to say. Ain't never known anybody who tried to kill themselves before."

"You don't have to say anything," Kai says. "You've never said anything to me in all the years we've been in school together. Why start now?"

I scratch my head while I look at the Irish chick. Then I stare at Wendy. Everybody's quiet. Even her. Which is not normal.

"Sorry," I say, eventually ending the silence.

"You don't need to say sorry," Kai says.

"No... I mean, I'm sorry that you felt sad enough to want to kill yourself. That's.... that's... well, I'm sorry that's how bad you felt. I can't imagine what that must be like."

"Yeah, I'm sorry, too, bro," Stevie says.

Then Stevie holds out a clenched fist and Kai stares at it before clenching his own and bumping it off Stevie's. So I do the same.

"So what you two doin' round here?" The Irish chick says really, really quickly in her really, really cool accent.

"Chillin'," I shrug. "What are you guys doing?"

"Just talkin'," Wendy says.

"Cool."

"Wanna join us?" the Irish chick says.

"What... and, like, just talk?"

"Yeah," she says, nodding.

Me and Stevie stare at each other. Then he coughs into his elbow again.

"Yeah... okay... cool," I say.

Without saying anything, everybody decides to just sit where we had been standing; in a circle on the freshly cut grass right next to the monument.

"So ah... what should we talk about?" Stevie says, picking a blade of grass from the dirt before stretching it until it snaps.

"Oh, I know what we could talk about," I say, "Who you guys think Sarah-Jane Zdanski is interviewing on Thursday?"

SEVEN

SARAH-JANE STRODE to wardrobe with her ponytail swaying behind her and a gray overcoat and red cheerleader's uniform draped over her arm.

She had refused to meet with the guest who had called by hair and makeup; not because she didn't personally respect Patrick Klay, but because she had long decided that meeting guests prior to interviewing them would have a negative impact on the interview itself. Not liaising with your subjects prior to interview was taught as a moral journalistic approach in most media colleges, though it was by now considered old-school, what with a number of television hosts now pre-interviewing their guests, so they can decide what questions will specifically be asked, and what answers should be expected in return. Sarah-Jane, though, had long decided that she would take the old-school approach to interviewing, even when she was a desperate-for-stories reporter back in her earliest days at PBS.

"Tell him I'm sorry," Sarah-Jane had said from the large chair in front of the brightly lit mirror, "but I'm only speaking to guests once the cameras are rolling."

"Less than one hour until you go live," Phil whispered as they continued to walk toward wardrobe, stalling every now and then to point down the maze of dark hallways, wondering if that's the route they should be taking.

"Jeez. We that close to going live already? I'm not even dressed yet," Sarah-Jane said, as she continued to stride in front of Phil, leading him nowhere, her ponytail bouncing from side to side. "'Scuse me!" she then said, stopping a young woman in the hallway. "Where's wardrobe? We're a little lost."

"Your next left, then take two rights," the young woman instructed.

Even though they had been offered precise directions, Sarah-Jane and Phil still took another wrong turn before eventually finding themselves outside a door they had last knocked on just over two hours ago. It struck Sarah-Jane, as she rapped her knuckles against the door, that they had been a helluva long two hours.

"Hey," Isla said, thumbing the straps of her overalls after she had answered the door. "I've got your dress all set out for you. Your makeup looks awesome."

Sarah-Jane stiffened her lips at Isla, because she had since let it sink into her mind that, like Barbara — Walter's secretary — Isla, too was an enabler in the big boss's elite-level misogyny. Or rape, Sarah-Jane thought it to be—having sex with somebody who doesn't want to have sex with you.

"Here," Sarah-Jane said, holding the gray overcoat and red cheerleader's uniform toward Isla, "I don't want you to ask me to wear any of these items again."

Isla let the clothes fall into her hands as her eyes widened behind her blue-framed glasses.

"It's just... I follow orders and—"

"Well follow this order," Sarah-Jane said. "Next time Walter or Barbara instruct you to dress me in some slutty uniform, you tell them I said they can go and shi'e."

Isla squinted.

"Shy?"

"Shite!" Sarah-Jane said, producing her best Scottish accent and kicking the sound of the T off her palate as forcefully as she could.

Isla glanced over Sarah-Jane's shoulder to see Phil eyeballing her intimidatingly while scratching at his patchy beard. Then she opened the door wider and invited them inside.

"Well," Isla said, walking over to the rack on the far side of the room and draping the uniform and overcoat across the top of it. "Maybe you should just tell him that yourself."

"Isla," Sarah-Jane said, placing her hands to her hips. "Don't do his dirty work for him. You're better than that. You've *got* to be better than that."

Isla didn't turn around to face Sarah-Jane, deciding, instead, to slide garments across the rack, even though she wasn't looking for anything in particular.

Sarah-Jane had been playing the events of the past two hours around in her head since she'd left hair and makeup with her blonde locks swept back into a tight ponytail.

Although there was undeniably a sense of strength within her voice, Sarah-Jane was still carrying a weight of worry in her stomach; worry about the ramifications of her refusing to take part in her boss's games. She had assumed that if she turned down Walter Fellowes's advances, then he would surely just cancel her show. But, buoyed by the knowledge that thirty million Americans were due to tune into her debut tonight, she felt she likely held the upper hand. After all, Walter Fellowes firing his new anchor after she had just broken all CSN viewing records would surely make news on other networks. Reporters would inevitably want to interview Sarah-Jane, to ask why she had lost her job at CSN after such a groundbreaking launch. And if that were the case, then surely she would have to be frank and honest. *I lost my job because I refused to have sex with my boss.*

Howie burst through the door, making Isla finally spin back around from hiding her face in the garments hanging from the rack.

"What took you so long in hair and makeup, Sarah-Jane," Howie snapped. "There's only fifty minutes until you're live. Let's get you into that black dress. Hey," he said, pointing his finger. "Why is your hair in a ponytail? I told Mollie we needed a throwback, blowback, like you had in the teaser commercials."

Sarah-Jane pressed her hands to her hips.

"And I told Mollie that I wanted *my* hair in a loose ponytail."

Howie dipped his chin into his neck, a stunned frown forming across his forehead.

"It's important the viewers see the woman they were tuning in to see," he said, as calmly as he could, in an effort to reduce the tension that had just begun to enflame.

"They're not tuning into see my fucking hair, Howie," Sarah-Jane said through gritted teeth. "They are tuning in for the story."

"No. No. No." He shook his head while wiggling a finger. "I have been in national television production for twenty-five years. I've been an executive producer for over a decade. I know what works, and what doesn't work when it comes to live broadcasting."

"Excuse me," Phil said, tapping a chubby finger to Howie's shoulder. "It's her hair."

Howie stood still for a long moment, flaring his nostrils at Sarah-Jane while everybody else in wardrobe stared at him, wondering how he was going to react to Phil's tapping of his shoulder, and his authority being questioned.

"Fine," he decided to eventually say, "anyway, we don't have time to get you back to hair and makeup. You need to get moving. I've left a copy of the manifesto, as I said I would, on your desk. Mikey will have a copy of it with him in the control room as he is directing you. I know you don't get to the issue of the manifesto until after the third commercial break, but promise me you'll take Mikey's directions when it comes around. Don't cast any aspersions... Mikey will take you through it."

"I know what I'm doing," Sarah-Jane said.

And then wardrobe fell silent again while everybody stared at Howie, wondering, once again, how he was going to react to his authority being questioned. He reacted by, at first, twisting his neck to take in Phil as he glared at him from over his shoulder, then spinning back to nod once at Sarah-Jane.

"Well, I'm gonna wait outside for you to get dressed, then I'll walk you to set." Howie spun, then walked around the bulky frame of Phil without acknowledging him, before exiting out the door he had just come in from, leaving the three folks left in wardrobe to awkwardly glance around at each other.

When Sarah-Jane's eyes met Phil's she shrugged her shoulders, then began peeling off her clothes. Isla — who was somewhat frozen stiff by the tension that had quickly erupted — snatched the black dress hanging from the back wall and walked it toward the new host. The little black dress was cut square across the top from the height of the collar bones, but it did only travel downward as far as the mid-thighs, and therein passing Walter's test of female anchors teasing either their tits or their legs anytime they appeared in front of his cameras.

After she had stepped into the dress, and placed her arms through the short sleeves, she turned her back to Phil and held her ponytail to one side so he could pull her back zipper all the way to the top. Then she flattened down the front of the dress, stepped into her high-heeled shoes and let out an audible sigh; relieving wardrobe of the tension that seemed to rise up as soon as her and Phil knocked on that door.

"You look amazing," Isla said, pressing her lips together at Sarah-Jane's reflection. "Camera's gonna love this look."

Sarah-Jane gazed at her own reflection, then nodded her agreement.

"Isla," she said, flicking her eyes to the grungy wardrobe manager's reflection, "somebody has to put a stop to the male dominance around here. Walter plays you. He uses you to get his female employees ready for him to sleep with them. If you stop, it'll all stop."

"I'll lose my job," Isla said.

"You're abetting in the sexual abuse of other women. Think about that."

Sarah-Jane spun around from the mirror, her ponytail whipping after her.

"I... I uh... I'm..." Isla stuttered.

"Somebody needs to put a stop to this. This behavior can't continue."

"I... I don't know what to—"

"Just do your fucking job, Isla. Dress the anchors before they go on air. Don't dress them to go up to Walter Fellowes's office so that he can take his little dick out and—"

"Hey," Phil said, butting in. "Forty minutes."

He reached his hand to cup Sarah-Jane's chin and then winked at her.

"Okay," she said, before exhaling slowly through her pressed lips. Then she spread her arms out wide. "Thank you for getting me dressed for tonight."

Within seconds of Sarah-Jane and Phil stepping back outside, they were already lost in the maze of dimly lit hallways until they eventually overheard Howie's camp voice barking out instructions.

He was gripping copies of the manifesto, handing them out to crew members and lecturing them that the subject was going to arise straight after the third commercial break.

"You look great," he said as he watched Sarah-Jane approach, her high heels clicking. "Would have preferred you in the blown out, throwback hairdo, but..." He looked to Phil and when he noticed the stern look on the producer's bullish face, the smile on his own faded sharply. "Here, you take one too," Howie said, handing Phil a copy of the manifesto. Phil took it, folded it in four and then placed it inside the pocket of his double-breasted jacket. Howie nervously cleared his throat, then leaned into Sarah-Jane.

"Thirty-five minutes till we're live," he said. And as he said it, Sarah-Jane noticed that her hands were beginning to get clammy and her stomach was rolling. "You uh... wanna take up your position in the studio?"

She closed her eyes, did some meditative breathing exercises she had, a long time ago, learned in a class, and when her eyes eventually popped opened at the tail end of a long exhale, she nodded once.

"Yep," she said.

So, Howie pulled the curtain aside and waved her and Phil through the gap where her studio was now a hive of activity; with cameramen all standing behind their large cameras, a floor manager with an overly large headset on holding a meeting with

two junior producers, and all of the lights on the stage quite literally sizzling.

Then the door on the opposite side of the studio cranked open,
and one-by-one, in shuffled each of tonight's panel of guests. They
all glanced at Sarah-Jane, some of them nodding at her, some of
them pursing their lips at her, and then they all stood still in the
shadows, behind camera number one.

"Holy shit," Sarah-Jane whispered out of the side of her mouth.
"I think I'm gonna throw up."

Then she spun around, whipped the curtain back open, and
raced away as fast as she could toward a restroom.

JOHNNY EDWARDS

My hands are so sweaty. Must be twenty years since I last asked somebody to be my girlfriend. And even then I wasn't so sure about it; not like I am now. I knew I was hot for Patricia when we started dating; knew that the gleam off her legs would make my dick twitch every time she wore a short skirt. But I also knew that I didn't really like her; that I didn't enjoy being in her company. It's a miracle we lasted sixteen years. If it wasn't for her ending up pregnant two months into us dating, I'm not sure we'd have made it to month three. But with Lucy, it seems to be the exact opposite. I'm actually not so physically attracted to her that I wanna tear her clothes off and screw her. I'm attracted to her mind; to how funny she is; to how smart she is. I love being in her company. I've actually been daydreaming of sitting down and just talking with her since the moment she waved goodbye to me outside The Shamrock bar last week.

I pause, holding in a deep breath and then, after I finally exhale, I rap my knuckles on the wood panel of her front door.

My heart flips when I hear her footsteps shuffling their way toward me, followed by the clunk-clunk of a chain being slid and released from its lock.

"Oh," she says, looking surprised as soon as she pulls the door open. "It's a Sunday morning. Shouldn't a Republican be at church on a Sunday morning?"

I puff out a laugh. She's so quick. So funny.

"Well, I thought I'd skip out on my slice of Holy Communion this morning just to come see you."

She stands aside, inviting me in, and as I rub my hands together to get rid of the sweat, I glance at the two dark walls either side of me.

"Nice place," I say.

"Yeah, right," she replies. "So..." She places her hands on her hips. "What can I do you for?"

"You look nice," I say. "Bright big smile you got there."

She actually looks really cute in just a T-shirt and pajama bottoms. Much cuter than she did on our dates. I think there's an extra glow to her when she's all natural. That's certainly another opposite trait from Patricia.

"Well," she says, "I got some really good news yesterday and I..." She swings her hips from side to side and then begins to nibble on her bottom lip instead of finishing her sentence.

"Let me guess... You realized you were in love with a Republican?"

She grunt laughs. And for some reason I produce the exact same laugh as if I'm copying her. I sound like a teenager again.

"Well, it's a secret for now, but..."

She grins. A massive full-toothed grin. She really is glowing today. I'm not sure why I've never noticed she was *this* pretty.

"Wow, you really look great," I say.

She drops her smile and then looks around, as if she isn't familiar with her own home. This is getting awkward now. *Really* awkward. I need to get to the point.

"I really like you, Lucy," I say. I clap my hands together once as I say that and it creates an echo in her hallway. Then I find myself guffaw-laughing like a teenager again.

"Oookaaay," she says, stretching out the vowels as long as she can.

"As in, I like you so much that I would like to ask you... to..."

"To?" she squints at me while shaking her head.

"To be my girlfriend."

"*Girlfriend?*"

She holds her hand to her neck. Holy shit! Have I just made a fool of myself?

"Is that not the next step?" I ask.

A cringe rolls down my back because I've just realized I've played this way too forward, and so I find myself stabbing my fingernails into the palms of my hands.

"We're not teenagers, Johnny," she says." We don't have to label our relationship."

"Relationship?" I say, eyeballing her. "So there is..."

"No, listen," she says, taking a step toward me and pressing her hand to my chest. "You and I... we can't... it wouldn't work."

"I've never bonded with any woman the way I've bonded with you," I say. "Not even my ex-wife."

She makes a sorrowful face; so sorrowful that the cringing ignites again inside of me and then intensifies.

"I know we bonded a little," she says, bringing her hand up to cup my cheek. "And I really like you, too. But we can't be in a relationship together. We don't even share that much in common."

"We share *sooo* much in common. It doesn't matter that I'm a Republican and you're a Democrat. It's bullshit to think we couldn't be together because of that—"

I'm silenced by her hand moving around to my mouth, where she presses a stretched index finger to my lips.

"I'm not turning you down because you are a Republican, Johnny. I like you as much as you like me. I think we get along great. It's just... we're in different places in our lives. Tomorrow," she says, her finger still pressed against my lips, her eyes, large and beautiful, staring up at me, "I'm undergoing IVF. I'm trying to get pregnant."

My stomach churns and a bubble of air catches in my throat.

"Pregnant?"

"It's all I've wanted... for years, Johnny. A child of my own. I've just never met anybody... and now I'm forty-one it's just the wrong time for me to be getting into a relationship. And this is the best chance I'll ever have to get pregnant. I need to do this... I need to do it alone."

I try to swallow down the ball of air in my throat. But it's not moving.

"You don't need to explain," I say to her, mirroring her by pressing my index finger to her lips.

Then we both just stand there, inside her narrow, dark hallway, staring at each other. Then I begin to wonder if she is thinking what I'm thinking: that our lives would have been so different if we had met when we were younger.

After producing a long, silent sigh through my nostrils, I bend forward a little and kiss her forehead, before moving to her front door.

"You'd better get your ass back to that church quick so you can get your slice of Holy Communion!" she says.

I smile back at her. And then I pull her door closed with my heart bubbling and cracking, as if it's just been tossed onto a barbecue grill.

"Oh hey," I say, pushing the door back open and beaming a great big, fat, fake grin at her. "I hope the IVF works for you."

LUCY DECKER

"Oh, I don't know the father," I say to the nurse, who immediately scrunches up her face in both apology and embarrassment. "It's okay. I'm doing this alone. I like that I'm doing it alone."

I feel bad that she feels embarrassed, so I squeeze her shoulder as I sit up in the bed before getting to my feet.

"Well, it's all done. It's just a waiting game now," she says.

"So, ah... how long is it until I could find out if this all worked?"

"As in, when can you take a pregnancy test?"

"Uh-huh," I say.

"Well, realistically, you can conceivably get detection as early as seventy-two hours from now, but it's probably best to wait two to three weeks to get a more definitive answer. The longer, the better."

"Seventy-two hours it is," I say, grinning. She grins back at me.

"I'm gonna keep my fingers crossed for you," she says. She crosses her fingers in front of me before I step toward her to hold her in an embrace.

"Thank you," I say. Then I step back and cross my fingers, too.

I can't believe I was seen to so quickly. Though I guess that's what private health care can do for you. If you've got the money in this country, all you have to do is make an appointment. I only phoned yesterday and when, by chance, the man on the other end of the line asked when I was next due to ovulate, I did a quick calculation inside my head before spitting out, "Tomorrow, actually. You don't have a space for me tomorrow, do you?"

"Can you pay all of the money tomorrow?" he asked.

"Yes, yes, it's all paid up," I replied.

"Perfect... how does ten a.m. work for you?"

It actually didn't work for me. I should be in school today. But I called Principal Klay's assistant first thing this morning as I was driving to the health clinic and told her I wasn't feeling too well. She did what she usually does when staff call in sick, she scoffed audibly down the line. So I fake coughed as loud as I could and then said, "So if you can just pass on the message please," before I hung up.

It feels so surreal that there is sperm inside my egg right now. I'm so excited, so elated. As if I'm a totally different person to the one who was making a mini mountain out of wet tissues in my living room just a few nights ago. I owe all of this excitement to Zachary. And Mia. They're my superheroes. I made my mind up as I was tossing and turning in bed last night that if I get pregnant — and there is a big chance I will; much, much bigger than when I was inserting the sperm myself — I will name the baby after them. If he's a boy, he's going to be Zachary. If she's a girl, I'll call her Mia —after my twin. It's the least I can do.

"I'm sure this is all okay, but just thought I'd ask to reassure myself," I say to the nurse as I am pulling my jeans up. "I'm supposed to fly on a couple of long-haul flights to Europe at the end of next week, that's okay given that I could be in the early throes of pregnancy, right?"

"I saw that on your notes... you have nothing to worry about, Lucy," she says. Then she crosses her fingers again, before turning to the TV hanging from the ceiling in the corner of the ward.

"So tune in on Thursday night when I will reveal exactly who the interviewees will be," Sarah-Jane Zdanski says, flashing both her perfect teeth and her enviable cleavage at us.

"Wonder who she's interviewing," the nurse mumbles, nodding up at the TV.

"Oh, I think I know who it is."

"You do?" she says, turning to me as I bend down to tie my sneaker laces. "Who?"

"Ah... trust me, she's building something up that isn't that special at all," I say.

Then I stand back upright, hug the lovely nurse again while I whisper another "Thank you" into her ear, then I throw my purse strap over my shoulder and leave the clinic ward, a smile spread wide across my face, my fingers firmly and painfully crossed, and healthy sperm already nestled inside my egg.

MERIC MILLER

I sit staring at the blank page in front of me cos I can't think what this week's newspaper should be about. I keep getting distracted by nothing, staring at the door of my office hoping that she'll walk through it any second.

She said nothing to me yesterday. Not a word. Though we didn't have American History, so we weren't sitting beside each other at any point. But even at lunchtime her and Wendy just sat with their backs up against the fence, talkin' and talkin'. At least Brody and Stevie weren't with them. That hurt me the other night when I was riding back from Esbon after paying Madam Aspectu that hundurd bucks and I saw the five of 'em sitting around by the monument, laughin' and jokin'. None of it made sense. I hope she's not gonna become all friendly with them. I ain't never been friendly with them. Any of them.

I slam my fist to the desk. Damn it! It's fucking Tuesday already and she hasn't said one word to me about the psychic reading she had on Saturday night. She's supposed to have realized that I am the one by now. Aspectu told me she would make sure it happened.

Maybe Caoimhe will open up to me on Thursday... when we sit together in American History. She'll prolly hold my hand, tell me that she wants to be my girlfriend. She prolly needs time coming around to what Apsectu told her. S'why her and Wendy were talking while they were sitting with their backs to the fence at lunchtime yesterday. They musta been talking all 'bout me.

I look at the digits in the bottom corner of my computer screen and decide it's time to leave. Caoimhe's clearly not gonna come down to chat today. She's likely left the school already. It's almost four p.m.

I race out the back door, to where my bike is resting against a wall, and then hop on it and begin pedaling as fast as I can to nowhere in particular. I never quite know where I'm riding to in the evenings. I just keep pedaling and pedaling to fill in the time. S'not much else to do around here. S'pecially if you've got no friends.

Then a thought pops into my head. I keep hearin' her high-pitched voice over and over as if she's screeching right next to my ears.

"Fuck it," I say as I begin to pedal faster and the wind picks up, blowing my hair away from my eyes.

I leave my bike resting against the wall before I bend over in two, with my hands on my knees, as I try to catch my breath.

"Sorry," I say to a man passing me. "Do you know what time it is?"

He looks kinda funny at me, then hooks the sleeve of his jacket to one side and stares at his watch.

"Five ten," he says.

Then he walks off as I remain bent over, still trying to try to catch my breath.

Five ten. That means it took me over an hour to ride here. I'll be exhausted by the time I get home tonight. This better be worth it.

Bloom Avenue is a busy street, with a big bar that is blasting out a Bon Jovi song, and a casino with bright lights blinking on and off next to it. I take my bike from the wall and wheel it down the sidewalk, past a group of adults who stare at me before they begin to laugh. I hope they aren't laughing at me.

I cross over to the quieter side of the street, to where the walls are sprayed with bad graffiti. And that's when my heart stops.

"What the fuck?" I say to myself.

Mom. Standing on the corner of the street with another woman, dressed like I ain't never see her dressed before. A skirt so short you can almost see her thong, her oversized pink purse tucked under her arm.

I stand against the wall, staring at the two of them as they share a cigarette, until a car pulls up to the curb next to them.

Mom points her thumb at her own chest then at the woman beside her before walking over to the car and bending down to talk into the driver's side window.

Then she waves back at the woman she was talking to, flicks the butt of her cigarette to the sidewalk and gets into the car.

BRODY EDWARDS

I keep tapping my pen against the desk while Stevie chokes into his elbow beside me. Again.

"Jesus, dude, you got AIDs or something?" I say.

He looks up at me, his eyes all red, and then he blows out his cheeks.

When Decker walks in, I instantly remember how all up in my face she was last Friday, spitting and yelling at me, and so I immediately sit up more straight. But I don't know why I do that. Cos I'm not afraid of her. She doesn't frighten me, even if she thinks she does. Sad thing is, I used to like Decker. She was prolly my favorite teacher until she got all pissed with me for no reason.

"There she is," Stevie whispers, nudging me. "Bushy pussy, huh?"

I giggle, and then hold my fist out for a bump.

"Where were you on Monday, Miss Decker?" Nicole shouts out. "I wanted to come find you, I have information on who Sarah-Jane Zdanski is interviewing tonight. Were you ill, Miss Decker, on Monday?"

"No, Nicole," Decker says, as she leans down to place her bag beside her desk. "I wasn't ill."

"Then where were you, Miss Decker?" Hawkins asks.

"I was... I was otherwise engaged."

"She was getting an AIDs test," I blurt out.

And then the whole room falls silent. Normally I get a laugh. Or sometimes the students will make an "Eewww" sound. But right now everybody is silent. *Everybody*. Even Stevie.

Then Decker's shoes click off the floor, and slowly make their way toward me.

"Brody, I wanna see your mother up here first thing in the morning," she says.

"No, Miss... you can't."

"I want to see your mother!'" she grunts, with her teeth closed, "In my classroom first thing in the morning. Do you understand?" She bends over me as I fold myself into my desk, resting my head on my arms.

"Yes, Miss Decker," I mumble.

"I've warned you about how you speak to me."

I glance up at her. She looks really angry with me; her mouth is turned down and her face is all red. Then she finally spins on her heels and makes her way back to her desk.

"Lover's tiff, huh?" Stevie whispers. And then he coughs into his elbow again.

"Okay," Decker shouts, just as the bell rings to signal the start of class. "You were saying you think you know who Zdanski is interviewing tonight, Nicole, huh? I think I might know, too."

"Who is it, Miss Decker?" Caoimhe shouts in her cool Irish accent from the back of the classroom. Caoimhe's actually pretty cool; certainly for a chick with lotsa freckles. I enjoyed being around her and Wendy and Kai the other night. We sat by the monument talking for over an hour. Though they haven't said anything to me or Stevie in school this week. Maybe they didn't like us. I don't know. I liked them, though. Sitting around talking was actually pretty cool.

"Well... let's just keep it a secret, shall we, Nicole?" Decker says, winking before she turns to begin writing on the chalkboard.

"Nicole looks hot today with that ponytail,' Stevie whispers to me. "Think I might fuck her again."

"Did you fuck her?" I whisper back. "Thought you said she just gave you a blowie?"

He shrugs his shoulders.

"Been with too many chicks to remember, dude," he says.

Then he coughs into his elbow again.

CAOIMHE LARKIN

I slide into the seat next to Meric and stare at him, just to see if he'll glance back and offer one of his awkward smiles. But he doesn't. He just keeps his eyes down at the edge of the desk, like he doesn't know who the hell I am.

I feel bad that I haven't spoken to him all week. I've just had too much going on, especially with Wendy's Mom. We've been up to the hospice every evening after school. Except for Saturday. That's when we hung out with Kai and Brody and Stevie down by the center monument.

Nicole shouts out, distracting me from my memories of giggling on Saturday.

"Where were you on Monday, Miss Decker?" she asks.

As Miss Decker turns to answer her, I take the time to nudge at Meric's elbow.

"Hey," I whisper. He looks up at me through his fringe. "Have ya had a good week?"

He huffs through his nose. Then it goes silent before Miss Decker erupts. I'm not sure what's happened. All I know is she has stomped her way over to Brody's desk and is shouting at the top of her voice at him, her finger pointing in his face.

"What he say? What he say?" I whisper to Meric.

Meric shrugs. And then he goes back to staring at the edge of his desk again while Decker lets Brody have it; her face red, her pointed finger now shaking.

"Did *you* have a good week?" Meric whispers to me.

"Yeah. Well. No. Kinda," I whisper back.

"How did your psychic reading go on Saturday?"

I don't answer, because Miss Decker has spotted us whispering and is staring down at us, just as she was about to start the lesson by discussing the Sarah-Jane Zdanski interview that's on tonight. Apparently she and Nicole already know who's being interviewed. Sure beats the hell out of me, even if me and Wendy and Kai and Brody and Stevie had about fifteen guesses each on Saturday. Brody tried to tell us with a straight face that he thought Sarah-Jane Zdanski was going to interview Michael Jordan because that's how much build up these interviews have had. Then we all fell back on the grass into fits of laughter, even though it wasn't really that funny.

"Well?" Meric says.

I turn and lean toward him.

"I forgot all about going to the psychic," I whisper.

"Excuse me!" Miss Decker calls out. "Caoimhe and Meric, what are you two talking about?"

I decide to take the hit, only because it's so unusual for Meric to talk in class. And it was me who started talking to him anyway. All he wanted to do was stare at the edge of the desk.

"Sorry, Miss Decker," I say, standing up. "We were just talking about... about, well...." I pause.

"About what?" Miss Decker asks, holding her hands to her hips while everybody twists their necks to stare back at me and Meric. I don't want her to shout at me like she just shouted at Brody. And I certainly don't want my Mam called up to the school.

"Ehh... about psychics," I say as I hide my neck by dipping it into my shoulders.

Everyone laughs. At least it sounds as if everyone is laughing.

"Psychics?" Decker says. And as she says it, her lips twitch into a half-smile. "What about psychics?"

"Well..." I say, staring down, like Meric does, at the edge of the desk. "I was supposed to go to one on Saturday night and I forgot. I was just telling Meric that I forgot to go, that's all."

"Do you believe in psychics, Miss Decker?" Nicole shouts out after shooting up her hand.

"'Course not," Miss Decker says.

"Huh?" I say, lifting my gaze.

"Well, listen," she says, brushing down the creases of her blouse, "I don't want to tell people what they should or shouldn't believe in. Each to their own. Do you believe in psychics, Caoimhe?"

I look around the class at all of the heads turned toward me and decide to just shrug my shoulders.

"Dunno," I say.

"Out of interest, how much does the psychic charge you to be able to tell you your future?" Miss Decker asks.

I shrug again.

"Forty dollars."

"Forty dollars?" she says, her voice going all high-pitched. "Listen Caoimhe, if somebody could really tell the future of another human being, you think they'd just charge forty bucks?" Then everyone laughs again, and I sit down feeling mortified. "Trust me Caoimhe, if somebody could really tell the future, they'd be on Oprah sharing their phenomenon with the world, they wouldn't be working outta some rented tent somewhere, charging forty bucks."

Most of the students turn back around, but some continue to stare at my red face.

"Hey," Miss Decker says, pointing at me and winking. "I like you Caoimhe. I think you're awesome and bright and super intelligent and I love having you in this class. In fact, I like you so much I've just saved you forty bucks."

Everybody laughs again. And so I join in this time. And as I laugh, I feel relieved. Not relief because I can forget about rebooking an appointment with Madam Aspectu. And not relief because my embarrassment has magically flushed itself away. But relief because for a flash of a moment there I thought I might have

to not like Miss Decker. When I love Miss Decker. Really love her.
I think she's an awesome teacher. I love how she teaches. I love
how she has just taught me in the space of two seconds there how
bullshit psychics are. How did I never cop that on? Forty bucks for
having a super power? Of course that doesn't make any sense.

"Anyway..." Miss Decker claps her hands twice. "Let's move
on with the lesson. The Sarah-Jane Zdanski interviews are on
tonight and I want you all..."

WENDY CAMPBELL

Sure is quiet here without Momma breathing so heavy and Sally's cartoons blaring loud from the TV.

I lean over the sofa and turn on the lamp to hear the sizzle of the bulb as it strains to shine. Then I look around our tiny home and can't help but compare it to the one I've just been in.

We went back to the Larkins to have dinner this evening after me and Caoimhe spent two hours up with Momma in the hospice straight from school. She wasn't sitting up today and didn't speak so much, but she is still doing a lot better than she was when she was lying here on this stinking makeshift bed.

Sally is loving life with little Aine. I think they might be best friends the rest o' their lives. A bit like me and Caoimhe. When I was over in the Larkins's house earlier, Sally and Aine were playin' hide and seek in the backyard, only stopping to take bites out of the burgers and fries Mrs. Larkin had made for us all before they were back out running and giggling and hiding again. I know we're gonna lose Momma real soon, but I can't help thinkin' we have so much to look forward to. Momma might not, but me and Sally sure do. We have our whole lives ahead of us.

I press my finger on the television and hold down the button until the screen flashes all the way up to channel number nine. Then I sit back into the fold-up sofa that I thought Momma was gonna die on, before I lean a little forward to snatch at my school notebook and pen. Even with all the drama going on around me, I'm actually excited for this. I enjoy Miss Decker's classes. She makes learning really interesting; makes me think differently like no other teacher does. Me and Caoimhe and Kai and Stevie and Brody had a good laugh talking about American History last Saturday down by the monument. In fact it was this very moment we were talking about for almost an hour, until it got dark and we all decided it was time to go home.

"Coming up in two minutes," Sarah-Jane Zdanski says straight into the camera, "my exclusive interviewees will finally be revealed. Stay tuned, and don't go anywhere."

KAI CHAYTON

I drape my new yellow dress across my bed and then step back three paces so I can take it all in.

It's so cool that I don't feel nervous. I'm just gonna do it. I'm gonna wear that sexy little number into school tomorrow and become the new me for the very first time. I'm a little nervous to see what some people's reactions will be, but mostly I'm just excited about it. I'm looking forward to my new chapter. My new life. My new me.

I spoke with Miss Decker today. She held me back after class, told me she was proud of how I was holding up after I'd returned to school this week. She said I look much happier. She's right. I do. I know I do. I can see it when I look in the mirror. In fact, I don't even need to look in the mirror to see it. Because I can genuinely feel the happiness inside of me.

"Kai, you just need to be the person you want to be. Don't let anybody hold you back," she said to me as she rubbed my shoulder. She's an awesome teacher. Always has been.

So, I decided, there and then, that I *was* gonna be the person I wanted to be. To hell with what anybody else thinks. I'm gonna dress how I wanna dress. Starting the moment I get dressed for school tomorrow morning.

"Kai," Momma yells out as I'm standing with my fingers stroking my chin, lost in how pretty my yellow dress is.

"Yes Momma?"

"It's about to start."

I race down the stairs to see Poppa in his armchair, staring over the evening newspaper at me. I pause in the doorway and nod at him and I think he kinda nods back. It looked like a nod to me.

"Thank you, Momma," I say.

I turn to my backpack in the corner of the room, and take out a notebook and a pen.

"So who do you think she's interviewing?" Momma asks.

"No idea," I reply.

"I heard everybody in town talking about it today," she says. "You know Winnie Deffley who runs the catering company? Well, she seems to think Sarah-Jane is interviewing somebody local; like from Lebanon. Cos there sure is a lotta whisperin' goin' on."

I smile at Momma as I stretch over her to reach for the remote control, then I sit back into my favorite armchair — opposite Poppa — from where I turn up the volume on the TV.

"Well, we're about to find out, Momma," I say.

The news jingle blares loudly, so loudly, that I take the volume down, and then there she is: Sarah-Jane Zdanski—looking so darn sexy in a low-cut dress that Poppa folds over his newspaper and sits more upright in his chair.

MERIC MILLER

The page is still blank. All bright. All white. Well... mostly white. I've scribbled two words and have drawn a small box in the corner, but that's all I've managed all week. And now that I'm comin' so close to the deadline, I can't concentrate with Mom snoring all up in her bedroom. I'm supposed to have this newspaper written and printed before first class starts tomorrow morning. But I just don't feel as if I'm in the right mood for it this week. It'll be the first time I'll have let Principal Klay down since he gave me the job as editor. But what's the point at this stage? Ain't nobody read the darn newspaper anyway.

I normally have the sports section all done by Wednesday. But I didn't have the concentration this week to get a quote from Coach Quill. Prolly 'cause I kept thinkin' bout Caoimhe the whole time. I just kept playin' over and over in my head how her psychic reading with Aspectu mighta gone. Though now I know she didn't go. And that she will never go again. Not now after what Decker said to her in class today. Maybe I should write about that on the front page of the newspaper for tomorrow: Miss Decker is a cunt! Or perhaps I could write the same about Caoimhe. I saw her last Saturday when I was riding back from Esbon; sitting in the grass by the monument, laughin' and jokin' with Stevie and Brody and Kai. In fact I keep seeing it over and over again in my head. S'why this darn newspaper hasn't been written this week.

I ball my fists up, then grab the page and bunch it up into a ball before throwing it across my bedroom. My breathing is scaring me. It's gettin' really noisy. Almost as noisy as Mom's snores. So, I snatch at my door and walk straight into the living-room. To drown out the noise of the snores comin' from Mom's bedroom, I punch my finger at the button on the TV, and before I even have a chance to sit down I can already hear her sexy voice. I forgot this was on tonight. Not quite sure how I forgot, 'specially as Decker didn't shut the hell up talkin' about it in class. Though I guess all's I was doin' in her class was staring down at the edge of the desk, seeing Caoimhe laughin' and jokin' with Stevie and Brody and Kai over and over in my mind again.

"Well, the work you have been doing is absolutely incredible," Sarah-Jane Zdanski says, beaming a smile at the luckiest dude in the whole world who is sitting next to her. Her knees are almost touching his. He's gotta have a hard-on. Who wouldn't if they were that close to SJZ? "Do you feel burdened by the expectation, Senator, or is that something you thrive on?'" she asks.

"Well," the gray-haired man says, rubbing at his chin. "I have to say I am conscious of the expectation but..."

Who the hell is this guy? This is the interview everybody's been gossiping about for weeks? Some ugly, old-ass gray-haired dude I never saw before my whole life?

"Well, we are so grateful for all you do." I tune back in when Sarah-Jane begins to speak again. "So now is the time for you to make your big announcement, Senator Edgar Owen. Are you ready?" She stands up, waves her hand for this Senator dude to follow her toward the camera. Jeez, she looks so good in that dress. It's so tight. So tight it's as if I can see all of her.

"Okay," the Senator dude says to the camera, "it now gives me great pleasure to announce that the school chosen by all members of the State committee to win the Kansas State School Grant for an overseas trip to Europe, 1997, is.... It's Median High School, in Lebanon, North Kansas."

"What the fuck?"

"Congratulations students of Median High School," Sarah-

Jane says. "We will be adding — to our panel here — the lucky Principal of that victorious High School after this quick word from our sponsors. Don't go anywhere."

I ball my fists up again. Only because I know they're all gonna have so much fun in Europe. I shudda stolen four hundred bucks from Mom's purse or some old lady in Esbon and gone on the trip. Though what would the point of that have been? Me traveling thousands of miles and spending hundreds of dollars just to be ignored by everyone—like I am in school every day...

Motherfuckers.

I breathe in and out through my nose, making almost the same noises Mom is with her fuckin' snoring.

Then I snap at the TV, turning off the commercials because I can't concentrate, not with the annoying noise of my own breathing.

In. Out. In. Out.

They're getting faster. And louder. Gruntier. My hands are beginning to sweat.

I turn quickly on my heels, then push at Mom's bedroom door to see her grunting her loud snores from the back of her throat with her mouth wide open. Then I bend down, pull at her oversized pink purse, taking all of the money out of it and tossing it on to her bed. I feel for the cold steel of the butt of her gun. Then I storm back out to our living room where I stare at the blank TV screen that I can actually see myself in while I press the barrel of the gun against my temple.

"Fuck this shit," I say.

Then I curl my finger around the trigger. And squeeze.

EIGHT

PHIL GRIPPED Sarah-Jane's loose ponytail while she continued to pant and sigh and spit into the toilet bowl.

She had yet to vomit, but that wasn't from a lack of trying. She was desperate to relieve her stomach of the knot it had been entangling itself in. It was unusual for Sarah-Jane to feel such strong pre-broadcast nerves mere minutes from airing live. But, it was also unusual for her to be mere minutes from airing live to thirty million Americans. She had been super proud when she heard the first ever live broadcast she did for PBS had been watched by three hundred households. Tonight she would quite literally be appearing in front of an audience one hundred thousand times that size.

She slapped her hand to her mouth and then swiped at it, before eventually standing back upright, and leaning into her lap dog.

"Sorry," she whispered.

Phil circled his hand around her back before he reached both arms around her waist so he could squeeze her tightly against his double-breasted jacket. When she had remained unmoving, her cheek resting on his shoulder, for what he considered a worryingly long time without her saying a word, he hooked the left cuff of his sleeve and then tipped his head to the side so he could see past the loosest strands of Sarah-Jane's ponytail.

"Eighteen minutes," he whispered.

She immediately leaned away from him and held the tips of her index fingers to the inner corners of each eye, before eventually blowing her frustrations out through her lips.

"I'm not nervous because of the audience figures... this is just such a big story for us, y'know?" she said. "Me 'n' you, this one's personal, right?"

Phil nodded. Then he squeezed her to his double-breasted jacket again. "You've got this," he whispered. "I believe in everything you do."

She leaned away from Phil again and stared into his narrow, dark brown eyes, then she pressed a palm on either side of his face so she could bring their noses close enough to touch. It was unusual for Phil to say something so frank and so deep. But as Sarah-Jane knew better than anybody else; when Philip Meredith spoke, it was because something needed to be said.

So, Sarah-Jane sucked down the tears that were threatening to spill from her eyes, then grabbed at his chunky fingers.

When they both swung open the toilet door and found themselves back in the maze of narrow hallways, Howie happened to be striding by, pinching the hooked microphone of the headset he now had on as close to his lips as he possibly could. He immediately stopped, then sneered back over his shoulder at the two of them.

"I've been looking for you all over the place!" Neither of them said a word. They both just stood still, staring at the executive producer while gripping each other's fingers. "What were you in the restrooms for? Throwing up?"

"No," Sarah-Jane said, tilting her head to one side. "I was having a shit!"

Howie looked her up and down, then flicked his eyes to Phil.

"What does he do in there with you... wipe your ass?"

"No," Sarah-Jane said, shaking her ponytail, "no wiping necessary. He licks me clean."

Phil scratched at his patchy beard while Howie shifted his feet awkwardly, a snarl hinting on the edge of his top lip. Then he flamboyantly flicked the cuff of his left sleeve to one side and tutted.

"Only sixteen minutes till we go live. Make your way to the set."

"S'where we were going before you stopped us," Sarah-Jane said. She gripped Phil's fingers tighter then dragged him around Howie and toward the curtain that led them into the bright lights of the studio.

When they both stepped into the shadows of those lights, the faces of the guests she was about to interview immediately looked up at her again, some of them pursing their lips, some of them half-smiling, one of them offering a nod and a stiff wave. Her stomach began to roll itself over again, threatening another race to the restroom. But she pressed a palm gently to her navel and then closed her eyes so that she could run through her meditative breathing techniques again. Standing next to interviewees in the wings had never made her feel nauseous before. And she realized there and then, as she was sucking in one of her meditative breaths, that she won't even feel close to this level of nauseous-ness when she has to interview George Clooney in two weeks' time. She'll be excited. Yes. She'll be excited and likely a little horny. But she won't feel sick. Not like she does right this minute.

She swiped her clammy hands down the sides of her little black dress, and when the guest who stiffly waved at her tried to approach, she spun away and stepped to the side, pretending not to notice him. Phil had to hold a hand to the man's chest to stop him following through with his intended greeting.

"Sarah-Jane doesn't speak with interviewees until the camera's rolling," Phil whispered.

It was Patrick Klay's chest Phil's hand was pressed against. The man who had tried to call by hair and makeup earlier to meet with the host.

"But we've met before," Klay said. "It's not as if we're meeting for the first time."

Sarah-Jane overheard the whispered conversation, but pretended not to as she took a step onto her stage, where she stood with her back to the shadows, the lights beaming at her ponytail while she pressed a hand to her stomach and continued to suck in deep, lungfuls of breaths before releasing them ever so slowly.

"Okay," Howie screamed as he stepped into the studio through the gap in the curtains, still pinching the end of the hooked microphone hanging from his head set. "Fifteen minutes until we go live. Can all floor staff and control room staff take their positions? The interviewees... if you can remain standing where you are, behind camera number one, we will sit you around the desk when we are only five minutes from going live."

Bodies instantly began to shuffle behind the cameras of the deathly quiet studio before those cameras began to wheel forward, toward the edge of the stage Sarah-Jane now was stood on with her back to everybody, staring at the neon blue light displaying her family name. She knew all of her family were proud of her. She certainly hadn't been starved of congratulatory phone calls in that regard. Even aunts and uncles she hadn't met had called her up from Krakow to anoint her as the family jewel—the one who had made a name for herself. Both of Sarah-Jane's parents were Polish immigrants; who met and fell in love on the boat they traveled to America on in search of loftier ambitions back in the spring of 1966. Her brother, Dean, was born two years after the Zdanskis had arrived and married in Massachusetts, but by the time Sarah-Jane came to be — in June of 1972 — they had already moved and settled in Kansas, after her father had landed his own franchise with the car showroom brand he had gotten his first job with in America. She grew up meeting every stereotype a beautiful girl is supposed to meet if Hollywood movies reflect real life. She was courted by every guy at school; she won, by a landslide, the valedictorian; she refused every advance of second dates through college simply because she genuinely thought herself more beautiful than anyone who approached her; and she ended up becoming somewhat a local celebrity—reporting for PBS. And that was all, of course, before she landed a big job and an eighteen-story tall billboard in the heart of Times Square.

She pursed her lips at her family name lit in neon blue as the knot in her stomach began to unwind itself.

Then she felt Howie step up on to the stage behind her, and when she glanced over her shoulder, she saw that he was fiddling with his fingers. He offered her a nod of his head before gently poking a flesh-colored oval nugget of plastic into her ear. Then he held both of her biceps lightly and stooped his neck so he could eyeball her at her own level.

"You got your own show on merit," he said. "You got this show for being you. So just be you."

As a smile began to form on her lips, she heard a light cough in her ear, then Mikey's Chicago accent.

"Y'all set SJ?" he said.

It irked Sarah-Jane to be called SJ, though she understood Mikey would be keen to short-cut his direction into her ear in as little detail as possible. And so instead of correcting him like she usually does when someone shortens her name to just her initials, she nodded her head once, while fingering her ear. Then she stepped back and perched her ass onto the edge of the sausage-shaped desk.

"The mic above your head will pick you up, SJ," the voice in her ear said, "so can you confirm, audibly, that you are all set, so we can pick your volume levels up in here?"

"Yes!" she shouted.

Everybody who had been shuffling around in the shadows of the studio to get into their positions stopped what they were doing and stared up at her.

"Sorry," she said, showing them all the palm of her hand. Then she lowered her voice to normal decibels. "Yes, Mikey," she said. "I'm all set."

"You sure you're not worried about anything?" he asked.

She fingered her ear again.

"You mean aside from those opening two lines?"

Mikey snickered into her ear, a noise that made Sarah-Jane's stomach threaten to knot again. But she didn't say anything, because she knew it was way too late to bring up the argument of the opening two lines once again. Not when there was only minutes left until she went live to the nation. Besides, she had already raised the issue multiple times and was shot down on each occasion; shot down by Howie; shot down by Mikey; shot down by Walter.

"How are all the guests doing?" she whispered to Howie as he rested his ass on the sausage-shaped desk next to her and folded his arms.

"Good. Mostly. Well... we've got researchers and producers talking to Abigail backstage now, calming her down. They think she may have taken some valium in her dressing room. She's showing signs of anxiety, but is still adamant she wants to appear on air. Don't worry about it. We'll address it as we go. If we need to, we can extend Patrick Klay's interview in the final part. We have lots of continuity questions for him... Listen," Howie shifted his feet and held Sarah-Jane's biceps lightly again. "Mikey is in your ear at all times. And I'm going to be standing right there at all times." He pointed just off stage, to the right of camera number four. "I'll have a full script in my hands. You literally can't go wrong. We produce this show as a team. Your role in that team is to just be you."

Her face broke into a wide smile then she held up an open palm for Howie to high-five. He winked at her, then stepped off the stage to stand in his position, just as everybody else, aside from the guests, had.

Knowing everybody was now staring at her from the shadows of the studio, Sarah-Jane held her arms wide and produced a subtle bow. Then her stomach began to instantly knot again, because she suddenly realized that bowing was a totally inappropriate thing to do. So, she held a flat palm above her brow, to block out the glare of the lights shining too brightly from above the stage, and peered into the shadows in search of a bullish-looking face with scruffy hair and a patchy beard. When she noticed he hadn't moved from where she left him, she waved Phil up to the stage, and as he was thudding himself up the step in the deathly quiet of the studio, gripping his boss's purse to his chest, Howie shouted out.

"Makeup!"

Mollie ran from the side of the stage, an open compact of foundation balancing on her flat palm, a thick makeup brush in the other hand. She stopped in between Sarah-Jane and Phil and lightly brushed around the host's cheeks before dabbing across her brow.

"Thank you for today," Sarah-Jane whispered.

"Just doing my job."

"You're doing more than your job. And I, for one, won't forget it."

Mollie was smirking when her brow suddenly dropped and she squinted closer toward the host's face.

"You smudge all that lipstick already?"

"Oh," Sarah-Jane said. "Might have. I wiped across my mouth."

Mollie plucked a lipstick tube from one of the many pockets of the apron hanging around her waist then subtly filled in the scarlet glow on the host's lips while Phil remained standing behind her, scratching at his beard and staring up his boss's name in neon blue splashed across the back wall of the set.

"There you go. I'll be back for touch up just before you go live. Break a leg."

Sarah-Jane winked at the only new confidante she had found since becoming a CSN employee, and when Mollie had tucked herself into a corner at the side of the stage, the host stared at her ex-producer slash cameraman, now full-time purse carrier.

"Not long now," he whispered.

She smiled nervously, then rubbed her moist palms together.

Do I need to stand here with everybody staring at me until we go live?"

Phil shrugged then shook his head, before pointing his hand toward the gap in the curtain.

"Where you going, SJ?" Mikey squealed into her ear as she stepped off the stage.

"We're gonna wait in the wings," she said without moving her lips as she passed by the guests. Then she ducked under the curtain to get back out to the quiet of the dimly-lit hallway.

Phil didn't say a word to her while they both rested their backs against the wall, because he had, by now, said all that needed to be said. He had no fears, no concerns at all, that Sarah-Jane was about to nail these interviews.

"I think it's just my moral pendulum swinging in my stomach. That's why I feel a little nauseous," she whispered.

Phil held a hand to her belly, and pressed it gently.

Then the last of the peace and the last of the quiet they were sharing got disrupted by a disgusting sound of somebody audibly clearing their throat. They both leaned off the wall and stared up the dimly-lit hallway to see Walter Fellowes shuffling his short legs toward them while slurping his tongue across his dry lips.

LUCY DECKER

It never feels right to place your hand between your legs while you're peeing. But, despite the horrible feeling of disgust as light mists of urine spray my fingertips, I've got a huge wave of optimism swishing around inside me today.

It's been four days since I had my IVF treatment. I could literally be pregnant right now. Chances are I *am* pregnant right now. Nurse said Friday morning is the earliest I can take a test, though she said it may be too early to detect. I had to get a special test to gauge this one so early in a possible pregnancy that cost two hundred and fifty dollars. But if it gives the result I am desperate for it to give me, the cost won't matter one little bit. I really can't wait much longer. If I'm pregnant right now then I wanna know right now. I really, *really* wanna know. Not just for my sake, but for Zachary and Mia, too. They paid for this wave of excitement that's rolling around inside me right now.

This pregnancy test is a lot bulkier and heavier than the ones I normally buy at the pharmacy. It looks more like a chunky TV remote control than a tiny electric toothbrush like the others do.

When I'm finished peeing, I shake the test into the toilet bowl while pulling up my pants and my panties with the other hand at the same time.

"Please. Please," I whisper to myself as I stare at the small screen on the front of the test.

I place it down onto a prepared sheet of toilet paper while I wash my hands.

After drying them, I stand in the middle of my tiny bathroom and stare down at the screen on the test again. If a blue plus sign shows, that's it—my dream has come true. If only a blue straight line shows, well then that means Zachary wasted all of his savings on my aging eggs. And perhaps he should have bought a Vespa instead.

"C'mon," I say to the test, as if it can somehow hear me. "Show me a blue cross."

In my impatience, I pick up the box the test came in and read the instructions again.

"Wait. What? Two hours? *Hours*? Why would it take two hours?"

Then I remember that the pharmacist had said that to me as she was taking my money. But it didn't register, because I was too excited. I assumed she said it would take two minutes for the results to show—just like every other pregnancy test I've tried over the years.

"Damn it," I say, slapping a palm to my bathroom wall tiles. Then I take a look at my watch. Eight forty-five. I gotta get going. I gotta get to class. I stare at the blank screen of the test again, then sigh. I'm wondering whether or not I should bring it with me to school. No... perhaps I should just leave it here. That way it'd be a surprise waiting for me when I get home. I don't wanna find out the result in school, do I? Seems a bit unromantic to me. Though I guess the whole process of trying to get pregnant has been as unromantic as getting pregnant can possibly get.

I decide to turn around, leaving the test lying face up on the sheet of toilet paper, and begin to stroll down my hallway, pulling on my coat and snatching at my bag before I open up the front door and leave; hoping that when I get back at around four p.m., there'll be a blue cross waiting for me on that screen.

BRODY EDWARDS

"Mom," I call out, rapping my knuckles against her bedroom door.

"What is it Brody?" she shouts back.

"I uh..." I scratch my hair. "You uh... you have to go to the school this morning. Miss Decker wants to meet with you."

"Who?"

"Miss Decker. My American History teacher."

"To meet? With me? For what?"

I hear her sweep the covers off of herself before she groans as loudly as she can.

"I'm not sure... I think... well, I think—"

"I can't do it. Not this morning. I got an appointment. You're gonna have to call your Dad. Let him do some parenting for once, huh?"

"Shit," I whisper to myself. "Okay, Mom," I shout.

I walk into our kitchen and pull at the receiver of the phone that hangs on our wall.

"Can you put me through to Johnny Edwards's room please?" I say to old Mrs. Ferguson.

"Hello," he says.

"Dad. It's me."

"You in trouble?" he says.

Wow. This guy can sniff out trouble. S'why he's such a great soldier I bet. S'why he was such a great left tackle.

"Kinda... yeah... well not really, no. I don't know."

"What?"

"Dad, one of my teachers wants you to come to her class today. First thing this morning. She wanted Mom to come, but Mom has an appointment and so..."

"So you *are* in trouble..." he says.

"Kinda. I don't know. Can you make it? It's gotta be now."

"Christ, Brody. I'm only home a few weeks and I'm already being called to your school."

"Sorry, Dad," I say.

"Who have I to meet with?"

"Miss Decker. She's nice. Or, used to be nice anyway."

"Lucy Decker?" he says.

"Huh? I dunno. Yeah. I think her name is Lucy. How d'you know?"

"I've just heard of her is all," he says. Then he sighs. A really, really long sigh. So long, I have to hold the phone away from my ear. "'Kay, I'll get there soon as I can. And Brody, you better not be in serious trouble."

Then he hangs up.

After blowing out my lips, I sling my bag over my shoulder and push my way out the front door.

"You better not be in trouble," Mom shouts after me.

I don't answer her.

I munch on a cereal bar as I walk up the street and when I finish it I begin whistling. I don't know why I'm whistling. I'm probably gonna have my ass handed to me by Dad later. If Decker tells him I've been saying all those sexy things to her, he might get real mad. Serious army soldier-type mad. He'll probably roar all up in my face like Decker did last week. Only this time it'll be a lot scarier. A hell of a lot scarier. Decker didn't scare me. But Dad will. I know he will. I've heard him shouting before. It shakes the whole house. He better not cancel my trip to Europe. I'll lose my shit if he cancels my trip to Europe.

I'm still whistling, probably 'cause I'm nervous, as I walk up the garden path, before holding my finger to the doorbell. Then I stand back and wait. And wait.

"Yo dude," he says, finally answering the door, wrapped up like a burrito in his gray duvet.

"What the hell, dude? C'mon, get ready, it's eight fifty."

He turns around to cough.

"I'm not going in today, dude," he finally says. "My Mom said I can stay home 'cause this cough ain't gettin' no better."

"Ah, for fuck sake," I say, realizing I have to face this day all on my own.

"Stop by after school, dude. I'll prolly be feeling better by then, and we can play some Madden. Or Mario. Whatever you like."

"My Dad is coming to school this morning to talk to Decker about the whole... y'know..."

"Oh fuck dude," Stevie whispers. "I forgot 'bout that."

I shake my head, then spin around and walk back down Stevie's driveway, sulking. This is gonna be the worst day ever.

"Good luck, dude," Stevie calls after me. Then he coughs again, before slamming his door closed.

KAI CHAYTON

Poppa had left for work before I walked down the stairs. Momma stared at me as soon as I entered the kitchen and tears came to her eyes, before she nodded once, and then spun back around to pretend to wash the breakfast dishes in the sink. She still hadn't turned back around by the time I'd poured myself, and then finished, a large bowl of Cheerios. Then I just said, "Bye Mamma," as I picked up my backpack and slung it over my shoulder, making sure the strap didn't touch the ribbons on my dress.

"Bye, love," she shouted after me.

And that was it. That was all she said to her son in a dress. My Momma sure is a woman of too few words. I've learned that over the past few weeks and feel a little silly for not learning it much sooner in my life. It's Poppa who does all the talkin' in our house. It's Poppa who makes all the decisions. Well, he used to. Not anymore. 'Cause I make decisions 'bout me now. This is my life. Not his.

The only thing poor Momma said to me last night, after I told her I was gonna start dressing like a girl this morning — long after the Sarah-Jane interviews had finished — was that she was worried about what other people would think. She is certain I'm gonna be bullied at school; that everybody is gonna laugh at me 'cause they wouldn't know how to identify with my change. I told her I didn't give a damn what anybody else thought. The only people I've ever worried about were Momma and Poppa. All I've wanted since I realized I should have been born a girl is for Momma and Poppa to agree with me. But they're taking their time coming to terms with all of this. I can't blame them. Of course I can't. It took two years for me to reach this point. I can't expect them to take this all in the space of a few days.

The cool of the wind brushing against my knees makes me feel all tingly. I've worn dresses before. But always indoors; always inside my home, or in the changing room of a department store— like I did the first time I tried this dress on two weeks back.

When I turn on to the street our school is on — a moment I thought about a hundred times in my head last night — I hear the hum of the other students before I see them.

I'm not gonna react. I'm not gonna say a word if anybody tries to bully me. Or laugh at me. I'm just gonna keep my head staring down at my Converse sneakers, get myself inside the school front doors, and then up those stairs to Miss Decker's room as quickly as I can.

Despite the craziness of my gender-change, I have actually been looking forward to this class this morning. I took lots of notes last night. Miss Decker is right. Sarah-Jane Zdanski was praising the senator as if she was in love with him. It was kinda gross, actually. There's definitely a relationship between the government and the news. Miss Decker is awesome teaching us things we otherwise would never realize. She's one of the main reasons I'm wearing this dress today. She told me that all I had to do was concentrate on being the person I was meant to be. So here I am. Me, being me.

I wonder if Decker knew Principal Klay was gonna show his face during the Sarah-Jane Zdanski interview last night. He appeared in the second-half of the show, thanking the senator for awarding Median High School the big prize. Europe. I can't believe it. I can't believe I'm gonna visit London and Paris and Rome next week. I'm bringing as much money as I possibly can. Cause I'm gonna buy myself the best wardrobe anybody in Lebanon, Kansas has ever owned.

"The fuck?" one of the seniors says, staring at me and then tutting, as I walk as quickly as I can up the school pathway.

I don't lift my gaze from my Converse. I just continue down the path, noticing a couple of heads turning as I go, before I finally run up to the double doors and push myself inside so I can breathe.

I feel relieved as soon as I hear the quiet of the reception area. Even if two girls' jaws have just popped open as they stand staring at me. They don't say anything, even when my eyes meet theirs. And so I walk up the stairs — to the sound of a bunch of ninth graders giggling as they come down in the other direction toward me. I ignore them, by continuing to climb, until I get to Miss Decker's door. I pause, take a deep breath, and then push myself through.

"Wow!" Wendy calls out. That's a nice response. Wendy is so cool. "You look awesome, dude."

I wink, then, ignoring all of the turning heads, I slide in beside her.

"Thank you, Wendy," I say.

"What the hell?" Brody calls out from behind me, and then, as Miss Decker looks up to snap at him, she glances at me and begins to stumble over her words.

Because of the awkwardness, I look down at my Converse sneakers again. Then Miss Decker claps her hands twice and, right on cue, the bell rings.

"I agree with Wendy," Miss Decker shouts over the noise of the bell, clasping her two hands together and bowing toward me. "You look awesome, Kai."

"Thank you, Miss Decker," I say, lifting my head high again.

"Brody, I hope your mother is coming up to see me. She's supposed to be here first thing this morning."

"Miss Decker, my Mom couldn't make it at short notice. She has an appointment so, ah... my Dad's coming up instead. He should be here any minute."

"Okay, well... wait... what? Your Dad?"

"Uh-huh." Brody says. And then it goes all quiet, which makes things awkward between them for a second. It's not awkward for me, though. It's awesome. Already the attention has been taken away from the boy in the yellow dress. This is great. Nobody seems to give a damn that I'm now a girl. I love this. I love being the new me already.

"Okay, so today we are gonna discuss the Sarah-Jane Zdanski interviews from last night," Miss Decker calls out. "Wait, hold on." She looks around the room. "A couple of guys are missing. Where's Stevie Jenkiss?"

"Oh, he's sick," Brody says. "Got a bad cough. He won't be in today."

"And Meric... anyone know where Meric Miller is?"

All students twist their necks at the same time, just to stare at the empty chair next to Caoimhe. Then we all seem to shake our heads, before turning back around to Miss Decker.

JOHNNY EDWARDS

It's as if she doesn't know I'm here; that I don't exist. She has kept her head down the whole time, staring at a notepad in front of her while I either take the time to look at the top of her head or re-read the triangular sign on the front of her desk that displays her position as the: "Assistant Principal."

I clear my throat. Loudly. And only then does she look up over her glasses at me, before pushing her lips to one side of her face.

"Yes?"

"I'm looking for Miss Decker's classroom. I'm the father of Brody Edwards. She requested to meet with one of his parents this morning."

She glances at the stars and stripes on my collar, then stands up and leans over her desk.

"Up those stairs," she says, pointing, 'and it's the first classroom you'll see straight ahead of you. Classroom 2C."

I don't thank her, because she left me waiting. So, I just shuffle off in the direction of the stairs and begin to climb them two at a time, pulling myself up by the rail. I see a door marked 2C straight ahead of me when I reach the top and when I walk toward it, I lean in, and listen.

"Wait, hold on," I hear her say. "A couple of guys are missing. Where's Stevie Jenkiss?"

"Oh, he's sick, Miss Decker," my Brody says. "Got a bad cough. He won't be in today."

"And Meric... anyone know where Meric Miller is?"

It goes silent. And in that silence I think about pushing through the door. But for some reason my nerves take over. I really don't want to do this. This is gonna be awkward as hell. So, I rub my hands together and take a deep breath. It's crazy that I can handle being in Iraq no problem, but entering the classroom of a woman I just might be a little in love with, who may or may not already be pregnant with another man's baby, well, that's a different challenge altogether.

"Okay," I hear her saying before she claps her hands twice, "take out the notes you took on the Sarah-Jane Zdanksi interviews last night. We're gonna have a big discussion about it today. I'll ask you all for your opinions in a couple of minutes, but first..."

Damn it. I mighta missed my best opportunity to push through the door during that silence. Now I've got the added awkwardness of dropping into her right in the middle of her lesson.

I cough into my balled fist as I look around the empty hallway, then I just rattle my knuckles off her door, before pushing myself through.

All of the students immediately turn to face me, including Brody who I stare at before glancing up at Lucy and offering her a thin smile.

"Oh, hello Mr. Edwards," she says. Then she waves me to the front of the class.

CAOIMHE LARKIN

There's a light knock at the door before it's pushed open and a man walks in wearing a white shirt with an American flag on the collar.

He nods at Miss Decker, then she waves him toward her.

Oh, I know... that must be Brody's Dad. Actually looks a lot like him. Brody's gonna get into a whole heap of trouble for telling Decker she was getting an AIDs test. I'd hate to be in his shoes right now.

As Decker and Mr. Edwards whisper to each other by her desk, I take the time to get out of my seat so I can go sit in the empty chair next to Brody, just so I can talk to Wendy in front of him.

"Hey babe," I whisper to her.

She turns around and winks at me. And so does Kai.

"Yellow is so your color, Kai. Whatcha think Brody?" I say.

But Brody has tuned out of whatever I'm saying because he's trying to lip-read what's being said between his Dad and Miss Decker.

"You coming up to the hospice after school?" Wendy asks, quietly.

"Sure," I say nodding.

"Wait. Who's in a hospice?" Kai asks.

A loud shout from outside the classroom distracts us, and when the door opens I spin around in my seat as quickly as I can to see what the hell is going—

WENDY CAMPBELL

"Is that your Poppa?" I say, turning around to Brody.

He ignores me, by leaning onto his desk, resting his chin on his arms while he stares up at Miss Decker and the man in the white shirt as they begin to talk.

"I think it is," Kai whispers back to me.

I grin at Kai and then twiddle the little yellow bows on his shoulder straps. He looks really cute. *Really* cute. It's a surprise—a big surprise, but he looks happy; happier than anybody could possibly be after trying to kill themselves a little over a week ago. In fact, I ain't ever seen Kai looking so happy before.

"Hey babe," a voice whispers from behind. I turn to see my newest and bestest friend sliding in to the seat next to Brody. "Yellow is so your color, whatcha think Brody?" she says, pointing at Kai.

Brody doesn't answer. He's too busy staring at the hushed conversation Miss Decker is having with his Poppa.

"You coming up to the hospice after school?" I ask Caoimhe.

"Sure," she says, nodding her head.

"Wait. Who's in a hospice?" Kai asks.

"Oh, it's—"

A loud shout from outside the classroom stops me from answering Kai, and we all swing our heads toward the noise. Then,

I hear Nicole screaming and I stare at her to try to understand what the hell is going on. When suddenly, Caoimhe drops to the floor beside me, and when I look up all I can see—

MERIC MILLER

The printer hums. Then stops. Hums. Then stops again. Only three more runs and I should be all good.

I don't feel nervous. I just feel ready. Ready to be listened to for once. It's about time my voice was heard!

I pick up the pile of newspapers, with my face front and center and smiling from ear to ear, then I grab my bag before heading out the door of my little office.

The hallways are all quiet now. First class has already begun. The only sound around here is coming from the squeaking of my shoes as I shuffle up the stairs.

Though I do hear a gunshot inside my head. I've actually been hearing it every few minutes. I imagine myself pulling the trigger last night, splattering my brains all over the living room. I was actually staring at my reflection in the TV, about to squeeze the trigger when I thought why the hell would I wanna do that? Ain't nobody in this world gonna give two goddamn fucks if I kill myself. They'd probably all just hear around the school that Meric Miller blew his brains out, then they'd go back to laughing and joking with each other down by the monument.

I drop a bundle of the newspapers on the large hallway floor when I get to the top of the stairs, before turning on to the open space near the front desk.

"You're a bit later than normal today," the principal's assistant says, staring over her glasses at me as I walk toward her.

I don't say anything. Not at first. I just drop the pile of newspapers on to her desk, then glance down at her.

"Everyone's gonna read this one," I say.

I spin away from her and, as my shoes squeak their way up the stairs towards Decker's classroom, I drop the backpack's strap from my shoulder, and feel inside it for the cold metal. When I take it out, I flick open the cylinder—as if I somehow feel a need to count them again. Eight bullets. Means I got seven shots. Then one for myself.

"Y'all gonna read this one!" I shout, slapping the cylinder of the gun back into place. "Y'all gonna hear from Meric Miller now!"

Then I sweep back the hair from my eyes, kick open Decker's classroom door—and aim.

NINE

BY THE TIME Walter Fellowes had shuffled his short legs toward them, gasping for breath, Sarah-Jane had glanced at her watch.

Seven minutes.

"Nervous?" he croaked.

"Excited," she said.

He cleared his throat disgustingly again as soon as he reached them, then licked his lips before swiping the back of his hand across his mouth. The slurp made Sarah-Jane's stomach tighten again. This was the last thing she needed; a pep talk from the network's toad-like owner, certainly not when she had been enjoying the final minutes of her own anonymity in the presence of a man who didn't speak unless something needed to be said.

"I hear you've been suffering with yer nerves," Walter said. "Thought I'd come down and have a word with you before you go on."

"I'm fine."

"Well, I'd like to talk to you..." Walter glanced at Phil, before shifting his beady eyes back to his newest on-screen beauty. "Alone."

"Uh-uh," Sarah-Jane said, shaking her ponytail from side to side. "Any time you want to speak with me, you speak with us." She flicked her finger between the chest of her little black dress and Phil's double-breasted jacket. "We're a team. You hired us as a team."

Walter cleared his throat, swiped across his mouth again, then reached into his inside blazer pocket and removed a tin box.

"Well," he said. "I guess this story is almost as much his as it is yours."

"Uh-uh," Sarah-Jane said, swaying her ponytail from side to side again. "Not *almost*. This story is as much his as it is mine. He just happened to be behind the camera. I happened to be in front of it. But we broke this story together. We arrived at that school together."

Timing can be everything in journalism. And on October, 24, 1997, Sarah-Jane Zdanski and Philip Meredith happened to be victors of the time lottery. All of their numbers came up. They were in the right place. At the exact right time. They skidded their white van with the PBS sticker peeling from the side of it onto the school lot and then raced, as quickly they could, to the entrance — a camera shuddering up and down on Phil's left shoulder — within twenty minutes of the shots being fired. They just happened to be waking up in the middle of middle America having stayed in a local motel the night before after interviewing the state senator and the school's principal for the local PBS network, exclusively revealing Median High as the victors of the state's school lottery. Nearest journalist to the story wins the time lottery. Sarah-Jane and Phil were only nine minutes away from this story. And the jackpot was huge.

Three local police officers were at the scene by the time they rushed to the entrance, after the cameraman slash producer had heard the original phone call made live by a teacher to emergency services through the receiver in his van while he was munching on a breakfast burrito. He dropped the burrito to the pedals of his van upon hearing a teacher scream down the line that she had heard multiple gunshots coming from the classroom opposite hers, then he raced into the motel to inform his colleague who was drying her hair. With no national reporters anywhere close to the vicinity of the middle of middle America, Sarah-Jane and Phil began to take total control of the story. And boy was it a *huge* story. Monumental. Mass school shootings didn't just happen every day. In fact, they rarely happened. Not like this. Eight shots fired, seven bodies confirmed within minutes by Sarah-Jane as she delivered the news to America straight down the lens of Phil's camera. Within the space of one twenty-minute period that morning — between nine-forty and ten a.m. — Sarah-Jane's beautiful face appeared on every major network in the country; from FOX News, to CNN, to MSNBC and then to CSN before cycling all way back through those networks over and over again. She handled the reporting of what was such a monumentally emotional and shocking story so coolly and professionally, that within twenty-four hours of the Median High school shootings, the owners of every major network were on the phone, lobbing all manner of offers her way. No offer arrived more attractive than the one sold, repeatedly in four separate phone calls, by Walter Fellowes at CSN: a quarter of a million a year to host her *own* panel show—*Zdanski*; a hard-hitting, all-encompassing cultural affairs program that would see her interviewing all popular public-interest guests each and every Thursday evening. Walter Fellowes knew exactly who the panel of guests should be for her debut show, and knew as soon as he conceived the idea that it would prove to be a ratings smash.

As he sucked and puffed to light the cigar he had just removed from the tin box, Howie's loud voice distracted him, shouting from behind the curtain.

"Only five minutes until we are live, ladies and gentlemen," the campy executive producer called out. "Can I ask the interviewees to take their seats around the desk on stage?"

Upon hearing the bodies shuffle, Walter took a step away from Sarah-Jane and Phil to pull at the gap in the curtain, so he could squint his beady eyes into the brightly lit studio. Then he exhaled a huge cloud of smoke, just as the first guest was taking her seat at the sausage-shaped desk. Patricia Edwards. She was the mother and wife of two of the victims—Brody Edwards and Johnny Edwards. Johnny was the only victim shot twice. It's not known why exactly, but it has been strongly suggested by investigators that he was charging at Meric Miller, even having being shot in the stomach, before a second bullet was fired through the bridge of his nose from close range.

Brendan Larkin sat in the chair next to Patricia. He was the father of Caoimhe Larkin; an Irish girl about to celebrate her sweet sixteenth birthday just three days after the massacre occurred. Her and her family had only moved to Lebanon two months prior.

Beside Brendan sat Tyrel Nelson— the father of Wendy Campbell. Though "father" should probably appear in quotation marks. Sperm donor is a more apt title to give him to describe his relationship with his beautiful, late daughter. Her mother, who raised her and her young sister Sally single-handedly, didn't live long enough between the atrocity and Sarah-Jane Zdanski's exclusive interviews with the loved ones of the victims of the Median High School shootings, and so her estranged ex-husband, whom she hadn't seen for fourteen years and who hadn't met with his daughter Wendy since she was just eighteen months old, was the only person who could appear on national television to mourn her tragic loss.

Next to Tyrel sat, with rigid shoulders and a strong, somber face, Nova Chayton—a man who had already appeared multiple times on TV for different news organizations since the shootings happened six weeks ago to inform the nation of the pride and love he had always held inside his heart for his "flawless" son, Kai.

On the far end of the sausage-shaped desk, the chair furthest away from Sarah-Jane Zdanski's twenty thousand dollar chair, sat Mia Hahn—the twin sister of the only teacher killed in the school shootings: Lucy Decker. It had been confirmed by eye-witnesses that Lucy was the last person shot, before Meric turned the gun on himself.

It's not known if Meric fired his bullets randomly or whether he knew who he wanted to take down during his rampage—though he couldn't have foreseen that US soldier Johnny Edwards would be in the classroom when he entered with his gun outstretched at nine-ten that morning.

There were some clues left by the shooter in his manifesto.

Meric had produced one final newsletter for Median High — announcing his "annihilation" of those who had continually failed to acknowledge his existence. What is clear from the manifesto is that Lucy Decker seemed an intended target, as her name was mentioned in unsavory terms repeatedly within the one-sheet newsletter. But while the names of four of his victims were also mentioned throughout the manifesto, so too were other names who weren't shot. What is abundantly clear, however, from the text of the manifesto, is that Meric Miller was yearning for attention. He had headlined the newsletter *Meric Miller, Serial Killer* and then placed an oversized portrait of himself, grinning a menacing smile, beneath that headline.

Sarah-Jane would get to the manifesto in part two of the show —when Meric Miller's mother Abigail was due to appear alongside distraught school principal Patrick Klay, who, coincidentally, Sarah-Jane had interviewed the night before the school massacre to reveal the winners of the state school lottery. Though Abigail Miller was still suffering backstage, and it was not yet clear if she would or would not appear on air.

"Three minutes," Howie shouted. "Where is my host?"

Walter exhaled a cloud of cigar smoke through the gap in the curtain, then croaked, "She's out here, talking to me. Don't worry. I'll have her in to you before cameras roll." He spun back around, cleared his throat disgustingly, then pressed a hand to his host's stomach. "You still got that knot in there?" he said.

Sarah-Jane closed her eyes gently, filled her lungs, then exhaled slowly before answering.

"I'm not nervous about the viewing figures."

"Oh, I know you're not nervous about the viewing figures," Walter said, before sucking on his cigar again.

"It's just... oh, I don't know..."

"I know," Walter croaked, while exhaling. Sarah-Jane shifted her marble eyes, just in time to see him slurp his wet tongue across his dry lips again. "I've hired sixty news anchors in my time and I know no anchor gets nervous because of the viewing figures. They're never nervous that something can go wrong. Why would they be? They're smart people. They know nothing can go wrong. They've got cue cards in large writing in front of them, a full script on their desk right under their nose, their questions printed out on little cards in their hands, a producer hunkered down beside camera four with a full script in his hand, and a director in their ear who knows every beat of the script by heart. Of course you're not worried that you might go wrong in front of so many people. You know nothing can go wrong. The only reason that knot is there inside your stomach is the same reason every news anchor gets nervous before their first major story. Your moral compass is swinging in your belly."

He sucked on his cigar again, and as he did, Sarah-Jane took a moment to glance over her shoulder at Phil's bullish, unmoving features, before she swung her beautiful face back around.

"I just don't think the opening two lines are necessary—"

"Just say the opening two lines," Walter said, leaning into her, before slowly whistling a cloud of smoke upward, between their two faces.

"It's about what those two lines represent," Sarah-Jane said, waving the smoke away. "Do we need to highlight right off the bat that we're putting these grieving folks up on a perfectly lit stage for America to gawk at?"

Walter chuckled, then turned to poke his head through the gap in the curtain again, to see all members of the crew stood or hunkered in their proper positions, waiting for the floor manager to begin his countdown.

"One minute!" Howie shouted.

"You seem way too focused on those who have nothing to gain, Sarah-Jane. You haven't mentioned anyone who does gain from this."

Walter turned back around.

"Gain?" Sarah-Jane said, squinting at him. "What do you mean gain? Not one of these guests gains from appearing live on national TV. The next hour and a half is hardly gonna relieve them of any of the anguish, or torment... or confusion... or grief... or whatever it is they are feeling, is it?"

"You're still focusing on those who don't gain."

Walter wrapped an arm around Sarah-Jane's shoulders and moved her forward to the gap in the curtain, before pulling it further across just in time for Howie to stare at them, shrug his shoulders, and then shout out: "Forty seconds."

"See those cameras," Walter said, pointing a stubby finger into the shadows. "Thirty million Americans are gonna be watching you for the next ninety minutes through those. Who gains? America gains. You gain. A quarter of a million a year contract. Your own show. Nobody has gained from this story more than you, Miss Zdanski. Except for CSN, of course. That quarter of a million you're earning a year, we're gonna make that back in the first sixty seconds of commercials we are going to air in..." he glanced down at his watch while clearing his throat disgustingly, "just twelve minutes time." He squeezed the beauty closer to him. "And your job for CSN, who pay you that quarter of a million a year, is to squeeze as much juice from this story as you can. I told you before. You are not in the news business. You are in the television business. You know that, right? We've spoken about that. That's what you get paid to do. So, go do your job... go squeeze some juice." He patted her on the ass, then spun around to shuffle his short legs back in the direction he had walked from while he continued to puff on his cigar.

Sarah-Jane turned to Phil, pressed a palm on either side of his face, then leaned up to press her lips against his before spinning on her high-heels and walking herself through the gap in the curtain, where she stepped up onto the stage while still pressing a hand to her stomach. She pursed her lips at each of the blank faces of the guests sitting around the sausage-shaped desk, then turned to face the lights.

"Ten seconds," Howie called out. "Makeup!"

Mollie raced onto the stage, balancing an open foundation compact on her flat palm and a makeup brush gripped in the other. She didn't say anything as she matted the glow from Sarah-Jane's brow before stepping off stage right on cue for the floor manager to raise his voice.

"And we go live in... five," he shouted, "four... three..." He signaled with his fingers, in front of the camera Sarah-Jane was looking at, the numbers two... and then one.

A tiny red light switched on just above the lens, and a motor could be heard humming within the mechanics of camera number one. Sarah-Jane pursed her lips tight and clasped her hands. Then she delivered the opening two lines she had always felt were highly inappropriate.

"Good evening, America. And welcome to the show."

...

This year, in America, there will be more mass shootings than there will be days...

THE SEQUEL IS WAITING FOR YOU...

THE FOOTAGE THAT SHOOK AMERICA

The Zdanski Show continues...

The sequel to *In The Middle of Middle America*

THE FOOTAGE THAT SHOOK AMERICA

—America Present—

Available now on Amazon in Kindle and in Paperback

DAVID B. LYONS

THE FOOTAGE THAT SHOOK AMERICA

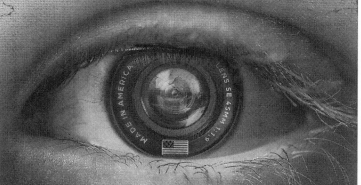

A BREATHTAKING MYSTERY SUSPENSE NOVEL

Watch an interview with author David B. Lyons now in which he discusses:

———

• The tells that Meric possessed the profile of a High School shooter

• Why the first two sentences of Sarah-Jane Zdanski's live broadcast are so powerful

• The significance of the last morning of the lives of these seven characters

———

Use the link below to watch the video now.

https://www.subscribepage.com/middleamerica

The end.

ACKNOWLEDGMENTS

This book was written during the Coronavirus pandemic—when we were all isolated from our loved ones.

We missed the O'Hanlons during that crazy year more than any other family. Barry, Eleanor, Emma, Ben and Grace — this one is for you. We're looking forward to making up for lost time...

I owe huge debts of gratitude to so many people whose support and insight made the challenge of writing this book an actual possibility (because it most certainly wasn't when I first conceived the idea). The biggest thanks goes to Hannah Healy — a consultant on this novel — who was instrumental in ensuring this story achieved its American voice. You're awesome. The wonderful Kathy Grams's feedback and insight on American voice was also super helpful. Thank you ladies so much for taking the time to give me fantastic notes on this manuscript while it was in development. Your finger prints are all over the pages of this book.

Margaret Lyons, Eileen Cline, Roz Casagrande, and Rosemary Rasmussen — thank you so much for reading early drafts of this novel and giving me really helpful notes on how it could become an even more improved experience for the reader.

A huge thank you goes to City of Lebanon, Kansas who gifted me some insight into the wonderful, colorful and characterful real town in which I set this novel.

I would also like to thank MiblArt for their unique design work on these covers and, of course, my editors: Lisa Gellar and Brigit Taylor.

And to you, the reader. I hope you enjoyed this read, even though the themes are ultimately very dark. I would highly recommend checking out the video link at the back of this book, so you, too, can join in the discussion.